LOST DAYDREAMING

a sweet romance

HILLARY SLAUGHTER

To Madey—I miss you every single day. Love you #55!

Trigger warning: This book contains content related to loss of a family member in addition to a parent battling cancer.

Chapter One

"WHY IS A SOAKING wet man wearing period clothing significantly sexier than any man wearing anything I've seen in modern times?" I asked my roommates as I reached for the bowl of popcorn. Thanks to the candle I'd lit at the beginning of the movie, the smell of pumpkin and cinnamon permeated the room, adding to the cozy fall feel of our apartment.

Once I'd secured the popcorn, I settled back onto the blue plaid couch, letting its familiar lumps welcome me into its embrace as I tucked my legs under me. At five feet, two inches tall, I was used to my feet not touching the ground and had found other ways to make seats—couches in particular—more comfortable.

"Wild guess here, Chloe, but maybe it's because basketball shorts don't quite fit the same as breeches and linen shirts?" One of my roommates, Audrey, responded without tearing her eyes from the screen. She absentmindedly petted her dog, Ruby, a brown shih tzu-mix curled up on the couch cushion between us.

"True. How do we bring breeches back in style? Because the things they do for his physique are impressive." I shamelessly ogled the man on the screen.

Mr. Darcy, as played by none other than Colin Firth, had just finished swimming in the lake at Pemberley, and none of us wanted to miss a second.

My week had been rough, filled with submitting an endless stream of resumés geared toward getting me out of Utah and onto my next big adventure. Hopefully to somewhere that provided a fresh start away from painful memories and pushed me toward fulfilling a promise I'd made to myself and my sister nearly a decade earlier. For every resumé I'd sent, however, I'd received just as many rejection emails. It didn't help that my mom was more than happy to greet each of my failures with unsolicited advice. My text thread with her was filled with helpful comments like: "Maybe it's a sign you're meant to stay in Utah," or "Bet you're wishing you got a teaching certificate after all," or "Your dad's office is hiring." I almost wished my brother and mom could get into an argument, just for a change of topic. At least then I could solve a problem instead of being the source of one.

To say life had been stressful was an understatement. So, when a rare Saturday arrived without me or my roommates having plans, I'd declared the day Pride and Prejudice Day complete with matching pink Costco lounge sets. We'd started the BBC version of *Pride and Prejudice* around lunch and had plans to follow it up with the Kiera Knightley version, most likely with ice cream in hand. That was assuming I could keep my roommates away from their significant others for an entire day.

A phone dinged, and Mallory sat up from where she'd been lying on the loveseat, her blonde ponytail swinging with the movement. "Chloe, how serious are you about making Pride and Prejudice Day an all-day affair? Ridge just texted and he—"

I held up a hand, cutting her off. "I don't want to hear it! Y'all promised me an entire day free from real men and wedding plans."

Of the three of us, I was the only single one, which was lonely, even when we were together.

Mallory was engaged to Ridge, her high school sweetheart whom she had recently reconnected with—years after they broke up, and their November wedding was fast approaching. While I was thrilled for her, I needed a break from all the wedding talk and gushing about how amazing her fiancé was.

Audrey wasn't much better. When she wasn't working as a yoga instructor, she was with her boyfriend Grey, the two of them snuggled close, teasing each other and generally being obnoxious levels of cute. I wouldn't be surprised if the two of them got engaged before too long.

Which left me, alone, trying to pull my life together after graduating with my English literature degree and having to leave my on-campus job now that I was no longer a student.

Audrey turned toward me, careful not to disturb Ruby. "Now wait a minute, I made no such promises. The whole movie day thing was pretty spontaneous. Besides, I told Grey we could go to dinner. He's found a new taco place he swears blows all other taco places out of the water."

Ruby slept on, oblivious to the important conversation going on around her.

"You did too promise when we started the movie. Besides," I held up a finger when I saw the protest building in Audrey's expression, "the taco place will be there another day." I reasoned, watching my day of girl-time evaporating before my eyes.

I reached to fiddle with the necklace that rested at the base of my throat, remembering too late I'd stashed it in my nightstand months ago to keep it safe and to try to finally let go of the memories it held. I let my hand drop, reaching for more popcorn instead.

I needed this day. I needed the distraction. The opportunity to think of something besides my failed job hunt and the promise I'd break if I didn't chase new adventures and opportunities outside of Utah. I needed something fun and low stress in my life, even if only for today. After all, everything would change in a few weeks when Mallory tied the knot.

Audrey bit her lip. "But then I don't get to see him today."

"Just think how much sweeter it will be to see him tomorrow," I said, trying not to give into the bright green puppy-dog eyes Audrey turned on me.

A knock on the door cut the discussion short, waking Ruby. I walked over to answer it, the dog following behind me to investigate. Standing on tiptoes to look through the peephole I found Derek, my longtime friend and the ultimate interrupter of girls' nights, standing on the other side of the door wearing jeans and a black jacket.

"No," I groaned, realizing the girls and I wouldn't be finishing even the BBC *Pride and Prejudice* today, let alone the Kiera Knightley version.

"It's Derek, isn't it?" Audrey called from the couch, sounding way too chipper about the interruption.

"Maybe," I said, turning away from the door, not yet willing to admit defeat. Maybe if I ignored it—

"You know he won't go away. He knows you're home. You're the one who shared your location with him," Mallory said, her head popping up above the loveseat like a gleeful prairie dog.

"Something I regret in this moment," I said under my breath, trying to keep my voice quiet enough that it would carry to my roommates but not through the door.

"Oh, come on! You know if you let him in, he'll probably take you to do something wildly fun." Mallory had a mischievous look in her eye as she glanced at Audrey. I didn't trust that look.

"Oo, yes! Like to try a new taco place," Audrey said, far too innocently, her expression matching Mallory's.

"Or he'll finally give into the attraction between the two of you and go for that kiss he's wanted since before we ever met you." Mallory waggled her eyebrows suggestively.

"I like that option even more! If Grey had looked at me when we first met the way Derek looks at you every time you answer the door, I would have kissed him immediately," Audrey said.

"No you wouldn't have. You could barely stand Grey at first." I hissed, feeling warmth creep into my cheeks.

Audrey shrugged. "If he looked at me with that much heat and interest, I would have been incentivized to like him much faster."

"Chloe? You going to answer the door or make me wait outside forever?" Derek called through the door, his voice filled with curiosity.

I stepped away from the door toward my roommates, keeping my voice low. "I've told you guys, Derek and I are just friends. And he's dating Tara now." At least, he'd been on several dates with Tara. They hadn't labeled it as a relationship or anything, but it was only a matter of time.

"We've told you, Derek wouldn't mind changing that 'just friends' label. Also, I don't think he's actually interested in Tara. I think he just asked her out to humor you since you've been saying the two of them would make a cute couple after you met Tara at that concert." Mallory persisted.

Audrey carefully studied her fingernails before commenting, as if she was considering getting a manicure and not meddling in my romantic prospects. "Which you've only been saying since you broke up with Mark because you can't risk both you and Derek being single at the same time. It might lead to something serious . . . like an actual relationship."

But I couldn't risk trying that kind of relationship with Derek. I liked him exactly where he was—in the friendzone. There was no reason or need to change that. Also, how did my roommates know things between Derek and Tara wouldn't work? I was a great, or at least good, matchmaker. I knew when my friends worked well together. I'd nudged Mallory and Ridge's relationship along, and now look where they were!

"Even if Tara wasn't in the picture, so what if he wanted to change things? *I* don't want to change things." I persisted, doing my best to keep my voice down, even as Derek knocked on the door again.

There were so many reasons why Derek and I were better off as friends; in fact, I had a whole list of them that I'd been adding to since we'd met during freshman year of college. For example, his place was here in Utah, and I had one foot—sort of—out the door.

Had I considered what it would be like to kiss him, especially when we were together late at night and Derek's hair was mussed and his expression sleepy after watching one too many movies? Absolutely. But I was never going to act on it. Derek was my best friend, and I couldn't risk that relationship.

"Best friends make the best kissers. Ask me how I know." Mallory threw me a wink and I groaned.

"I second that! Though Grey and I kind of skipped the 'just friends' part of things. Not that I mind." Audrey added far too loudly, her expression becoming dreamy, no doubt picturing locking lips with her bearded, flannel-wearing man.

"Shh, I don't need to hear about your love lives and—"

"You know I can hear your voices, right? I don't know what you're saying, but I'm guessing you're talking about me." Derek called through the door. I didn't have to look through the peephole to know he was smirking, finding the entire situation hilarious. That's what came from being friends for over seven years. We could sense how the other would behave without having to see them.

Which was probably another reason why a relationship with Derek wouldn't work. I wanted a guy who could surprise me with big romantic gestures like in the movies. I knew Derek so well I could *feel* him smirking without seeing his face. There would be no surprises in dating Derek.

I rested my head against the door and took a breath, using the moment to regroup after the conversation with my roommates before swinging the door wide open and gesturing Derek inside.

"You might as well come in. My evening just opened up," I grumbled, waving him inside.

"Hello to you too, though technically I was already your evening plans, but it looks like you forgot," Derek said, giving my lounge set and mussed pixie cut a once over before crouching down to greet Ruby.

"Hi, Ruby girl."

The dog rolled over, instantly exposing her belly for petting.

After a moment, Derek followed me further into the apartment and settled on the couch in the middle of our junk food debris.

He looked ready for a night out with his wavy brown hair tamed by gel. He shrugged out of his jacket, revealing a cozy cream sweater that I wanted to touch to see how soft it felt. Which was a totally normal, friend reaction. Not strange or overstepping or indicative of attraction at all. I was woman enough, and friend enough, to own Derek was an objectively attractive man. That didn't mean I wanted to date him.

It was then I fully registered what Derek was wearing and became suspicious. Derek's go-to outfits typically consisted of t-shirts, shorts, and baseball caps. He was clearly trying to impress someone.

"Don't mind Chloe. She's just mad because we're ruining her spontaneous plans," Mallory said, brushing past Derek and me on her way into her bedroom.

Audrey had already disappeared, presumably to change into something more appropriate for a taco date night. Now that Derek was here, I had no leverage to keep them sitting on the couch while wearing pajamas and eating junk food.

"Why are you dressed like you're going to a party?" I asked, slumping onto the couch. Just because I was twenty-five didn't mean I couldn't pout like a five-year-old.

"Because that's where I'm going. In theory, you're supposed to be going too." Derek grabbed a handful of popcorn, making himself at home. He'd spent so much time at my apartment he basically counted as an honorary roommate. It had been that way ever since we'd met, which was another reason why my roommates thought we should date.

A memory niggled at the back of my mind and I smacked my forehead as I remembered what he was talking about. "Tara's party's tonight, isn't it?"

"Ding ding ding. We have a winner," he said in his best impression of a game show host, pointing two finger guns my way. Sometimes his humor resembled that of a middle-aged dad more than a twenty-six-year-old bachelor.

"What if I said I can't go because I'm sick?" I fake coughed into my sleeve, underscoring my excuse.

Derek's eyebrows puckered in concern as he reached over to feel my forehead and test my temperature. His hand lingered a moment too long, and I leaned away.

"You feel fine to me. Not to mention, this seems like an awful lot of junk food to consume for someone who's under the weather." He paused, his lips twisting in thought. "Though the movie content seems to align with illness. No one operating at full capacity would willingly choose to watch this nonsense." Derek gestured to the TV where a frozen Elizabeth Bennet stood in Pemberley reevaluating her life decisions.

"Hey now, *Pride and Prejudice* is a classic and a commentary on romance in all forms," I said, sitting up and crossing my arms over my chest, forgetting my fake illness in my rush to defend Elizabeth and Darcy. I had an English literature degree. I would die on this hill.

"It's an idealized world that gives women unrealistic expectations of men." Derek responded without missing a beat. I wince at the rote response. Maybe I asked him to proofread a few too many of my literary analysis papers.

"Have you ever watched it?" I asked, raising an eyebrow at his tone as I turned toward him.

Derek leaned in close enough I could feel the warmth coming off his skin. If I lifted my hand only a few inches, I could appease my curiosity about the softness of his sweater. "No. And I won't. I don't need to be second-guessing my manliness when compared to Mr. Derby."

"It's Mr. *Darcy*, which you would know if you'd watched it. Or better yet, read it. You might even learn a thing or two to help your dating life." I arched an eyebrow, refusing to back down even though the space between us had dwindled to mere inches. This was how it was between Derek and me, bickering like siblings, nothing more.

Derek shook his head, an exasperated smile tugging at his lips as he nudged me with his shoulder, breaking the spell and moving to put a bit of distance between us. "Regardless, you're stalling and trying to get out of the party tonight. You're coming with me. It's up to you if you're going in your pajamas or something else."

"You're assuming you could get me out the door in my pajamas. What if I plan to stay here and become one with the couch?" I spread my arms wide and sank deeper into the worn sofa. I had bonded with this couch. When I wasn't searching for a job at the desk in my bedroom, I was sitting here watching and reading more romantic comedies and historical romances than was advisable.

"Then I'll recruit your roommates to help me kidnap you and force you to be social. You've been holed up in this apartment for days. You need fresh air and social interaction. If I didn't know better, I'd think you were turning into an introvert in your quest to escape Utah for new adventures." He quirked an eyebrow in challenge, giving a mock gasp of horror.

I shook my head at him. Despite my recent behavior, I could never truly be an introvert. Derek knew I thrived in social situations and hated being left alone for long stretches of time.

Or at least, I usually did. Lately, the effort to leave the house felt like too much. A feeling I'd only grappled with once before in my life—which was not a time I liked to think about, so I pushed the thought away.

"My roommates wouldn't help you. They're on my side." I argued, my lips tipping into a smug smile.

"We would help," Mallory called, coming out from her bedroom wearing jeans and a crew-neck sweatshirt advertising "Hagrid's Pumpkin

Patch." Her blonde hair framed her face, her wispy curls making me reconsider my pixie cut.

Maybe that's what I needed, a new hairstyle. Maybe it could snap me out of the funk that had haunted me since I'd graduated without a job and no clear plan for my future. Too bad that as an unemployed, recent graduate, I didn't have the budget for a new cut and color.

"Traitor! I thought you were my friend." I leaned further into the couch, as if slouching would prevent my friends from pushing me out the door.

"We are, which is why we can't let you spend another evening wallowing on the couch." Mallory came to stand in front of me, arms crossed over her chest, pulling out her best stern-teacher pose. "Give yourself a break. Do something fun. Who knows, you might even have a meet-cute or get a lead on a job or something."

She gave me a pointed look, tilting her head toward Derek in her not-so-subtle way of indicating what she meant by "something." If I had a dollar for every time someone hinted I should date Derek, I wouldn't need to find a job. I could move out of state and go on epic adventures around the world without any hesitation.

"Or you could just have a genuinely fun time and come back home refreshed and ready to try again." This comment came from Audrey who had come out of her room. I leaned my head back to see her standing behind my spot on the couch, her long brown hair piled in a slightly more tamed messy bun.

"Please, Chloe! I really need this distraction, and I don't want to go alone." Derek turned his wide hazel eyes on me, and I could see pain lurking in their depths, a pain I knew all too well.

Derek's dad had been diagnosed with cancer earlier in the year and, while his prognosis was good, it didn't change the harsh realities of battling a disease that turned your own body against you. And though Derek didn't live with his dad, most of Derek's time outside of work was spent helping with whatever his dad needed, which was an exhausting emotional struggle all its own.

Derek's pain was one I still felt and kept buried deep, so deep that no one here knew how much I was hiding. It was the pain of watching someone you loved battle for their life while you could do nothing but watch and cheer them on while still praying for a miracle.

Derek looked down at his hands, his voice quiet when he said, "Dad had a rough day today."

And there it was. The six words that would seal my fate and decide my plans. I couldn't leave Derek to face the party alone, not when I could be there to help him find something happy at the end of a hard day. It was what friends were for.

My expression softened, and I gave Derek's hand a squeeze before pushing to my feet and walking to my room. "Fine, but you owe me."

Chapter Two

TWENTY MINUTES LATER, I was ready to go. I looked reasonably cute in a denim jacket worn over a sweater with elbow patches and paired with jeans and some ankle boots. Thankfully my hair had decided to cooperate, the longer portion in front swooping off to the side instead of curling into random waves and sticking up in odd places.

I took a deep breath, steeling myself for the evening ahead, not sure if Derek would want to talk about his dad or not. Not sure if I wanted to talk about his dad or not.

My stomach tightened at the memories I did my best to avoid, even as my hand reached toward my nightstand and the photo I kept hidden inside. The decade-old family photo contained a lifetime of memories, memories I didn't talk about but that I couldn't stop thinking about no matter how much time passed. I pulled my hand back, fisting it at my side as I took a deep breath, ignoring the photo for now. Instead, I pushed open my bedroom door. I couldn't grapple with those emotions on top of everything else tonight.

When I walked out of my room, Derek flashed me his customary grin, dimple and all, and I wanted to wrap him in a hug and promise him everything would be okay. But I knew better; I couldn't make those promises. Instead, the best I could do was go with him to this party and put on a brave face, channeling my most bubbly, upbeat self.

I stepped into the living room, bracing myself for the night ahead.

"You look nice," he observed, pushing up from the couch and walking to the door.

"I was shooting for fall vibes," I said, running my hands down my sides, a nervous habit I'd been trying to break as I prepped for interviews. Nothing said "hire me" like fidgeting on a video call. Though this habit was a bit easier to hide than reaching to play with an invisible necklace.

"I'm not sure I know what that means. Is that when everything you eat, drink, and wear has been sprinkled with pixie dust from the pumpkin spice fairy?" Derek asked, pausing by the door.

"Something like that," I responded as I walked to the fall candle that had been burning on the kitchen counter. Closing my eyes, I considered for a moment.

I wish for a job and some direction for my life, preferably outside of Utah. I recited the words to myself before blowing out the flame, the smoke trailing up into the air and carrying my wish with it.

"You know, wishing on candles only counts for birthdays," Derek joked as he held the door, careful to keep Ruby from slipping outside.

"Says who?" I asked as I walked past him, pausing to lock the door once Derek had also stepped outside, my roommates having left while I was changing. I ignored the warmth coming off Derek, wrapping my arms around myself to fight off the chill.

"You're literally the only person I know who makes a wish on every candle she blows out," Derek said, leading the way down the stairs to his car.

"That's so sad. Think of all the wishes you're missing out on!" I wasn't the only person I knew who did it.

Memories danced across my mind of a bald head and arguments over whose turn it was to blow out the candles my mom lit around the house. Each remembered image was filled with a girl who had a near-identical grin to mine, but I pushed the memories down, locking them safely away in the emotional box I tried to keep closed. That road down memory lane was full of pain and tears I did my best to avoid. Some things were better left in the past.

The night outside was dark, the cool air making me shiver and distracting me from memories I didn't want to think about. Too much colder and I'd need a coat every time I left the house.

Derek unlocked his car, and I climbed in, immediately adjusting the seat so that it wasn't leaning all the way back.

"Looks like you've spent time with Axle lately." I gestured at the seat. Left unsaid were the reasons why Derek's brother Axle would be in Derek's car: hospital visits, running errands for their dad, vent sessions when the emotions became too much.

"Only the two of you could fight over something as insignificant as how far back to lean the passenger seat." Derek pulled out of the parking lot, turning towards Tara's house.

"He started it! Who needs to lean back that far? Is he taking a nap every time he rides in your car?" I asked. I had been waging war against Derek's brother for control of the passenger seat position for as long as I'd known him. At six feet, three inches tall, Axle claimed he'd hit his head on the ceiling if the seat wasn't leaned all the way back. At just over five feet tall, I tended to think his adjustments were excessive. I personally liked to see where I was going when riding in a car.

"Is it really that hard to adjust the seat?" Derek's voice was laced with humor as he asked the familiar question. We'd had this discussion repeatedly over the years.

"It's the principle of the matter." I shrugged. "At this point, the only thing that can resolve it is death."

"Should I be worried this thing will escalate until you murder my brother? I mean, I get that he can be annoying, but murder seems excessive." Derek's jaw twitched as if fighting back a smile.

"Orange really isn't my color, so murder is unlikely. Though not having to worry about finding a job and paying rent could be a nice benefit of prison," I said, doing my best to keep a straight face, even as the corner of my mouth tipped upward.

"Ah yes, the color orange. The reason most people avoid committing crimes."

Our banter continued, and I relaxed into the comfortable rhythm. With the heater finally warmed up, I could stay in Derek's car the rest of the night, riding around, the city outside my window a blur of lights. Here my job woes and family drama didn't exist. I hoped Derek's worries could also fade for a couple hours tonight.

All too soon we reached Tara's place, a two-story house built sometime in the 90s. If I hadn't known which house was Tara's, the yard full of Halloween decorations, including two giant skeletons, would have been a dead giveaway.

I stepped onto the curb and paused, taking a moment to remind myself I liked these people and wanted to spend time with them. Normally I was a social person, eager and ready for the next party or adventure. But lately, the thought of socializing felt exhausting. It was one too many things in a never-ending list of expectations.

I self-consciously glanced down at my outfit, smoothing my hands down the front. Deciding the jacket was too much, I slipped it off and stashed it in Derek's car, braving the cold in the name of fashion.

"Are you sure I look okay? Maybe I should have gone with a flannel or a graphic tee, something to really show the Halloween spirit." I didn't own any Halloween shirts, but that was beside the point. Maybe I could have borrowed one from Mallory and her stash of holiday attire that only an elementary school teacher would own.

Derek shook his head. "If you're underdressed, what does that say about me?"

It was only then I realized that, without my jacket, we matched. All Derek was missing was the elbow patches and we could have been twins.

A laugh escaped as I shook my head. "What are the chances?"

"Probably higher than you think since you cheated and saw my ensemble before picking your own." Derek winked at me before following me up the stairs. "If anyone asks, I'm going to tell them we're going to a dance together. What's the one where you wear a matching shirt with your date? Sadie Hawkins? Harvest? Homecoming?"

I shrugged. "I didn't go to any high school dances, so I have no idea. Though I'm pretty sure homecoming is formal."

"You know, one of these days you're going to tell me why you never went to dances. You're too pretty and fun for no one to have asked you out. Either that or all the guys you went to school with were exceptionally dumb," he said, making me laugh.

"Maybe I just never wanted to go." I hedged, biting my lip and playing into the lighter tone Derek had set with his teasing.

Derek grabbed his chest, gasping in mock outrage, accepting my answer at face value without pushing. That was part of why I'd let Derek as close as I had. He never pushed, he just accepted that there were parts of my life I didn't want to talk about, and he left the door open for me to share if I ever changed my mind.

"Never wanted to go? That's a tragedy! We have to fix this right now. Back to the car. We're finding a mediocre high school dance for you to crash, complete with awkward slow songs and tacky streamers. Otherwise, your life will never be complete," he said, doing his best to school his features into a serious expression. But even in the dim light of Tara's front porch, I could see a smile trying to break through.

I draped my hand across my forehead, assuming a dramatic pose as I leaned against the doorframe. "You're right! How have I survived this long? My life will forever be haunted by not getting asked to a mediocre high school dance."

The door opened, startling a shriek from me as I stumbled into Tara's entryway, just barely avoiding falling to the floor.

Tara stood there, holding the door open and wearing the perfect yellow flannel, her face pinched in a confused expression. "I thought I heard voices. What are you guys doing outside? Everyone's in the living room."

She waved down the hall where I could hear chatter from several people, soft music playing in the background.

"We were discussing high school dances and how essential they are to the growth and development of a young teen," Derek said without missing a beat, his face and tone serious. Though I didn't miss the wink he cast my way.

Tara shrugged, her curly brown hair bouncing with the movement. "Maybe, though my dance experience left me more self-conscious than developed. But who knows? I went to prom with the kid next door who still picked his nose when no one was looking, so maybe it was better for everyone else."

"That's fair. Do you think Chloe and I look dance ready?" Derek asked, pulling me into a side hug.

"Definitely! Though casual dances are usually girl's choice. Did you pop the question, Chloe?" Tara asked with a quirk of her eyebrow before she gestured for us to follow her into the kitchen. Her quick wit and easy conversation were part of the reason she and I had become friends at a concert last year. They were also part of why I'd pushed so hard for her and Derek to date.

"Careful," I muttered under my breath, grabbing Derek and forcing him to hang back with me. "You don't want to make Tara jealous."

"You don't have to worry about Tara. We decided we're better as friends. Besides, I think she's going to give things with Kevin a go."

"That's too bad," I said, the words tasting disingenuous at the combination of relief and disappointment I felt. If Derek wasn't dating Tara, I had one less reason to give people for why we weren't dating. "Tara and Kevin? That's an interesting combination."

I tried picturing Tara, the bubbly schoolteacher, with Kevin, the stoic former-football player, but couldn't quite make the pair fit in my head.

"Hope it works for them. I'm sorry that leaves you back at square one, but I know you. You won't be single for long. Has anyone else caught your eye?" I nudged Derek with my elbow, ignoring the twinge in my stomach that came with the thought of Derek dating someone else. It was a sensation I'd started experiencing more and more of late, and I wasn't quite sure what to do about it. I'd spent the last seven years tamping down any and all potential feelings for Derek to the point that simply considering changing that practice felt ridiculous. Yet, a part of me couldn't help but wonder what would happen if I took the risk and gave into something I'd been fighting since freshman year of college.

Derek shrugged, leading the way down the hall to the party. "Maybe, but I don't think she sees me that way." His voice held a hint of sadness.

"Her loss," I said, following him into a cozy open-concept kitchen and living room decked out in Halloween décor. "Maybe you'll get lucky and meet someone tonight."

"What if I don't want to meet someone else?" Derek's words were so quiet, I wasn't sure he meant to say them out loud. And yet I couldn't unhear the longing behind every syllable as I joined our friends.

Chapter Three

THE PARTY WAS ALREADY in full swing when we entered the kitchen. People stood in clusters talking while a group on the couch played a game that involved the TV and their phones. I recognized most of the people present, though there were a few new faces in the mix.

Someone called Derek's name, and I found myself standing alone in the kitchen, absorbing the scene and trying to decide who to talk to first.

The number of Halloween decorations Tara had managed to add to the space was impressive. Paper bats hung from the ceiling and fall foliage draped the cabinets, giving the whole party a fun, cozy vibe. An essential oil diffuser sat on the counter, emitting an aroma that smelled delightfully like fall with hints of clove and cinnamon along with other scents I couldn't identify.

"I was starting to think you two got lost in the hall. Trying to squeeze in a different high school experience?" Tara waggled her eyebrows and made a kissing face.

I shook my head, my cheeks heating at the thought of making out with Derek. The mantra that we were only friends was losing its bite, especially now that I knew he and Tara weren't a thing.

"We just wanted to make a grand entrance," I winked, trying to take control of the conversation before Tara could get any ideas. "We're friends."

"You forget I've been on dates with the man. I don't think he'd mind if you gave him a chance at something more than friends," Tara said, leaning against the counter.

"You're reading too much into it." I shook my head, perhaps a little too emphatically.

"Why haven't the two of you ever dated?" Tara asked, her expression filled with curiosity.

It was a question I normally brushed off with a quip about how we were better off friends, but my current life struggles had me feeling open and vulnerable.

I fiddled with my sweater sleeve. "The timing was never right. One of us was always dating someone and then we just reached a point where being friends was easier and more comfortable."

"He's not dating anyone now," Tara said, gesturing toward Derek who stood with a group of guys, his head thrown back with laughter. "And last time I checked, you were also single."

My stomach gave a funny twist at the thought of Derek and I giving being more than friends a shot.

"I'm moving out of state as soon as I find a job. It's better to just stay friends." I persisted, shaking my head.

She studied my face for a moment before accepting my response.

"Fine, but you're still here right now. And, while things didn't work out between me and him, he's genuinely a good guy who will make someone very happy." She gave me a significant look before a mischievous grin stole across her features. "Just promise me, if you ever do decide to let that man out of the friendzone, I'm the first person you call."

I sputtered, not sure how to respond to the comment.

Tara laughed at my expression and nudged me towards the table, where an assortment of finger foods waited, arranged on a bright orange tablecloth. "Fine, no more dating talk. Go eat something. I made too much food and do not need all these leftovers."

Accepting the easy out from the conversation, I walked to the table and grabbed a plate despite not really being hungry. I took in the spread, debating if I wanted anything from the veggie platter or if I'd rather go straight for the chips and less healthy options when I felt someone standing behind me.

"It's kind of overwhelming, figuring out where to start." The voice was deep, with a nice rumble that immediately snagged my attention. I looked up and up and up, before finally finding the prettiest pair of blue eyes I'd ever seen. They were light and piercing. Combined with his thick, dark hair and an infectious smile, the guy reminded me of Zac Efron from his *High School Musical* days.

I'll be your Gabriella Montez. The thought flashed through my mind before I could fully process it. I could immediately picture me and this man peer pressured into a New Years karaoke number. Forget that this was a Halloween party. Maybe we could do Halloween karaoke. Was that a thing? More importantly, did I know all the words to the "Monster Mash"?

"Hi. I'm Chloe." I stuck out my hand for a handshake and inwardly cringed. Who shook hands at a party?

He took my proffered hand without hesitation, giving it a gentle squeeze. He seemed to hold on a bit longer than necessary, and warmth shot up my arm into my cheeks. If this was what a meet-cute looked like, I was fully on board. Who knew finger foods could be romantic?

"Nate. Nice to meet you." His voice was deep and rich, the kind perfect for narrating my favorite romance audiobooks, and I felt my legs turn a bit to jelly at the sound.

He had the best smile, perfect white teeth flashing and contrasting nicely with tan skin. I got lost in his eyes for just a moment, scrambling to think of what to say next. I really was out of practice if I couldn't find words to follow an introduction. Normally, I could flirt with the best of them, but right now my pulse was racing, my cheeks flushing, and I had no words.

Instead, my brain decided to continue pondering on our perfect musical number. Now that I knew he had a deep speaking voice, I could do better than the "Monster Mash." Unfortunately, the only other Halloween song currently coming to mind was "The Purple People Eater" and if there was any song less sexy than the "Monster Mash" it had to be that one.

"And I'm Derek." Another hand pushed its way between us, forcing me to let go of Nate's hand. I turned to find Derek standing just behind me, his lips forming a firm line, no dimple in sight.

I'd been so absorbed pondering which musical number would best accompany this moment that I'd missed Derek coming to join me. Nate gave Derek's hand a quick, firm shake before turning back to me.

"I don't think I've seen you before at Tara's parties. I definitely would have remembered," I said, pulling out my best flirty smile. Too bad I didn't have long hair. I could have really used a hair flip right about now.

Nate shrugged. "I just moved to the area. I knew Tara growing up and definitely wormed my way into an invite. She's my only hope if I'm going to make friends while living in Utah for the next six months."

My ears perked up at the clearly short timeline. A move with an end date meant he was likely looking for something temporary and fun. Both things I could do.

"Lucky us!" I said, batting my eyelashes and trying my best to convey just how interested I was in turning this conversation into something more. Preferably something that involved just the two of us. "What brought you to Utah?"

"Work," Nate said, his arm brushing mine as he reached past me for a cookie. Was that on purpose or an accident? Either way, I could work with it. He smelled divine and I wanted to lean in, try to identify his musky scent.

"Sorry, let me get out of your way." I said, resting my fingers on his arm and pretending to take a step back.

"You're not in my way. I like exactly where you are." Nate tossed me a slow grin and my insides somersaulted.

"What do you do for work?" Derek asked, jostling me from behind as he reached for his own cookie. The motion forced me to take an awkward step to the side, breaking my contact with Nate.

While I would be lost without Derek's friendship, I wouldn't mind if he got lost right now. Couldn't he see I was making a move? We needed to work on his wingman skills.

"I work in cybersecurity. My company just opened an office here and asked me to come out and get things off the ground," Nate said, with a nonchalance that made it sound as if his move for work wasn't a big deal, but it sounded like a big deal to me. I would love to have a job where they trusted me enough to open a new location.

Of course, I would love to have a job, period.

"What exactly does that entail?" Derek leaned a hip against the counter, clearly settling in for a long conversation.

Derek continued in that vein of questioning, asking details about Nate's job and hobbies. So much for my plan to test the waters with Nate and lay the groundwork for a fling.

I bit back a groan, wishing I could nudge Derek out of the way. While I was grateful to learn more about Nate, I would be able to ask him those questions later if I could get his phone number. It would be even better if I could get him to ask me out.

I tuned out Derek and Nate's conversation, trying to think of a way to steer Nate's attention back to me. Biting my lip, I considered my options. Maybe if I spilled something on his shirt, I could use it as an excuse to help him get cleaned up. Learn how firm his chest was. Though knowing my luck, Derek would step in to help, producing a stain remover pen out of thin air.

Twist an ankle? Not really feasible since I was holding still. Reach past him for my own cookie? That would put me closer to Derek than Nate. Fake a fainting spell and aim myself right at his chest? Seemed a bit extreme and probably wouldn't leave him with the best impression.

Coming up blank, I refocused on the exchange in front of me.

"I'm actually having a group over to my place for a movie tomorrow night. You guys interested?" Nate asked, his eyebrow quirked in invitation. "Another chance to celebrate Halloween."

I placed a hand on Nate's arm, giving it a gentle squeeze as I smiled. I could definitely work with a movie night.

"Absolutely! I love all things fall. A movie sounds perfect, especially if there's popcorn." I also wouldn't complain if some type of pumpkin spice beverage was available.

"I can make popcorn happen." Nate shot me a grin that made my toes curl and had visions of snuggling during a movie dancing through my head. "If I can snag your numbers, I'll text you the details."

I schooled my features, doing my best not to show my excitement as I rattled off my number. Maybe this exchange wouldn't be a complete bust after all. He then took Derek's number as well. While the invite might not be for a date, like I'd hoped, at least I'd have a chance to see Nate again before the week was out. Not too shabby for a party I'd considered bailing on earlier.

I poured myself a glass of diet Coke, adding a lime zest packet and taking a satisfied swig as I watched Nate walk away and join another cluster of people. The view from behind was almost as good as the front.

Derek muttered something about needing the restroom, a strange expression on his face that I brushed off, certain it was concern for his dad and some of the emotions from his day playing out now that he had some down time. I refused to think that it could be anything else, even as my many conversations with my roommates about Derek played through my head. There was no way the frustration on his face had anything to do with me. No matter how many times my friends pointed out Derek's interest, he and I were meant to stay friends.

Not liking where my thoughts were headed, I scanned the room, catching Tara's eye and waving her over. I snagged her arm as she got close, pulling her in. I needed information about my new acquaintance, and I hoped Tara could deliver.

"What's the story with Nate? Tell me everything." I whispered.

"Isn't he adorable? If I'd known the obnoxious kid down the street would grow up into that hunk, I would have reconnected with him sooner. Though he's got nothing on Kevin, he's definitely one of the cutest guys here." She gave a small sigh, clearly distracted by Kevin who was playing the game with the group on the couch.

I jostled her arm, needing her to focus for a moment. I needed information now if I was going to use the movie night tomorrow to my advantage.

Tara took in my expression and gave a small laugh.

"You interested in Nate? At the moment, he's very much single." Tara wiggled her eyebrows suggestively. "Though he'll only be here for a few months."

"He's gorgeous! And can actually hold a conversation without constantly checking his phone." I gushed. It was a low bar, to be sure, but dating in the twenty-first century came with its own set of challenges.

"You talked to him for maybe three minutes," Derek interrupted, having returned from the restroom. His expression was still stormy. "Give him a few more minutes and I'm sure he'll prove himself to be human."

I waved Derek's comments away, not wanting him to bring reality crashing in just yet. I didn't need a relationship with a foundation that could stand the test of time. Just a decent enough guy who would be down for a good time until I found a job and moved away.

"Good thing I'll see him again tomorrow night. It'll give him the chance to prove you wrong." I lifted my glass to my lips, letting the carbonation and caffeine work their magic while I daydreamed of snuggling with Nate while watching something cozy. He probably wasn't a Hallmark fan, but that didn't mean he wouldn't be up for suggestions.

The car ride home was quiet as I relished my victory. Forget about my family and my failed job hunt. Not only had I been in fine flirting form, but I gave my number to a guy I was interested in, and he'd already texted me the details about the movie night. It had been months since someone had caught my attention like Nate had, and I was going to enjoy every moment. I could picture it now, our story laid out like a movie montage. We'd hit it off watching the movie, flirting the whole time and driving everyone else nuts as we talked. Maybe we'd grab hot chocolate afterwards, turning the night into a date. Next he'd invite me over to carve pumpkins, which would result in a flirty and only mildly disgusting pumpkin guts fight that would end with a toe-curling kiss. I could all but hear the Andy Grammer soundtrack playing in the background as each movie-worthy moment played through my mind.

Then, once I found a job, we'd say goodbye and move on with our lives. The perfect mix of romantic and no-strings-attached.

"Nate seems cool," Derek observed, bringing my daydreams to a halt. "Though I'm surprised you wanted to join for the movie night. Since when do you watch horror?"

I nearly did a spit take, sans liquid. "Horror? What do you mean, horror?"

Derek adjusted the temperature on the dashboard. "I'm not sure if they've picked a slasher movie or something more psychological, but they're definitely watching a horror movie. Nate was talking about it right before he invited us." He glanced at me, taking in my reaction. "Though clearly you weren't paying attention."

"Derek, that's not funny. You know I don't do scary." I crossed my arms over my chest, my seatbelt digging into my neck as I turned to glare at him.

Derek raised a hand as if taking an oath. "I'm not the one planning this thing. I'm just sharing what I know. It's not my fault you slipped into one of your daydreams while we were standing there."

"But . . ." I trailed off, not sure how to finish the sentence. Looking out my window, I watched the streetlights blurring outside the car as we drove closer to my apartment. I'd been so absorbed in my thoughts while Derek and Nate had been talking that I'd somehow missed a critical detail. I did romances. If I was feeling particularly brave, I might even give action or adventure a try. But I wasn't built for horror. Just the thought of watching a scary movie sent my pulse racing.

"Don't worry. I'm sure Nate will understand you backing out," Derek said, casting me a soft, knowing look when I stayed quiet for too long.

My hackles rose, my defensiveness immediately triggered at Derek's kindly meant comment. Too many people had been telling me what to do lately, and I was not adding him to that list. From my mom telling me what jobs to apply for to my friends telling me I should stay in Utah and everything in between, everywhere I turned there was someone with well-intentioned advice trying to direct my life. I was tired of it.

"Who said anything about backing out?" I asked, schooling my features into a neutral mask, even as my pulse pounded in my ears.

"Cee, you hate all things scary. Watching Scooby Doo with my nephews puts you on edge. Why on earth would you want to watch a horror movie with a guy you just met?" His tone was filled with incredulity.

Freaking out while babysitting Derek's nephews when his sister was in town was not one of my finest moments. Who knew cartoon zombies could be so scary? But that was beside the point. There was an opportunity to flirt with a cute guy on the line. I was not giving up this chance to pursue something good in my life right now—not when I felt like I was failing at everything else.

And maybe Nate would think a girl snuggling into his side and hiding her face for an entire movie was attractive and not clingy. Terror could be cute, right?

"Maybe I'm turning over a new leaf. Nothing in my life is changing by watching exclusively chick flicks. Perhaps it's time I try something new." I tried for a nonchalant tone as I clenched my hands into fists in my lap to keep them from fidgeting, pretending this movie was something I wanted to watch. In reality, my stomach twisted at the thought of spending hours watching some psychotic monster chasing and murdering unsuspecting people.

"Since when?" Derek's voice was full of skepticism, his face pinched in concern.

"Since right now. Starting this Halloween, I'm going to be brave and do all the haunted things I'm invited to." I forced a level of bravado into my voice that I definitely did not feel.

Derek pulled into the parking lot outside my building, turning to face me as he removed the keys from the ignition. I knew the words were a mistake as soon as they escaped my mouth, and his quirked eyebrow confirmed it.

"Want to bet?"

With those three words, I knew I was in trouble. I'd been making bets with Derek almost from the moment we met. It had started simple, one calling the other's bluff with silly things like asking for someone's phone number or trying a new ice cream flavor. Slowly the stakes and bets had escalated, leading us to this moment where I was going to have to commit to attending all things scary for the rest of October.

I'd never backed out of one of our bets and I couldn't start now. Losing would mean I'd owe Derek a favor of his choosing, and the last time I'd lost, he'd made me run a 5k with him. I felt the ghost pain of shin splints just thinking about it. I refused to give him the satisfaction of winning another bet. At this point it was a matter of pride.

Forcing down my hesitation, I nodded. "Absolutely. Usual terms?"

A slow smile stole across Derek's face, making my stomach clench in dread. "Just to clarify, you can't refuse any invitation you receive to a scary activity from now until Halloween?"

I swallowed, my throat suddenly dry.

"Unless I already have other plans," I qualified, though that exception wasn't much of a cop-out. With my unemployed status and my roommates in full twitterpated mode, I currently had no plans beyond finishing *Pride and Prejudice* with a diet Coke and my own carton of Ben and Jerry's ice cream.

"I can work with that," Derek said, clearly enjoying this moment far too much.

He stuck out his hand and I gripped it in mine, praying my October wasn't about to become significantly worse. "Deal."

Now I just had to come up with a lot of non-scary plans for the next two weeks. Piece of cake.

Chapter Four

THE NEXT NIGHT, I pulled up in front of Nate's house and took a deep breath, smoothing my hands down the floral blouse and wide-legged jeans I'd spent way too much time picking out. I may or may not have landed on flowers because chances of me accidently matching Derek were near zero with the bright pink and purple floral print, even if it didn't give off fall vibes.

The house I'd parked in front of was new construction in a beautiful area near the foothills of the mountains in Pleasant Grove. The smattering of Halloween decorations covering the front lawn told me I had the right house. Nate and Tara apparently had the same decorating tastes. From a series of fake tombstones that contrasted with the blue siding to an inflatable ghost dancing in the breeze, it was abundantly clear Nate had a favorite holiday.

"That's *not* a deal-breaker," I muttered to myself as I climbed the porch steps past some jack-o'-lanterns that erred more on the side of creepy as opposed to cute. "Especially not for a relationship that will only last a couple of months at most."

I paused on the top step, hesitating to knock as I considered what awaited me on the other side of the unassuming white door. I could do this. I could watch a scary movie and not embarrass myself by screaming like a child at the first sign of a monster or bad guy. Or maybe I could convince them they didn't actually want to watch a scary movie. *Casper* would make a good alternative.

I was so absorbed in my thoughts, muttering encouragements to myself as I lifted my hand to knock, I didn't hear someone come up behind me.

"Talking to yourself again, Chloe?"

I jumped and whirled around with a small shriek, my hand coming to rest on my chest. I could feel my heart pounding a million miles a minute and I hadn't even gotten to the scary part of the night yet. I spotted Derek walking up the driveway as I tried to take deep breaths to calm my racing heart. He wore jeans and a hoodie, making him look relaxed and comfortable. If I'd worn the same outfit, I would have looked like a slob who'd given up on life. While my repeated failed attempts to land a job outside Utah pushed me closer and closer to that reality, I hadn't given up yet. At least not tonight.

Of course, tomorrow morning when I was dressed in sweats with wild hair searching for employment, Derek would be in slacks and a polo, climbing the corporate ladder as an accountant. That was the difference between me and Derek. He had his life put together, graduating from college with honors in just four years and landing a job immediately after graduation. I, on the other hand, had taken seven years to get a bachelor's degree because I couldn't pick a major and went on an impromptu study abroad partway through my third year.

"Talking out loud helps me process information," I said, sticking out my tongue at him as I walked to the edge of the porch to wait for him.

"Is that why you do it everywhere?" He asked, humor filling his tone.

"I don't do it everywhere," I huffed, my racing heart forgotten as I defended myself. I rested my hands on my hips, pretending it looked intimidating. In all likelihood it made me look like a child throwing a fit. One of the many perks of being vertically challenged. But the pose made me *feel* intimidating, which had to count for something.

"Just the grocery store, your car, Target, in front of near stranger's houses." Derek stopped a stair below me, making us nearly eye-level with each other.

"Nate's not a stranger," I said, shaking my head. It was a weak defense, but I could only pick one battle at a time, and my potential short-term love interest had to take precedence over my tendency to mutter to myself. At least for today.

"I said 'near stranger.' If he was a complete stranger, I'd be worried," Derek said, leaning in close enough I could feel his warmth.

Not sure how to respond, I took a small step back to put distance between us and changed the topic.

"I didn't think you'd be here. I know scary movies aren't really your thing," I said with false confidence.

He shrugged, crossing his arms over his chest in a stance that oozed confidence. "I had to make sure you didn't back out on our bet."

"And miss out on a chance to have you owe me a favor? Not a chance. I can't wait to make you watch *Pride and Prejudice* with me. I'm thinking we'll do pedicures at the same time, really go for girls' night vibes." I channeled all the bravado I didn't feel as I led the way to the front door, Derek's footsteps sounding on the cement patio as he followed me.

I pretended my insides weren't twisting themselves into knots at the thought of watching a horror movie. I reached to ring the doorbell, but hesitated before my finger could make contact. The breeze outside brought with it a chill that, under normal circumstances, I'd be eager to escape by rushing inside. But not knowing what awaited on the other side of the door gave me pause.

Nate's texts about the evening had lacked details about the movie we'd be watching, though I highly doubted it would be something more my speed like *Young Frankenstein* or *Hocus Pocus*. To be fair, those movies also made me jump. Especially *Hocus Pocus*. The Sanderson sisters were terrifying.

Derek gave a small chuckle before reaching around me to ring the doorbell.

"How long are you going to keep this up? I know how you feel about all things scary." He whispered in my ear. His breath tickled my neck, causing my arms to break out in goose bumps. It wasn't an entirely unpleasant sensation, which I did my best to ignore.

"Nate said it was more intense than scary. I can do intense," I said, stubbornly crossing my arms over my chest and glaring at my friend over my shoulder. Nate had said no such thing, but maybe if I manifested it hard enough, it would be true.

"I know you can do intense, but I also know you don't particularly like to. Remember, I've watched *The Hunger Games* movies with you."

"Those are literally movies about kids trying to kill each other. They're meant to make you jump," I said, turning around and poking him in the chest to emphasize my point. Had his chest always felt this warm and firm? Muscles I hadn't realized Derek possessed left me questioning what exactly he did with his spare time away from me and his job when he wasn't helping his dad.

"We've also watched the Harry Potter movies. Not to mention a handful of Marvel movies. Intensity is not your friend." Derek took a step forward, getting into my space and forcing me to drop my finger.

"Maybe I've developed a recent appreciation for intense movies." I persisted, refusing to give in and let Derek win the argument. "You don't know how I spend all my time." Something about Derek always brought out my petulant side. A side of myself I didn't feel comfortable showing most people.

"I mean, that's always a possibility, but I also know you try to leave the room whenever Ursula comes on in *The Little Mermaid*, so I'm gonna guess things haven't changed that much." Derek stepped back to lean against the porch railing, relieving the electricity that had been building between us. He smirked as he gauged my reaction. "Not that I'm complaining. All of this is just working to my benefit. I'm thinking I need someone to bake pies for Thanksgiving, and you know how I am in the kitchen. Dad really wants fruit pies this year." He paused for effect. "From scratch."

Before I could respond, Nate pulled the door open, a giant grin stretching across his face. "Come in! I'm so glad you guys could make it."

Nate's hair was mussed, and he wore a faded blue t-shirt that did excellent things for his arms and chest. Though to be fair, most shirts would do wonderful things for a physique like his. His muscles were not secret muscles that required chest poking to discover. The man could wear an Uncle Sam costume to sell mattresses on the side of the road and still look good.

We followed Nate into the house, and I paused, taking in the clean white walls, tasteful décor, and vinyl floors. If Mallory were with me, she'd be salivating at the well-lit entryway and open concept first floor with its high ceilings. The space could have featured in a home show.

"Wow! Your house is..." I trailed off, at a loss to describe what I was seeing. This did not look like a bachelor's house.

"Is it too much? My mom and sisters helped me decorate. I always worry that it's over the top, but I'm also lazy and hate furniture shopping," Nate said, rubbing the back of his neck and ducking his head. "Besides, it's a rental so I needed stuff that I could easily resell after my six months are up."

"Maybe a little—" Derek started, but I cut him off.

"Not at all! It's beautiful. So homey. It feels like a magazine." I assured, gushing as we walked down the stairs.

"Glad you approve." Nate gave me a wink and a wide grin, clearly appreciating my approval. "Though downstairs is more my speed." Nate waved us towards the basement. "A couple of the guys came over early to play video games, so everyone's down there waiting for us."

The upstairs and downstairs could not have been more different. While the upstairs was tasteful artwork, fluffy rugs, and couches that looked like they'd just been delivered, the basement looked like someone spent all their money on the TV and gaming consoles, which were clearly top of the line. In contrast, the couches gave distinct secondhand vibes, looking like they were rescued from curbs and thrift stores.

"It looks . . . well-loved," I said, the words I really wanted to say stuck in my throat. This resembled the bachelor's pad I'd been anticipating. All that was missing was crumpled up food wrappers and it would be a direct throwback to some of my guy friends' college apartments.

"Make yourselves comfortable."

Derek immediately settled onto one of the couches next to one of Nate's friends, but I paused a moment, taking in the setting and my seating options while Nate continued talking.

"This movie is one of my favorites. Chloe, you can sit by . . ." He trailed off, seeming to notice for the first time that there were only two couch spots left and, much to my dismay, they were not on the same couch.

Two guys and a girl I vaguely recognized from Tara's party sat on the couch closest to Nate, leaving the only open spot a seat on the other couch next to Derek.

"I guess you can sit by Derek. Though I was hoping to hear your thoughts on the movie. It's definitely a classic!"

I made a noncommittal sound as Nate sat down. I hesitated a moment longer before making my way to the other couch.

A scuffed coffee table littered with miscellaneous snack foods sat in front of the couches, eliminating the option to sit on the floor in front of Nate's couch. Not that I wanted to spend the duration of the movie on the floor, but if it meant I could be close to Nate, it could have been worth it.

"Sorry Nate won't be able to comfort you when the monsters jump out," Derek whispered as I settled in next to him. Nate hit play on the movie and the opening scene filled the TV screen.

"Quiet, I'm trying to watch the movie." I shushed, my cheeks flushing at the possibility someone might have overheard Derek's comment.

The other occupant of our couch, a guy with a blond ponytail wearing a slasher movie t-shirt, appeared too engrossed in his phone to notice our existence, let alone our conversation. But you could never be too careful. I'd played the dating game long enough to know seemingly innocuous conversations could come back to bite you if you weren't careful.

"I'll keep my commentary on your lack of dating life to a minimum," Derek muttered under his breath.

"That's all I really ask," I whispered back.

A shriek from the TV made me jump, pulling me back to my present dilemma. I'd committed to watching a scary movie to impress a guy. A guy who, if one glance at Nate was any indication, couldn't care less about my presence as he grinned and muttered something to one of his buddies, elbowing him in the ribs. At least Nate had wanted to sit by me, even if it hadn't worked out. It was a tiny positive note that told me I hadn't completely misread the interest in Nate's eyes the night before.

"More into intense movies, huh?" Derek asked, nudging me with his shoulder and pulling me from my thoughts.

"It just takes me a moment to warm up," I muttered, scooting into the arm of the couch in an effort to put as much space between myself and the TV as possible. As if that would make any difference. There were still scary creatures filling the screen, and a couple of hours standing between me and the opportunity to leave without losing my bet with Derek.

Though if I escaped partway through to use the bathroom and didn't come back until the credits started rolling, did that count as bailing? Because the images on the TV screen had me genuinely considering that option.

Derek studied me for a moment, his expression shifting from teasing to concerned. "You know you don't have to—"

He broke off when I jumped, closing my eyes when another shriek came from the TV. I wasn't completely sure what was happening, something involving monsters and lots of running, but the sounds coming from the TV had me convinced this movie was definitely more scary than intense.

I felt the couch cushion next to me dip and I peeked an eye open to see Derek settling in closer to me, his presence providing much needed reassurance.

"Don't worry. I'll protect you from the monsters," Derek said quietly, draping a reassuring arm around my shoulders.

"Promise?" I asked, curling into the comforting warmth of his side. We often sat like this when watching movies on my couch, making it feel natural to sink into the position, his familiar scent adding to the comfort.

"What else are best friends for?" Derek asked, a note of something I couldn't identify in his voice. It almost sounded like longing, but I couldn't focus on figuring it out right now.

I closed my eyes and relaxed under Derek's arm, pretending not to notice how his warmth made my heart race in a way that had nothing to do with the movie in front of me. Maybe if I didn't watch, the monsters wouldn't get me. I just had to be careful I didn't settle too close to Derek. I didn't want anyone getting the wrong idea. After all, I had a guy to impress. Just as soon as the movie was over and horrible sounds were no longer coming out of the TV speakers.

Chapter Five

"Time to wake up, Sleeping Beauty. All the monsters have been vanquished." The voice calling to me was accompanied by gentle shaking. I fought against the wake-up call for a moment, reveling in how comfortable I felt. I was in a warm, manly-scented cocoon and I did not want to leave.

Other voices and shuffling sounds drew my attention, and I sat up with a start, nearly knocking my head into Derek's chin.

"Watch it!" Derek said, laughter lacing his tone as he leaned away from me, trying to dodge flailing arms as I disentangled myself from his side. At some point, he'd draped a blanket around me, making it difficult to push up from the couch and act like nothing had happened.

No one, Nate in particular, would think we were more than friends, right? It was an innocent accident, nothing more. Friends could sleep on friends' shoulders. It was a totally normal thing.

"Look who decided to join the land of the living! You totally missed out on a classic," Nate said with a wink, coming over to my couch and offering me a hand up. Miraculously, the blanket cooperated, and I stood with ease. I resisted the urge to run my hand over my face, not wanting to draw attention to smudged makeup and mussed hair. Pixie cuts and naps rarely played nicely with each other.

"Guess my survival instincts kicked in. Instead of fight or flight, I sleep." I joked, forcing a laugh and hoping Nate would find the humor in the moment too.

He laughed along with me, slinging an arm around my shoulder as if I'd made a good joke. It was more of a gesture between buddies, but I welcomed it and the chance it gave me to finally connect with Nate. Tonight had not gone according to plan and I wasn't quite sure how to salvage it. None of my rom-coms had covered what to do when you fell asleep on the wrong guy while watching a movie.

"She's kind of like one of those fainting goats. One good scare and she's oblivious to the rest of the world." Derek came up behind me and I resisted the impulse to elbow him in the stomach. Just what every girl wanted, to be compared to a defenseless farm animal. He really was the worst wingman ever.

"Fainting goats can be cute." Nate grinned, dropping his arm and I felt a combination of joy and regret. He'd called me cute, but the lost contact and barnyard animal comparison were less than ideal when trying to convince someone they wanted to date me. "I will say, that survival mechanism is something I'd pay to see at a haunted corn maze. It would be worth it just to watch the employees scramble, figuring out how to react when you curled up in the corner for a nap while they're trying to chase you with chainsaws."

Everyone else chose that exact moment to pay attention to our conversation, joining in with jokes and laughter. My cheeks heated, but I played along with the gentle ribbing. If I knew anything about guys, it was that you had to be able to take their teasing.

"It's not a corn maze, but next week they have friends and family night at the Halloween lift ride." The blond guy who'd shared a couch with me and Derek said, his voice a deep, unexpected growl coming from his tall, lanky frame. "We should all go! James is doing it again this year and he said it's their creepiest year yet."

"Dude, that sounds amazing! Who's in?" Nate fairly vibrated with excitement at the possibility.

A glance around the room showed that everyone present was up for the adventure. Derek was the only one who seemed the least bit hesitant, but he quickly schooled his features when he noticed me looking his way. I bit my lip, pondering my options.

I hadn't specifically been invited, so it didn't count as going against the bet if I bowed out. I just had to make sure Derek didn't—

"You're coming too, aren't you, Chloe?" Nate turned bright blue eyes on me and I was helpless to say no, and not just because of the bet. Those baby blues could convince me to do just about anything. "I'm guessing this movie wasn't really your thing, but from what I've heard, the setting makes the lift ride worth it if nothing else." He quirked an eyebrow and I could have sworn I saw interest on his face despite my nap from earlier.

While the haunted part of the night sounded awful, the idea of taking a cozy lift ride with Nate while surrounded by mountains sounded very appealing.

I forced a smile, praying disappointment didn't show in my expression. "Of course, I'll be there."

Maybe I could fake an illness or something that night to get out of it. That wouldn't count against my bet with Derek, would it? I couldn't control if I was sick . . .

"You really are pulling out all the stops to impress this guy," Derek mumbled under his breath.

"Shush," I hissed back, as I pinched his side, making him flinch away from me. Nate had turned back to the others to solidify details for the lift ride, coordinating carpools. Hopefully no one else was paying attention to Derek and me. "People do crazy things for the potential of love." *And to keep from losing a bet.*

"Thanks Hercules, but you completely botched the quote. Not to mention I don't think he was talking about going out of your way to do things you hate. He was more talking about heroically giving your life for another person," Derek whispered back, stepping out of reach.

"Close enough," I shrugged, pretending like his observations didn't bother me. Though if faking weak ankles would get Nate's attention, I wasn't above trying it. I'd done worse to snag a guy's interest. Like taking a mountain biking class. I still had a scar on my elbow from a spill I'd taken, but the guy I'd been trying to date had been the one to patch me up, which had led to one of my best make-out sessions in college, so it had worked out.

"What night is the lift ride, again? I want to make sure I have it in my calendar." Derek spoke up, waving his phone, the calendar app open.

The group shared the time for meeting at the ski resort that hosted the lift ride in their off season.

"What are you doing? I thought you didn't want to come," I said as Derek entered the details into his phone, everyone else chatting around us and expressing their excitement for the outing. I wanted to snatch the device out of his hands and throw it across the room, anything to prevent Derek from furthering my purgatory.

"You literally just fell asleep in an effort not to watch a scary movie. Now you're committing to a haunted ski lift that includes monsters and witches after dark in the woods. I'm not missing this for the world," Derek said, stashing his phone in his pocket. He leaned over and snagged a handful of popcorn from the coffee table, his expression one of pure enjoyment.

Chapter Six

MONDAY FOUND ME SHOUTING at my computer in frustration. I'd received another round of rejection emails from potential employers. Most hadn't even bothered to give me an interview.

I rested my head on my desk, trying not to consider how much longer I could afford rent without a steady paycheck. Maybe if I started donating plasma again, I could make it work. Or I could look into doing food delivery. Just until I found a marketing or content development job out of state. Mostly I needed to find something that would keep me from moving back in with my parents. I'd moved out after high school and never looked back. I couldn't handle living under the same roof as my mom ever again.

My phone vibrated on the desk and I propped it up to look at the screen, not bothering to sit up. Expecting to find a text from my mom, I was surprised to see my brother's picture on the screen.

MAX: *Will you please tell Mom to let up? I'm going to a football game, not a rave. I'm seventeen. I can drive myself. Nothing's going to happen.*

I cringed, picturing the argument that had led to this moment. I had thought my role as referee between my mom and Max would end when

I moved out. Seven years later, and I was still playing peacemaker and trying to balance Max's determination to grow up and Mom's overprotective nature.

ME: *Can you ride with someone? You know she worries about you driving alone.*

MAX: *She worries about everything. If I ride with a friend, she'll worry if they're responsible enough to drive. You can't tell me she was this way before everything happened with Meg.*

I flinched, his words triggering a familiar ache in my heart. Leave it to Max to bring our dead sister into a conversation about his curfew and driving privileges. If he pulled the same card with Mom, it was no wonder I found myself in the middle of their arguments more often than not. Though to be fair, while Max had a tendency to push Mom's buttons, Mom had a tendency to overreact with punishments that didn't exactly match the crime. Such as the time she'd made Max help her clean out and reorganize the garage when he'd gotten a B on a test that she "knew he could have done better on."

I walked to my nightstand and grabbed the photo I kept in the drawer. Its scuffed silver frame and small size made it appear unimportant, but it was easily one of my most valuable possessions.

I studied the people in the frame, amazed as always that I was one of them. The people in the photo felt like strangers from another lifetime, as opposed to my family. A happy family of five sat in a living room wearing matching shirts in different jewel tones. Wide grins stretched across their faces, though the smiles couldn't quite hide the dark circles under my mom's eyes or the crinkles of worry in my dad's forehead. Us three kids clustered around our parents, oblivious to the changes that were lurking just a few short months away.

At the time, Max, the youngest, was in elementary school. His dark brown hair was shaggy, his smile wide, revealing missing teeth. He stood next to our dad, the men of the family filling the left side of the photo.

I was the middle child, the eight-year age gap between me and my brother evident in the contrast between his softened little kid features and my gangly teenaged frame that I was just growing into. I stood next to my mom, my smile holding a hint of self-consciousness. I was a sophomore in high school and had just gotten my driver's license. This was before I'd gotten brave and chopped my hair off into a pixie cut. Instead, it was styled in a bob that framed my face. A face that looked startlingly similar to that of the final sibling in the photo, despite the two-year age gap: Meg.

My sister had been the kind of person who others gravitated towards. People used to confuse us for twins, that is until the chemo stole her hair. In this photo she stood in the gap between our parents, a gray hat on her head, a tiredness in her eyes that I had come to expect that last year, especially towards the end.

I traced my fingers over the familiar faces, the accompanying pang of heartache reminding me why I kept this picture hidden. Not seeing it was easier than having the constant reminder in front of my face either from the picture itself or from the questions that always came when people saw Meg's lack of hair in the photo. And even though that time had been the hardest of my life, sometimes I wished I could go back. Tell myself to soak everything in, to write everything down, not realizing that in a few short years the details would fade from memory. If it wasn't for photos and videos, I feared I would forget more than just the daily details. Even now, I wasn't sure I'd be able to pick out her voice from a crowd, something I hated more than I could put into words.

So instead, I pushed the feelings down, keeping the photo in a drawer next to a matching silver box filled with mementos from Meg's last year, including the necklace that even now I was itching to pull out and put back on. The photo traveled with me everywhere I went: dorm rooms, apartments, vacations. But I never talked about it, keeping it tucked away in a drawer so that Meg was always close, but never up for discussion. It was a survival mechanism I'd developed in college, and it had worked for me so far, even if it meant keeping a big piece of my history and life from the friends I'd made since high school.

It wasn't so much that I hadn't wanted to tell them about Meg. It was more that talking about her hurt too much, and, instead of learning how to navigate the pain, I hid from it. Even now, my current friends and roommates had no idea about Meg.

I returned the photo to my nightstand, back where it belonged next to the silver box and slid the drawer shut on the photo and the emotions it brought to the surface. Life was hard enough without dwelling on the past.

ME: *This has nothing to do with Meg. I'll talk to Mom, but I make no promises.*

Deciding it was better to talk to Mom now instead of pushing the conversation off until later, I called her, pacing small circles around my room. Copies of favorite movie posters stared back at me from my walls as I waited. The phone rang twice before her familiar voice filled my ears.

"This is a pleasant surprise! How's the job hunt going?" Her voice sounded strained and breathless, making me think she was cleaning. Again. The mommy bloggers of the world could learn a thing or two from my mom and her obsession with cleanliness.

"It's going," I hedged, not wanting to open that can of worms. My life was not our topic of conversation for today. It wouldn't be our topic of conversation for a very long time if I had any say in the matter.

"You know, I'm sure your dad could put in a good word for you at his office. I heard they're looking for a new receptionist." A small grunt came through the line that I chose to ignore. I did not need a ten-minute discussion about the new all-purpose cleaner she'd discovered and how she was using it to deep clean the pantry.

"That job's not really what I'm looking for, Mom," I said, dragging my toes through the carpet as I continued to pace.

My parents couldn't wrap their minds around how I could possibly use my English degree for anything besides teaching. As a result, all their employment recommendations involved minimum wage jobs I could do without a degree and the writing and critical thinking skills I'd just spent thousands of dollars developing.

"I heard there are lots of positions open for substitute teachers right now. Could get your foot in the door, help you get experience so you can get a teaching certificate later." This statement was punctuated by some kind of screeching sound and a series of mumbled, four-letter words I was fairly certain she hadn't meant for me to hear.

"I'll consider it." I hedged, my voice coming out high-pitched and strained. I would have said almost anything to change the topic. "So Max texted." I rushed to get the words out before she could share another job suggestion.

The sudden quiet on my mom's end of the phone put me on guard as I waited for her response. I never knew how Mom would react when I broached these types of conversations. Usually, she was calm and even keel, listening to my logic. But every once in a while, especially if it was around holidays or certain anniversaries from Meg's life, Mom would be emotional, the wrong word leading to tears and monologues about the heaviness of life.

Finally, a sigh filtered through the phone, leaving me questioning which one of us was the parent in this relationship.

"Of course, he did."

"I just want to understand what's going on. Mom—"

"Before you start, you should know last time he 'just went to a football game' he was out past curfew because he went to a party afterward." The background cleaning noises resumed with vigor. "What if he'd gotten in a wreck on the way home? I wouldn't know where he was or why or—"

"Mom, you're spiraling." I cut in, hoping to bring logic in before she went too far down the panic rabbit hole. "Did any of those things happen?"

"No." This word sounded remarkably like it was spoken by a petulant child. I couldn't see her, but I could almost guarantee her arms were crossed over her chest and her expression pinched, a container of cleaner and a rag clutched under one arm.

"Did you already punish him for breaking the rules?"

"Yes." She gave a heavy sigh. "He was grounded for a month and had to deep clean the shed."

"How long ago did he do it? I haven't heard anything about him attending football games yet this school year." While I knew Max had a tendency to push his limits, I also knew my mom had a hard time letting go and forgetting past infractions. She didn't handle loss of control well.

"It was last year." She mumbled under her breath.

"Did he drink or do drugs or any other illegal activities?" I settled onto my bed as I listed each activity, my back pressed to the headboard.

"Not that I'm aware of." These words were spoken slowly, like she was confessing to a crime.

"So, if I'm understanding correctly, Max messed up a *year* ago, he was given consequences, and yet you're still holding it against him."

I waited a beat and when Mom didn't respond I continued.

"If it was me or Meg, would you have let us go?" My voice grew soft as I asked this last question, and I pushed away the memories the words attempted to invoke, doing my best to stay present. Pulling my pillow into my lap, I hugged it to my stomach for comfort as I waited for her response.

"You wouldn't have wanted to go." Mom pointed out. And while she wasn't wrong, those months spent hiding away from friends and activities after Meg's death were some of my biggest regrets. Something I more than compensated for with an overactive social life in college.

"That's not the point. If Meg had wanted to drive herself to the football game, even after breaking the rules the year before, would you have said yes?" I hated playing the Meg card, but I'd learned through the years that it was the only way to make Mom see reason when she got this way.

"Yes." The answer was barely audible, but as soon as she said it, I knew I'd won.

"Then why are you really telling Max no?" I closed my eyes, blocking out the world and the memories hovering on the edges of my mind.

The silence that followed my question was heavy with unspoken pain as I waited for her response. My fingers reached for my throat, wanting to fiddle with a necklace that wasn't there.

Finally, her voice rasped over the line. "Because he's the only baby I have left."

I knew what I wanted to say in response. That Max wasn't her only living child. I was still here too. But something had broken within her at Meg's death, and Mom had poured her whole heart into Max, leaving Dad and me to fend for ourselves.

"Don't hold Max so tight that he runs from you as fast and far away as he can after graduation," I said as gently as I could, pushing the words through the lump in my throat.

Max already had a stash of college pamphlets for schools out of state stacked in a bin under his bed, safe from Mom's cleaning frenzies. He'd sworn me to secrecy over their existence, and I kept waiting for a frantic call from Mom when she eventually discovered them.

"What am I going to do when he's gone, Chloe?" Her voice cracked with the quiet words. The sounds of scrubbing and cleaning had stopped filtering through the phone, a testament to just how scared Mom was of the coming change.

"What if instead of worrying the next year away, you spend it building memories with him? You can worry about him being gone after his graduation." I spoke slowly, feeling the inadequacy of my advice with each word. Max would move away from home in less than a year, and I had no idea how my mom was going to survive.

Mom exhaled a deep breath, and the sounds of cleaning resumed. I could picture her picking her rag back up and redoubling her cleaning efforts. I wasn't the only one in my family who had learned to push down her emotions when needed.

"You're right. He can go to the game, but he'll have an early curfew," she said, her voice clipped and no-nonsense.

My lips tipped up into a smirk, knowing Max wouldn't be thrilled with the stipulation, but also knowing he'd accept it if it meant he got to go out with friends.

"That sounds fair to me," I said.

"And he's coming with your dad and me on our Sunday drive this weekend. No excuses! We're going to create more memories together. Assuming I can get your dad to step away from work for a couple of hours." She gave a sniff that sounded suspiciously like she was pushing back tears, but I didn't point it out. Recognizing how much this phone call had cost her.

My mom thrived when she was in control. Unfortunately, life very rarely went according to plan.

We ended our conversation, and I slumped to the side with a sigh as I curled into a ball on my comforter. I was the glue that held my family together and, no matter how hard I tried, it never got any easier. Mom poured herself into caring for Max to the point of suffocation. Max pushed Mom away to the point of constant fighting. Dad lost himself in his work to the point that I worried, one day, my parents would look around and question if they even had a marriage anymore.

What will happen when I leave? The thought was barbed, sticking in my mind and haunting my every interaction with my family. I knew they needed me and yet, I'd made a promise to Meg years ago that I'd live my life for both of us, getting out of Utah and discovering more of what the world had to offer. I couldn't break that promise, not when I already felt like I'd failed her as my memory of her faded with each passing year.

Pushing up from my bed, I returned to my desk, settling into my chair cross-legged. I pulled up one of the job sites I'd become intimately familiar with over the last few weeks, resuming my job search. I had a promise to keep.

Chapter Seven

THAT EVENING, I HAD just settled on the couch, remote in hand and Ruby snuggled up next to me, when my phone lit up with a text. I groaned as I picked up the device from the coffee table. My fruitless job efforts had left me feeling frustrated and disillusioned with life, the tension in my neck likely a precursor to a headache later. Since both of my roommates were out with their significant others, my plan was to drown my emotions in too much junk food and the rest of *Pride and Prejudice.*

As I picked up my phone, I couldn't help but smile when I saw Derek's picture on my screen. It was a photo from freshman year that he'd begged me to delete many times over, but I couldn't quite bring myself to replace it. In the photo, Derek and I were wearing matching university gear, our cheeks smashed together as we grinned into the camera. His hair was longer, curling at the nape of his neck and nearly hiding his eyes. My hair was shorter, the most extreme I'd ever gone, with designs shaved into the sides of my hair and the top consisting of longer spikes.

DEREK: *Dad keeps complaining you never visit any more. How would you feel about stopping by to say hi?*

I bit my lip before responding, trying to decide if I had the emotional capacity to see Derek's dad, Chris, right now. I wasn't sure if I could handle seeing the clear signs of cancer in the stoop of his frame and the exhaustion in his eyes. Yet, I also couldn't say no to Derek's dad. Even battling cancer, Chris was the life of the party, making everyone feel welcome and at home with his loud laugh and bear hugs.

ME: *Be there in ten! Can I bring anything?*

Knowing Derek, he wouldn't ask me to bring anything even if they were completely out of food and toilet paper, but I still liked to offer. I knew what small offers of kindness could mean in moments like these.

I pushed up from the couch and headed to my room. I quickly changed into jeans and a sweatshirt, finger-combing a few strands of hair back into place and reapplying deodorant. At least, I was pretty sure it was a reapplication. At this point, I only put forth the effort to shower and apply makeup on days I had virtual job interviews, which were becoming fewer and farther between. This had unfortunately resulted in a handful of days where deodorant was forgotten until late in the day. Or, on one occasion I was not proud off, not applying deodorant until the next day.

When I walked into the living room, the only sign of Ruby acknowledging my departure was that she'd shifted on the couch, curling up in the spot I'd vacated. I walked over and gave her a pet, grabbing the snack foods from the coffee table. I stashed the food in the pantry and paused by the candle on the counter I'd lit earlier. I was going to have to invest in more fall candles. This one, which smelled like sugar cookies and cinnamon, was almost gone. And I needed all the wishes I could get at this point.

Closing my eyes, I blew out the candle, hoping the universe would somehow hear and grant my wish: that Chris would beat cancer.

Stopping by the front door, I slipped on my flip-flops, pausing long enough to glance around the apartment to ensure I hadn't forgotten anything. Satisfied, I headed to Derek's dad's house and the promise of an emotional roller coaster.

ell

I pulled up to the curb outside the familiar white house with its aspen trees and rose bushes. Only a couple dying roses clung to the branches in the fall breeze, as if refusing to give up the last remnants of summer. The aspen leaves rustled in the breeze, their bright yellow color making me smile.

I walked past the bright pink mailbox, one of the last home improvements Derek's mom had completed before she'd abandoned her family and left for warmer climates. I knew Derek occasionally spoke with her, but from what I could tell, those conversations were infrequent and usually left Derek in a foul mood. If I'd been in Chris's shoes, I'd have repainted the mailbox and sold the house, finding a fresh start as soon as the ink on the divorce papers had dried. Instead, he'd made a home for him and his kids that I envied. It was a place they were always welcome, and I'd lost count of the number of times I'd visited since becoming Derek's friend.

What would that be like, bringing friends I'd met since moving out to meet my parents? I tried picturing bringing Derek, Mallory, or Audrey to meet my family and couldn't make the pieces fit. All I could picture was awkward, stilted conversation and my friends trying to leave as soon as they sat on stiff couches in the too perfect living room, pictures of my family from before Meg died filling the walls.

I rang the doorbell, waiting in the last vestiges of sunshine, a slight breeze making me shiver.

"You know you don't have to knock," a voice called from behind me. I turned to find Axle loping up the driveway, a giant grin splitting his face. He looked like a younger, taller Derek, his shaggy hair dancing with his movements.

"I can't quite bring myself to just walk in. What if your dad's wandering around in just his underwear?" I joked.

Axle shuddered. "I've walked in on that before. I'm just glad he doesn't have a naked room like in that one Matthew McConaughey movie."

"*Failure to Launch?* I love that movie." It had been a minute since I'd watched it, but some movie scenes lived rent free in my mind, and that included any time Matthew McConaughey's shirt allergy acted up.

"Of course you do. Are there any romance movies you don't love?" Axle quirked an eyebrow, his lips tipped into a mischievous expression, hinting at the trouble he must have gotten into as a kid.

"Depends on if you're using the technical definition of 'romance' or the incorrect definition certain authors, producers, and directors like to throw around in the name of selling books and movies."

Axle shrugged, opening the door and ushering me inside. "Is there a difference?"

I sputtered in mock outrage before pulling Axle in for a hug. With him well over six feet tall, my hugs with Axle were always a bit awkward since I came to somewhere between his chest and belly button. Yet, from the moment I'd met him as a gangly teenager, I'd felt the need to fold him in a hug and give him at least one woman in his life, besides his sister, that he could depend on no matter what. Even if he did have a tendency to recline car seats way too far back.

"I see you found trouble!" Derek rounded the corner into the entry hall, a tiled area with space for the shoe rack and nothing else. The complete lack of wall hangings testified to the male occupants who had called this house home for many years without a female influence.

"Hey now! I accept Ax, Axie, and the Commander as nicknames. Trouble hasn't been on the list since I was at least 12," Axle said, trying and failing to hold a serious expression.

"'The Commander?'" Derek questioned. "I have never heard anyone call you that. You know if you give yourself a nickname it doesn't count, right? It just gives me more ammunition for teasing you."

"I didn't give it to myself!" Axle sputtered. "You don't know everything my friends call me."

"Just more evidence you shouldn't pick up strays," Derek said, turning to me with humor written all over his face. "You never know what they're named, and they could be carrying strange diseases. It's not natural for someone to be this tall and skinny." Derek gestured at his brother who looked a bit like Hiccup from *How to Train Your Dragon*, but without the Viking attire or accompanying dragon.

"He looked hungry, so I thought you could feed him before we let him loose again." I played along, taking off my shoes and following Derek past the family room and into the kitchen.

The kitchen was a bit dated with wood cupboards stained an almost orange color. The top of the cupboards was decorated with dusty fake plants a la Ikea and a couple of giant mason jars. I couldn't decide if the jars were intentional décor or if someone had put them up there to store them and never taken them down.

Axle came into the kitchen a few steps behind us and immediately opened the off-white fridge, rummaging for something to eat.

"I never say no to free food." He came up with a slice of pepperoni pizza in one hand and a baggie containing more slices of pizza in the other.

"Gosh man, use a plate." Derek shoved a blue plastic plate at his brother, who took a huge bite of the cold pizza in his hand before depositing the slice on the plate.

"I knew you had me covered." Axle dropped the bag of pizza on the counter next to his plate and pulled out a second slice.

I took a moment to study the brothers closer than normal, noting just how much they resembled each other. Both had hazel eyes, wavy brown hair, and a trim, slightly muscular build. Axle was a good three inches taller than his older brother and had grown his hair out. Derek was stockier, his commitment to exercise clear in the secret muscles I'd recently discovered in his chest and arms, though he hadn't hit body builder status. His physique was more that of someone who did their best to take care of themselves. Both brothers favored their father in looks with their tall builds and defined jaws, though there was a softness to their cheeks and around their eyes that I assumed came from the mother I'd never met.

If their sister, Gemma, were here, she'd fit the same mold, just shorter and more feminine. There was never any question the three of them were siblings.

"I thought I heard the circus was in town." Chris shuffled into the kitchen, a giant grin stretching across his face as he caught Axle in a hug. He'd been balding before starting chemo, but the treatments had caused the last of his graying hair to fall out. He was one of the few lucky men in the world with the head shape to pull off bald. He wore a faded college football t-shirt and gray, baggy sweatpants that hadn't hung so loosely on his frame the last time I'd seen him.

"Dad, you're supposed to be lying down," Derek chided gently. His hands balled onto the counter, knuckles white, as if trying to distract himself from the desire to rush over to his dad and force him back to his recliner.

"And miss out on seeing your girl? Not a chance!" Chris made his way to me, and I returned his embrace, saddened to feel just how much thinner he'd become in recent weeks.

"She's not my girl, Dad." Derek rolled his eyes and grabbed a washcloth from the sink, wiping up Axle's crumbs, his jerky movements a clear sign he was upset.

Chris had called me "Derek's girl" since the moment we'd met. He refused to accept that we were just friends, always playfully hinting at how much he'd enjoy having me as a daughter-in-law.

"Careful. Say that too many times and she'll start to believe you." Chris winked at me before pulling away and sinking into one of the creaky wooden chairs, clearly tired from the few steps required to get from the living room to the kitchen.

"I'm just waiting for him to propose, make it permanent." The familiar joke rolled off my tongue without hesitation, though this time it brought with it a certain level of curiosity.

What would it be like to date Derek? To let down that barrier and consider the possibility of being more than friends?

Derek seemed absorbed in his cleaning efforts, leaving his expression unreadable. If I could see his eyes, would I read possibility in them or exasperation at the often-repeated joke?

I shook my head, clearing it of the possibility. We were friends and that's what worked for us. I wasn't going to waste my remaining time in Utah on what ifs.

"What cooking show are we watching today, Dad?" Axle asked as he rinsed off his plate and deposited it in the dishwasher.

"That Halloween one with the cakes and pumpkin carving started last week. I thought it could be fun to give that one a try. As soon as my tastebuds grow back, I've got a whole list of recipes to test." Chris threw me a mischievous grin. "Maybe I'll even submit to compete on one of those amateur baking shows."

A long-buried memory clawed its way to the surface, Meg's earnest face as she refused to eat the nachos that only a day before had been the only food she would eat.

"When I'm done with chemo, you and I are going to make the biggest bowl of mashed potatoes, complete with butter puddles and chicken gravy," she said, setting down the plate of chips and cheese on the table next to her.

She'd looked at me earnestly from her place in the hospital bed as chemo dripped into her body through the port in her chest. When I'd first started visiting her in the hospital, the bags of medicine hanging from IV poles had given me pause. Now I barely registered their existence.

At least the chemo was clear. I hated seeing the dark red, almost black bags when she received blood transfusions because it meant her numbers weren't good and her next treatment would be delayed.

As I looked into my sister's green eyes no longer fringed by thick eyelashes, I prayed we'd make it to "someday" and that she wouldn't fade even more between now and then.

I should have wished harder on every candle I blew out.

"Dad, just because you've watched all these cooking shows doesn't mean you actually know how to cook." Axle's words pulled me back to the present where I stood by the cream Formica countertop in Derek's dad's kitchen, listening to the three men banter.

I took a deep, steadying breath, trying to regain my equilibrium after the memory, carefully schooling my features to hide the emotions fighting their way to the surface.

"I can cook," Chris insisted.

"I beg to differ," Derek responded without hesitation, finally depositing the washcloth in the sink and looking up from his cleaning. "Did you ever eat any of the food you made for us as kids?"

"It kept you kids alive, didn't it?"

"Dad, edible and enjoyable are not the same thing. And some of your food didn't qualify as either." Axle responded from where he leaned against the counter.

"If Gemma hadn't learned to cook, I think we actually would have starved. Or gotten scurvy," Derek said, his face schooled into a serious expression, though I could see him fighting a smile.

The banter continued and I relaxed into the familiar rhythm, wishing my family could be this way: united in the face of difficult things. While Derek had feared his dad's cancer diagnosis, I had watched it strengthen their familial bonds and bring these men even closer together. For my family, cancer had had the opposite effect, shattering us beyond recognition, leaving me as the last bit of glue holding our family together. Unfortunately, the glue was losing its stickiness. I wasn't sure how much longer I could hold things together. Especially when I moved out of state, additional hours of distance adding to the strain.

But I had a promise to keep to Meg, and while I hadn't been able to give her chicken gravy and mashed potatoes, I could give her this: me living my life to the fullest for her.

"Well, are we going to stay out here bashing my cooking or are we going to watch the show?" Chris asked, pushing up from his chair and leading the way into the living room, his voice laced with humor. "I don't have to put up with this nonsense."

Axle followed him down the hall into the living room, but I hung back, waiting for Derek. He paused next to me, and I reached out, looping my arm through his and giving it a squeeze.

"You okay?" I asked quietly, not wanting Chris and Axle to overhear.

He gave a giant exhale before nodding. "Fine. You know, just trying to hold my family together. Gemma called today. She's hoping to bring the kids back out to see Dad soon. It'll be good to have her help."

My stomach clenched. I hoped I was reading too much into the simple statement and prayed Gemma's visit wasn't an indication that Chris had taken a turn for the worse that Derek hadn't told me about.

"That'll be nice to have everyone together for a bit," I said, words feeling inadequate.

Derek opened and closed his mouth, as if wanting to share more but uncertain what exactly to say. I held my breath, waiting.

Instead, Chris's voice from the other room broke the tension of the moment. "Are you two joining us this century? Or did you find something better to occupy your time? Not that I'm complaining. I could use another daughter and a few more grandkids."

Axle's laughter rang out from the other room at his dad's comment. A blush stole onto my cheeks and I ducked my head, not wanting Derek to see my reaction. He inhaled sharply at his dad's words and immediately began coughing.

"You okay?" I asked, patting his back.

"Yep," he choked out, his eyes watering. "Just swallowed down the wrong tube."

I walked to the sink, grabbing a cup from the drying rack next to it and filling it with water. Derek had his cough mostly under control by the time I handed him the glass, our fingers brushing as he gratefully accepted the offering. Warmth from the contact shot up my arm, a sensation I wasn't sure how to process when it came from my best friend.

"Thanks," he said, sipping on the water and clearing his throat one more time. "Sorry about him. I really can't take him anywhere." He threw me a wink before leading the way into the living room.

I followed a couple steps behind, telling myself my blush and leaping heartbeat had nothing to do with the possibilities my brain was considering with Chris's comment. I just had an overactive imagination prone to daydreams. There was no way I was interested in my best friend. Was there?

I shook my head, trying to remind myself of all the reasons dating Derek was a bad idea: my upcoming move, the fact we were friends, my desire not to mess up one of the healthiest relationships in my life. Just because we both happened to be single for the first time in our friendship didn't mean I should open the door on the possibility. I had a fling I was attempting to start with Nate. I needed to refocus my attention on that. It was easier that way, cleaner when it came time to move. It meant I got to keep Derek as a friend and didn't have to worry about making something more work with distance thrown into the mix.

Chapter Eight

I STAYED WAY TOO late with Derek's family. I hadn't had the heart to tell Chris I had to go home, not when he kept giving me his giant grin and promising me the next episode would be even better. We watched an entire season of his current favorite baking competition show before Derek finally stood, yawning, and told his dad he had an early work meeting.

I followed Derek to the entryway, the floor creaking with each step as if agreeing with our assessment that it was time for bed. Derek opened the door and paused, flicking on the porch light as the cool fall air greeted us.

"Thanks for coming over," he said. "I know Dad really appreciated the visit."

"Anything for Chris," I said, fiddling with the cuff of my sleeve as I stepped past Derek and out onto the porch.

I hesitated, waiting to see if Derek would follow me outside or if he was staying the night. Following Chris's diagnosis, Derek had talked about moving home, but Chris wouldn't hear of it. So, they'd reached a compromise of sorts: Derek and Axle alternating spending the night in case their dad needed something. Though, even on nights when Axle stayed, it felt like Derek spent the night more often than not.

"Tonight's my night to stay with Dad," Derek said with a shrug. "Though, it's late enough Axle will probably sleep here too. I really don't get why Dad won't just let us move home. It would make things easier."

But I understood. And I knew, on some level, Derek understood too. For Chris, letting Derek and Axle move home would be one more thing stolen by cancer, another indicator of forced change.

So instead of commenting, I wrapped my arms around Derek, burrowing into his warmth and doing my best to communicate comfort and understanding. Derek returned my embrace, seeming surprised at first before settling into the hug, pulling me in closer. His familiar scent mingled with the fresh air of outside and I breathed deep.

We stood that way for a long time, neither of us speaking, both of us seeming to recognize that we needed this moment. It was something we'd done more times than I could count since becoming friends, but something felt different this time. Maybe it was the situation with Chris and my desire to show Derek my support. Maybe it was all the stress of life lately and my need for someone to help me hold it together. Or maybe it was a third reason, something I didn't dare put into words but that had been expressed by friends, roommates, and family members almost since the day Derek and I became friends.

I eventually stepped away, mumbling something about the late hour before digging my keys out of my pocket and walking to my car. The warmth and comfort of Derek's hug continued to play through my mind as I drove, something I chose not to question but just to enjoy for now.

—ele—

At home, I'd fallen asleep quickly, but was woken up too few hours later when my mom texted me a recipe for her new go-to DIY glass cleaner. I couldn't decide what was more humorous: that she thought I made my own cleaners or that she thought I owned even half the ingredients on the list.

I debated going back to sleep but recognized that a job wouldn't magically fall into my lap, despite my many candle wishes. I forced myself out of bed with a groan. I stayed in the shower longer than normal, hoping the warm spray would energize me. Once I was done, I stepped out and got dressed. Knowing I'd see Nate tonight at the haunted lift ride, I took my time with my hair and makeup, putting extra effort into my appearance.

If I was lucky, dressing for success might even be the secret to my finally finding a job. It hadn't worked in the past, but it only took once, right?

I spent the morning scouring job sites for new listings, even calling a few of the companies where I'd applied to see if they'd filled the position yet. After hitting one too many dead ends, my eyelids felt heavy, my bed tempting me back to its comforting embrace.

Promising myself I'd only close my eyes for five minutes, I curled up under my blankets and quickly fell asleep.

My phone ringing jerked me awake some time later. I had hoped my nap would leave me feeling refreshed, ready to restart my job hunt with fresh eyes. Instead, I felt like I was being pulled from a coma, my eyes feeling gritty and like they didn't want to stay open.

"Hello?" I rasped into the phone, not bothering to check the caller ID. Maybe if I kept my eyes closed a little longer, I'd feel less like death. Or maybe I'd wake up in a new world where I had a decent-paying job with benefits located near the beach. If I dreamed, it might as well be big.

"Is this the part in a romance novel where I'm supposed to ask, 'Who hurt you?' and then proceed to murder everyone who's ever so much as looked at you cross-eyed?" The humor in Derek's voice rang through the phone loud and clear, unexpected warmth filling my chest as I realized he was on the other end.

"Obviously. It's the only correct response when a woman in your life wakes from a nap and feels like she's traveled to a new dimension," I said, sitting up and smoothing my hand across my face, trying to rub away the grogginess. I likely had only succeeded in smudging my mascara. I'd have to redo my efforts to look cute before the lift ride tonight. Though, maybe if I looked enough like death, Nate would take pity on me and drive me home. Not that leaving early would impress him. But it would finally give me the chance to be alone with him.

"I'll keep that in mind the next time this happens. Currently, I have an extra movie ticket and less than twenty minutes to find someone to go with me. You interested?"

I paused. While my brain wasn't fully functioning at the moment, Derek's extra movie ticket felt highly suspicious. Knowing him, he'd bought two tickets to a scary movie in another attempt to win the bet.

"What movie is it for?" If I didn't like the answer, job hunting was an acceptable excuse not to attend, right? I was fairly certain it counted as "already having plans."

"Why? Don't you trust me?" Humor laced Derek's tone, and I bit my lip, past experience telling me to be cautious.

While Derek would never do anything to hurt me, he would push my buttons and do his best to drive me crazy. It was what best friends were for. An incident involving tiny plastic ducks hidden around my apartment when I'd lent him my key so he could water my plants came to mind. I was still finding ducks hidden in obscure places in my room.

"Derek, we currently have a bet going involving all things spooky. Of course I don't trust you." I settled against my headboard, pulling my blanket back around my legs.

His surprised laugh immediately brightened my day, making me wish I could record the sound and set it as his ringtone on my phone. He had a great laugh.

Which was a totally normal, friend thing to notice.

"It's nothing scary, I promise," he said, his voice sounding almost too sincere, like he was hiding something.

"And you have an extra ticket because...?" I trailed off. If he wasn't going to tell me the movie, the least he could do was provide a bit more context to settle the hint of unease that was dancing in my belly. I toyed with the corners of my blanket as I waited for his response.

As I sat there, another thought occurred to me. Why wasn't he at work? Yesterday, he'd claimed he had early work meetings. I glanced at the clock by my bed. Unless his meetings had started at 4:00 a.m., there was no way he was done with his workday already.

"Also, why aren't you at work?" He wouldn't take a day off just to torture me with a scary movie, right? I was mostly certain that was crossing a line for him. Probably.

Derek gave a big exhale, and I could picture him on the other side of the phone, head hanging down, running his fingers through his hair as he searched for the right words.

"Because I needed a distraction from Dad stuff and I had a slow day at work. So I requested the afternoon off, bought the tickets on a whim, and hoped you'd come with me. Please, Cee?" If his reason for the extra ticket didn't convince me to come, the vulnerability in his tone would have done the trick.

"I thought everything was going okay. Your dad seemed good last night, just a bit tired." I spoke the words slowly, searching my memories for any details I might have missed.

Had Chris taken a turn for the worse? I knew just how quickly things could go from okay to terrible. Though if that had happened with Chris, Derek wouldn't be planning a day at the movies. He'd be at his dad's side.

"You know Dad. Everything's great until it isn't." Derek gave a small laugh, the sound forced and flat. "Please, Chloe? I don't want to talk about it. I just need a distraction."

Heaviness filtered through the phone, the defeated, pleading note in his voice breaking my heart. And for just a moment, I considered telling him about Meg, opening my heart to someone in a way I hadn't since leaving home for college. I could tell him all the secrets I'd kept buried deep, locked in a part of my heart I refused to share with anyone because of the fear they couldn't handle it. But I hesitated. I couldn't add to Derek's emotional load by telling him about Meg, not right now. I couldn't fix things with his dad. And I refused to add to the heaviness with my own emotional baggage. Instead, I would do something about the weight I knew he was carrying and give him a moment of humor and escape.

"I don't know. I probably should get back to my very demanding life of being unemployed and trying to find a job that pays above minimum wage and utilizes my very in-demand English degree," I said, trying to bring some levity back into the situation as I kicked off my blanket and stood up, certain my hair looked like it had never met a brush or comb before.

"So that's a yes?" I could hear Derek's eagerness through the phone and bit back a smile as I walked into the bathroom to repair the damage to my appearance from my nap.

"What time and which theater?"

Chapter Nine

FIFTEEN MINUTES LATER I was standing in front of the theater a couple blocks away from my apartment, watching the parking lot for Derek. Only a handful of cars filled the lot, and it was easy to spot his black SUV as soon as he pulled in and parked in the spot next to my car.

When Derek reached me, I greeted him with a hug, taking in his familiar scent as he squeezed me just a little too tight. While he did a good job at putting on a brave face, I knew better than to believe everything was okay. I held on an extra moment, wishing I could take away some of his pain, shield him from all the unknowns that came with a family member battling cancer.

"For my sanity's sake, please tell me which movie we're seeing," I said, trying to distract him from the exhaustion etched around his eyes. I was about 60 percent sure he was telling the truth when he promised the movie wasn't anything scary, but there was still 40 percent of my brain that wasn't convinced.

"I really want to help with your newfound Halloween obsession, so I thought we could check out the latest slasher movie," Derek said without missing a beat, gesturing to a movie poster on the outside of the building that depicted a man in a mask carrying a wicked-looking knife that was dripping blood.

"As fun as that sounds, I'm out of here." I turned on my heel and jokingly started walking towards my car, knowing I wouldn't follow through with the threat.

While he'd talked a big game at Nate's, Derek didn't love horror, though he'd tolerate it in social situations. However, if watching a scary movie really would help him, I'd stay. It was what best friends did.

I'd just need the biggest diet Coke and bucket of popcorn available. I'd also need a blindfold and earplugs. Really, just the essentials.

"Kidding!" Derek snagged my elbow and turned me back towards the theater, guiding me inside the lobby where we were greeted by the smell of fresh popcorn. "Though if I wasn't, would that have counted as you losing our bet?"

I shook my head. "You didn't disclose it was a scary activity from the beginning, so I submit it doesn't count."

"I don't think that argument would hold up in a court of law." He quirked an eyebrow and I snorted at the mock-serious expression on his face.

"A court responsible for enforcing bets between friends? Can't say I've heard of that before." I elbowed him softly in the ribs, tempted for just a moment to pull his arm around my shoulders and burrow into him as we waited for our turn at the concessions counter. It was an impulse that had me taking a slight step away, unsure what to do with my growing attraction to Derek.

I tried picturing Nate, with his Zac Efron-blue eyes, but I had a hard time picturing him as I took in Derek's familiar hazel eyes and dimple.

"The Friendship Court has been around for ages. Very handy in tension-filled situations like ours." He gave a sage nod, and I was impressed with his ability to keep a straight face.

"I don't know how our friendship would fare in a legal battle. Maybe there's a more civilized way we can settle things?"

"Like fisticuffs?"

"I was thinking pistols at dawn, but your option works too. Though that means we'd have to miss the scary movie this afternoon while we settle our dispute." I snapped my fingers in mock disappointment, pivoting as if to leave.

"Good thing we're going to a chick flick instead then." This time Derek waved to a cardboard cutout off to the side with two of my favorite actors wrapped in an embrace on a beach at sunset.

The line shuffled forward, quickly approaching the cashier, but I tugged Derek to a stop, forcing him to face me.

"Now I'm really worried. You're voluntarily watching a romance without me having to coerce you into it? Who are you and what have you done with my best friend?" I was only half joking. Derek only willingly watched romance when he lost a bet or when there was absolutely nothing else going on.

Derek gave a small shrug and sad smile. "After my early meetings, I had to take Dad to the doctor today. That's the real reason I took the afternoon off. The news wasn't what we'd hoped."

My heart ached at the revelation, and I gave his arm a squeeze, studying his face. Now the exhaustion and pain I'd seen around his eyes earlier made sense. Those setback days packed a punch and often required time to process. I could give him time to process. I could give him junk food and distraction and anything else he needed to get through this afternoon. If he asked, I could even give him this evening, away from

Nate and the Halloween lift ride and our latest bet. Whatever he needed to feel better. It was what best friends were for.

"Say no more! I'm pretty sure this calls for popcorn *and* chocolate." I turned toward the front of the line, pleased to see there was only one person left in front of us. If Derek needed a distraction, I was more than happy to deliver. "Whoever paired popcorn with movies was a genius. It really is the perfect combination. Almost as good as diet Coke and lime."

∼ele∼

Two hours and a happy ending later, Derek and I squinted into the sunlight of late afternoon as we exited the theater and started back toward our cars, the fall breeze carrying with it a bit of chill that left me grateful I'd thought to grab a hoodie on my way out the door.

"That was a solid seven out of ten chick flick," I said, content in my cheery bubble of witty banter and swoony kisses. Where did I sign up for a romance like that? Probably the same place that handed out jobs for recently graduated English majors who didn't want to teach.

Not that I'd known exactly what I wanted to do when I chose English as my major. I just knew I needed a degree, so I got one. Now I had a degree *and* no idea what I wanted to do with the rest of my life. Maybe I could find an independently wealthy man accepting future wife applications. Where was a modern-day Mr. Darcy when you needed one?

"What qualifies as a ten out of ten?" Derek asked as we stopped outside my car. He leaned against the side of my car, waiting for my response.

"Probably *The Proposal* and *You've Got Mail*. Though almost anything with Meg Ryan and Tom Hanks gets full points by default," I said, mimicking Derek's pose as I leaned against his car, facing him.

"What about *While You Were Sleeping*?" Derek asked, his lips tilting up in a slight smile. I was relieved to note the tension around his eyes had lessened while we were in the movie though it still hovered in the set of his shoulders.

"It's definitely up there right next to *Return to Me* and *My Big Fat Greek Wedding*." I nodded sagely, as if there was some kind of science to my chick-flick rating system beyond me simply liking the movie.

"What about *Groundhog Day*?"

I pulled a face, pushing away from Derek's car with a shake of my head. "That one's a hard pass for me. Repeating the same day over and over again gives me anxiety. Though, it's kind of what my life has felt like lately." I tried not to dwell on that too much. Something had to give soon, otherwise I'd lose my mind. Maybe I should give *Groundhog Day* another chance. It might teach me how to escape my current situation.

"Job hunt not going well?" Derek's expression was full of sympathy. He knew better than most how hard I was trying.

"That's an understatement if I've ever heard one. Every job I apply for wants at least three years of experience. I just got my degree. How am I supposed to get experience if they won't hire me?" I unlocked my car and pulled open the door, hesitating. My gut said Derek needed more from me than a cheesy movie and my company today, but he had to be the one to start the discussion. From the moment of his dad's diagnosis, we'd had an unspoken rule that he'd talk about it if he wanted to, and I wasn't going to change that.

"Give it time. You'll find the right fit." Derek hung back, indecision written all over his face.

Taking a breath, I closed my car door and placed a hand on Derek's arm, watching his face. His eyes seemed to light with surprise and another emotion I had always been afraid to identify. Though the possibility hadn't felt quite as terrifying of late.

Shaking away the thought, I pulled my hand back and refocused on the conversation in front of me. Something told me Derek wanted to talk, even if he was dodging the conversation at the moment.

Settling against my car, I carefully studied Derek's face. "Are you sure there's nothing else you wanted to talk about? Did Axle break your passenger seat with it leaning all the way back? Because if that's the case, I may reevaluate my stance on wearing orange."

Derek gave a sad smile, too small for his dimple to appear, as he shook his head and scuffed the toe of his shoe in the gravel of the parking lot. "I wish Axle was the problem." He hesitated, seeming to sink in on himself, as if trying to hide from the words he was about to say. "I told you I took the afternoon off to take Dad to the doctor and that the news wasn't good." He took a deep breath, as if steeling himself. "He's going to have to do a few more rounds of chemo than anticipated."

My face pinched in instant concern and Derek rushed to reassure me, resting a warm hand on my shoulder.

"He's fine! As fine as anyone battling cancer can be. They just want to be extra sure they've gotten everything before they do surgery." He paused, his Adam's apple bobbing as he swallowed down his emotions, a hint of moisture in his eyes. "It's just a lot to take in. Dad's my rock, has been since Mom left, and it just kind of hit me. What am I going to do if this doesn't end well? What if the treatments don't work? What if he gets sicker? What if...?"

Guilt niggled at me. I should have been the one comforting him after the hard news of the day. The panic and pain on Derek's face spoke volumes, echoing the fears of a past me I'd worked hard to bury deep.

"What if he's just fine and everything ends well? What if you have decades more to celebrate with your dad?" I asked, refusing to think about how those same questions and reassurances had proved false for me and my family.

Derek gave a pathetic shrug of his shoulders, refusing to meet my eyes.

I pulled him in for a hug, feeling him take a shuddering breath as he resisted, then settled into the embrace, accepting the offered comfort. We stood there for a moment, me on tiptoes, Derek holding on tight, his face buried in my neck and his breath warm against my skin. I could only imagine what we looked like: me in all my five-foot-two-inches, doing my best to convey all my support for this over six-foot-tall guy.

"Derek, you can't spend the next months living with those what ifs. Otherwise, you're going to drive yourself insane," I said softly as he straightened, swiping at moisture that lingered in the corner of his eye.

"You're right. I know you're right. It's just … hard." He paused for a moment, as if there was more he wanted to say. Instead, he stepped away and started walking around his car, hands stuffed in his pockets. "But that's why we went to a chick flick. Only happy endings allowed, right?" His voice was filled with suppressed pain, and I did my best not to flinch.

Only happy endings allowed. I had made that my mantra since Meg passed away, used it to justify not sharing my heartache with friends, but somehow hearing it from Derek in this moment brought with it a certain sting I wasn't sure how to navigate. I knew how to be the one facing hard things. Helping my best friend through his hard moment was a different game entirely. It left me feeling insufficient and at a loss for what to do.

"Right," I said, the word tasting sour on my tongue as I opened my car door once more. If I was braver, I'd tell Derek, tell all my friends, about my sister and the list of sad endings that had filled my life. But it felt like the time to tell him had passed years ago and I couldn't add to his burden now. Instead, I pulled on my brightest smile and called after Derek. "Only happy endings allowed. Which means if this free lift ride doesn't end with Nate at least asking me on a date, I want a refund."

Chapter Ten

LATER THAT NIGHT, I stood in line with Nate and his friends, doing my best to ignore the actors dressed as monsters around me. The other carpools had been full, so Derek and I had driven together. He claimed it was to ensure I actually came, but after our conversation earlier, I was fairly certain he just needed the company.

When we arrived at the Halloween lift ride, I was filled with anxiety and regret, emotions that only grew when I caught sight of the actors working the lift. I'd been prepared for cheesy witches and hokey vampires, but whoever was in charge of costumes had gone above and beyond, purchasing masks, fake gore, and makeup that definitely didn't come from the discount Halloween section of a grocery store.

If Derek hadn't spent most of the car ride threatening to force me into doing a half-marathon or some equally terrible physical activity if I lost the bet, I would have insisted he drive me back home the moment I spotted the first actor. Instead, I stood on a mountain up Provo Canyon shuffling my feet in an effort to stay warm despite the many layers I'd donned the second I climbed out of the car. The smell of smoke tinged the air thanks to a series of fire pits spread out sporadically in an attempt to keep participants warm. Nate stood at the front of our group, his circle of friends separating me from him and any possibility of flirting.

He had said something about saving me a spot on his lift chair when he hugged me in greeting, so the interest signals weren't completely one-sided. Unfortunately, the signals were definitely stronger on my side. Though I wasn't too hurt about group dynamics. The monsters seemed more interested in Nate and the group he was currently talking to, sneaking up behind the group to try to startle them.

Maybe, if I hung back and tried hard enough to ignore them, the monsters would leave me alone.

As soon as I finished the thought, I felt the presence of someone standing behind me. A chill snaked down my spine that had nothing to do with the cool mountain air.

"Derek," I squeaked, my voice high-pitched and unrecognizable, "please tell me the person standing behind me a bit too close is Nate trying to get to know me better."

Derek looked over, jumping slightly and nearly dropping the blanket he held.

"How bad is it?" I pushed the question out through gritted teeth, determined not to freak out. Was that a breeze? Or did I feel someone's breath on my neck?

"That depends," Derek trailed off, inching away from me and my unwanted shadow, his eyes wide in panic.

"On?" My voice was approaching decibels only dogs could hear, my heart pounding at a speed that surely wasn't healthy.

"How you feel about murder clowns."

I froze, refusing to turn and give a face to the fear tightening my chest. If I waited long enough and didn't react, the actor would have to move on, right? Find another unsuspecting victim to terrorize. I focused on breathing deep, wishing I had paid more attention to Audrey's yoga breathing videos as the chilly mountain air filled my lungs.

As if the monsters in my vicinity had developed a sixth sense for detecting peak levels of fear, I heard a twig snap, and I caught a glimpse of something dark and furry out of the corner of my eye. Definitely not the murder clown walking away.

"Derek," I pushed out between still clenched teeth, my entire body tensing. "I think my murder clown made a friend."

Knowing my luck, he'd probably attracted the monsters that had been targeting Nate and his friends at the front of our group.

This time Derek refused to turn my way, staring straight ahead at the lift ride and the handful of people that stood between us and escape from my menagerie of monsters. He seemed off somehow, taking deep breaths of his own, though Derek's fear didn't seem triggered by the monsters circling like I was some kind of Halloween homing beacon. Instead, his eyes were locked on the ride, his hands fisted at his sides, his shoulders stiff.

"I'm glad he learned how to tap into his social skills and make connections," Derek said, a strained smile teasing at his lips at the joke, his dimple flashing in his cheek, even as his jaw remained tense. Something was off. Maybe all this Halloween stuff freaked Derek out more than he'd let on, though that didn't make sense. Why would he make the bet with me and join in every activity if that was the case?

"Not funny," I hissed, trying to stare ahead instead of taking in the monsters I could feel drawing closer. How hard was it for someone to die of fright? What were the risk factors? I'd have to do some research before committing to any more ridiculous bet activities. If this all became bad for my health, I had grounds to back out right?

Feeling like I was going to pass out, I took one more deep breath and turned to face my nightmares head on. A clown with a bloody smile and a looming werewolf grinned back at me. The werewolf took my eye contact as his cue to throw his head back and howl. I flinched back at the sound, hoping they'd had their fun and would leave me alone.

Instead, as I moved back, I bumped into another person, stepping on their foot. Assuming it was Derek finally coming to my rescue, I mumbled an apology as I turned. An involuntary shriek escaped as a man in a mask with a chainsaw greeted me instead of Derek's teasing hazel eyes and familiar smile.

I wasn't sure how it happened, but I managed to push away from the mass murderer in front of me and nestle myself into Nate's group all within the span of a few seconds. Nate and his friends watched me with a mix of humor and surprise. But if enough people stood between me and Mr. Chainsaw, I might be able to escape. I could run, not fast, but I just had to be faster than everyone else here. One girl had worn heels. If worse came to worst, I could push her down and make it to the parking lot. I'd ridden up the mountain with Derek and couldn't really get away after that, but that type of logic had no place in my brain as my flight mode was fully triggered.

At least I knew now that fainting wasn't my actual response to danger. Though if I fainted, maybe I'd have an excuse to leave. Maybe they'd even send a sexy paramedic to save me then I wouldn't have to do any more scary activities because he'd instantly fall in love with me and I'd lose all interest in Nate.

One could dream.

A grin split Nate's face as he spotted my tormentor.

"Dude, you look awesome!" Nate called, coming over to give Mr. Chainsaw a giant hug. Apparently, Nate also had terrible survival instincts. "Hug the enemy" had to be right up there with "sleep" when it came to worst options for surviving a zombie apocalypse.

After a bit of back slapping that I hadn't realized was possible while holding power tools, Nate and Mr. Chainsaw broke apart. Nate waved me over with excitement and I cautiously came forward, allowing Nate to pull me closer with an arm around my waist. While Nate's reaction was a good indicator this man wasn't actually a chainsaw-wielding murderer, my body was having a hard time accepting that as adrenaline continued to pulse through my veins. If it wasn't for my many layers, Nate probably could have felt my pulse racing, which, unfortunately, had nothing to do with finally getting close enough to Nate to touch.

"Chloe, this is my friend James. He's the one that told me about the lift ride. Though not soon enough for me to join in the fun." Nate dropped his arm from my waist and elbowed his friend. I immediately missed the added warmth and reassurance of human contact.

James reached up to remove his mask. Underneath was a very average, if a little sweaty looking man in his mid-twenties.

"Nice to meet you, Chloe. Nate mentioned meeting you at Tara's the other night." James held out the hand that wasn't currently holding a chainsaw and I gave it a quick shake before withdrawing and taking a step back. At least Nate had mentioned me to his power tool-carrying friend, though I would have much preferred to meet James in a nice, well-lit setting. Like a restaurant or hiking or bowling. Really anywhere besides a dark mountain filled with monsters right before I climbed onto a haunted ski lift.

"It's nice to meet you too," I said, pretending I wasn't terrified to turn around and see another one of his buddies hiding behind me. Who was next? Big Foot?

"I hope you enjoy the lift ride. They really outdid themselves this year," James said. I had to fight down the words trying to escape that would express exactly how I felt about this ride and how much I dreaded learning what "outdid themselves" meant.

James and Nate continued to talk for a few more minutes before it was our turn to climb onto the lift. Apparently, the clown and werewolf had had their fun and moved onto tormenting someone else. I was not sad to see them go. And while I should probably be embarrassed about my overreaction to James's sudden appearance, he had given me the nudge I needed to move over by Nate.

When we reached the front of the line, an Asian woman in her early twenties gave simple instructions, explaining that only three people could fit on a chair at a time. Our group of eight immediately began breaking into smaller subgroups.

"Nate do you want—" Before I could finish the sentence, Nate joined the group of guys in front of me, clearly having forgotten about his invitation from earlier. Instead, he left me alone with Derek who was being oddly quiet, his steps growing slower as he approached the lift ride.

Disappointed at another failed attempt to spend time with Nate, I followed the worker's instructions and stepped up to a set of yellow painted footprints on the ground of the loading zone. Derek stood next to me on his own set of painted footprints, his posture tense, making me think the murder clown scared him more than he'd indicated.

The black chair came behind our knees and we sat back, pulling the safety bar down across our laps as the lift kept moving, pulling us up the mountain. The lights of the ski lift provided dim illumination, keeping us from plunging into full darkness as we moved. Derek spread his blanket across our laps, and I settled onto the seat, grateful for the added warmth. I kicked my feet back and forth as we moved above the trees, the scene of dark pine trees both beautiful and eerie. My movement made our chair bounce slightly, a sensation I found oddly soothing. I needed to do something to relieve the nerves building as we climbed closer to the first vignette of the lift ride.

"Can you not do that?" Derek asked through clenched teeth.

"Do what?" I asked, surprised to find Derek white-knuckling the safety bar in front of him, every muscle in his body stiff.

"Swing your legs. You're making the chair bounce and—" Derek broke off, squeezing his eyes shut, his breath coming out in a tense whoosh.

"It's perfectly safe. I was on this lift for the full moon ride this summer. It was gorgeous! The green trees and bright moon. We even saw some deer bedding down for the night." I babbled, surprised when Derek didn't respond. Normally he loved talking about all things outdoors, especially if it involved wildlife.

Instead, he continued to grip the safety bar like his life depended on it, his eyes squeezed shut as we made a slow, steady ascent. His lips formed a thin tight line, and his jaw locked as if he was grinding his teeth.

"Derek?" I prodded gently, nudging him with my elbow, a thought niggling in the back of my mind that seemed like the only logical conclusion, even as it felt impossible given how often he hiked mountains and did other adventurous activities.

"Yes?" He bit out through tight lips. If he didn't relax and take a deep breath soon, he was the one who was going to need a paramedic.

"You don't happen to be afraid of heights, do you?" I asked the question slowly, certain I had to be mistaken. I'd known Derek for seven years, surely I would have realized he was afraid of heights before now. Though, as I thought about it, we'd never done anything remotely like this. He'd always had an excuse, a reason to stay safely on the ground when friends wanted to do adventurous things like ropes courses, ziplines, and roller-coasters.

Kind of like how I'd never mentioned Meg by finding ways not to talk about my family with Derek and my other friends.

"Define 'afraid?'" Derek asked, pulling me from my thoughts. "I can go on tall buildings, hike mountains—" The chair bounced slightly and Derek cut off, his lips pressing together.

"Is this why you never come to the amusement park with me?" I asked, pieces falling into place. I typically went to the only amusement park in Utah about once a year with a group of friends and Derek always was busy when I extended the invite. I hadn't thought too much about it until now.

Mr. I-Climb-Mountains-For-Fun was terrified of heights. Who knew? It served him right for forcing me to confront my fears through this ridiculous bet. It only seemed fair he had to do a bit of the same.

"It's not heights themselves that scare me. It's when there isn't something secure underneath me. A mountain isn't going anywhere," Derek said, his words coming out clipped.

"Unless there's an earthquake or landslide," I mumbled under my breath, trying to hide my amusement at the situation. I shouldn't find this funny, but there was a certain irony in this moment that I was enjoying a bit too much.

"But those are flukes, and chances are slim they'll happen to me. Falling off a rollercoaster or ski lift happens far more often!"

While I wasn't sure statistics supported Derek's logic, I wasn't about to point it out. He was a finance guy; if anyone could find and understand the numbers, it was him.

"Whatever you need to tell yourself to make yourself feel better. And to think, you were giving me a hard time about being scared of slashers in the woods." I waved behind us towards the base of the ski lift ride where the murder clown waited.

Derek peeked one eye open at me, exasperation clearly written across his face. "How many times have you come across actual serial killers in your life as opposed to being forced to ride in death traps that could fall out of the sky at any moment?"

"I don't know how many serial killers I've met in my life. It's not like they walk around with a name tag listing their hobbies." I pointed out. "Just because I didn't know someone wasn't a serial killer, doesn't mean they weren't one!" I insisted. "Nate's friend James definitely gave me serial killer vibes." Someone who found that much enjoyment in scaring people while carrying power tools had to be a bit suspect.

"Not everyone who carries a chainsaw is trying to kill someone," Derek said, relaxing his grip on the safety bar and sinking into the chair a little more.

"And how many lift rides have you been on that broke and fell out of the sky, plunging you to your doom?" I shot back, quirking my eyebrow as I went back to swinging my legs. If he was going to mock my fears, I was going to return the favor.

"It only takes one." He tensed up again and I felt a little bit bad, but not enough to take the words back. Or to hold completely still as we continued our ride.

"That's what she said," a high-pitched voice squawked from below us, drawing us out of our conversation.

I'd been so caught up arguing with Derek, I'd forgotten about our potentially haunted surroundings. Beneath us, a group of witches pranced around a cauldron in a clearing, spotlights casting eerie shadows on the scene below.

"Don't forget to add the dead man's tongue, Dorcas!" One witch called.

"What about the hair of a damsel in distress?" Another asked.

"He can provide that!" I called down, curious to see if the witches would react.

The witches cackled, looking up at us, the dim lights highlighting their patchy green makeup. Apparently, the costuming skills had been focused on the actors down at the entrance and not so much the ones up higher on the mountain.

"Want to throw us a strand?" A witch, whose shoulders and deep voice indicated she was actually a he, called.

"Happy to!" I reached towards Derek, who leaned away from me with a laugh.

"I'm not providing ingredients without knowing what they're cooking," Derek said, loud enough for our audience. I caught the hint of a smile on his lips, telling me I'd finally succeeded in distracting him from his fear.

"Beauty potion. You don't wake up looking like us. It takes work! How else do you think we've become so irresistible?" This came from a purple-haired witch with a crooked black hat on her head.

"Speak for yourself. This beauty is all natural." This came from the first witch with the deep voice.

The witches' chatter and cackling followed us as our lift continued moving up the mountain towards the next vignette.

"Maybe I should ask them for some of their beauty tips. Might help me snag Nate," I said to Derek, my lips stretched wide in a grin I could feel throughout my whole body. I had not expected to be so thoroughly entertained on this haunted ride.

Derek's laugh quieted, his expression turning into something soft and filled with sincerity as he looked at me.

"You don't need magic to make you irresistible. Just keep being you."

Chapter Eleven

Heat stole into my cheeks as I processed Derek's words. Before I could respond, our lift chair leveled out as we came to the midpoint station. Faint, eerie circus music played from somewhere, making the hair on the back of my neck stand up. One look around had me biting back a shriek as a clown popped up in front of us. I had definitely exceeded my yearly quota for clown exposure.

"Will you play with me?" The clown asked in a high-pitched voice, its head tilted at an odd angle as it stared at me. While I'd thought the clown down at the base of the mountain had been scary, this one's makeup made that one look tame and huggable by comparison.

A bang from the side made me jump and I looked over to where another clown had been hiding behind a metal barrel.

"No! They're here to play with me!" The clown on the side said. This one was covered in makeup that made it look like the clown was crying blood.

I cringed into Derek's side, desperate to put as much space as possible between me and the demonic clown.

"Ahh!" An actor jumped out with a yell, this one dressed like a giant sock monkey, banging cymbals together with a clash.

That was all I could take before I squeezed my eyes shut, biting my tongue to keep from screaming, and doing my best to ignore the sounds the clowns were making as I held Derek's arm in a death grip. I felt the chair continue forward, shifting to climb further up the mountain as we left the laughing and calling of the clowns behind.

"Why did it have to be a sock monkey?" I muttered, refusing to open my eyes until the sounds of the clown section had fully faded behind us.

"You're afraid of sock monkeys? You're the one who was giving me a hard time about heights! At least my fear could actually kill me," Derek said, and I tried to ignore the humor lacing his tone. After all, I'd been the one mocking his fear of heights a few minutes earlier. Turnabout was fair play.

"That's how they get you. They lure you in with their creepy button eyes and then, when no one's looking, they strangle you in your sleep," I said with a shudder. The sock monkey trend from my childhood had definitely left its mark on me.

Derek just laughed, bringing a hand up to rest on mine where it continued to grip his bicep.

"If I promise the sock monkey is gone, will you stop trying to cut off all circulation in my arm?"

I cracked my eyes open and released Derek's arm, relieved the clown station was far behind us. Below, projections of talking jack-o-lanterns covered some of the trees. Otherwise, it was quiet. A slight breeze teased my hair, making me shiver. I relaxed into the seat, trying not to think of what the next vignette might contain. As long as it wasn't more clowns, I'd survive. Probably.

Without warning, our chair stopped moving with a jerk, leaving Derek and I suspended above the trees.

"We're not moving. Why aren't we moving?" Derek asked, looking around for a moment, before sinking back, his grip strangling the safety bar.

"Maybe they had to stop it to help someone off?" I offered. "I'm sure they'll have us moving again soon."

Derek muttered something unintelligible.

"I missed that. What did you say?"

"Distract me," Derek said, turning to face me with desperation in his eyes.

"Excuse me?"

"I'm trying really hard not to think about the deadly drop beneath us right now. I'd even go live with the clowns if it meant I could get off this stupid ride." His voice was strained, his breaths starting to come in panicked gasps.

"Okay. . ." I considered our surroundings as I tried to think of anything I could use to distract Derek. My phone was stuffed in my pants pockets, and I highly doubted he'd handle it well if I sent the chair rocking while I tried to pull it out. Not to mention, I didn't think I had service up here, so pulling up random videos on social media wasn't really an option.

"Describe your ideal date." The request popped out of my mouth before I could think too much about it, desperate for anything to ease the tension rolling off Derek in waves.

"Is this one of those moments when I'm supposed to quote *Miss Congeniality*?" Derek pushed the words out through clenched teeth. I was starting to worry the furrows of fear and worry on his forehead and surrounding his eyes would become permanent if he held them much longer.

"I mean, it's never wrong to quote a rom-com, but I genuinely want to know. What would you do on your ideal date? Besides a ski lift ride, obviously."

Derek snorted and considered the question for a moment, looking up at the sky and the speckling of stars that could be seen above the trees. I hoped the view above us would distract him from the drop below.

I reached for his hand where it sat on the safety bar and gave it a squeeze. I was surprised when Derek released the bar and intertwined his fingers with mine as if I could help him hold himself together until we were able to get off the mountain. I liked that he felt he could trust me in his moment of fear.

"I don't know. Probably something simple, like a hike and a picnic or going for ice cream and talking. Really just something that would let us get to know each other better, enjoy each other's company." He gave a shrug, the gesture causing our chairlift to rock. His eyes slammed shut, his lips returning to their tight line as his hand flexed in mine. "Not riding a chairlift to our doom."

"What kind of food would you take on the picnic?" I asked, trying to work with the information he gave me.

"I don't know. Probably sandwiches or something." Derek snapped back, his chest rising and falling in rapid succession.

My distraction wasn't working and the catcalls from other lift riders trying to figure out what was going on weren't helping. I rubbed circles on his wrist with my thumb, hoping he'd find the motion soothing.

Personally, I found the sensation of our intertwined hands more inviting and enjoyable than holding hands with my best friend probably should be.

"You hate sandwiches. You always dissect them before eating because you say the pieces taste better separate. Is that really the impression you want to leave your date with?" I prodded, hoping to keep him talking.

"Fine! I'd take fried chicken, then. Fried chicken is good cold or warm and is perfect for a hike." His tone was exasperated, but at least his breathing was starting to slow.

"Wouldn't you get messy eating it?"

Derek cracked open one eye and quirked an eyebrow at me. "We've just hiked a mountain together. I doubt this mystery date woman would be worried about a messy face after walking through dirt for a couple miles."

"She would if she's trying to impress you."

"If we're hiking together, chances are good she's already impressed me enough that I wanted to be alone with her in the woods." Derek persisted, his other eye opening, though his chin stayed tilted upwards as he trained his gaze on the stars above.

"Just like that, you've turned this romantic tryst into a slasher movie." I pointed out, humor lacing my tone.

Derek snorted, the tension easing from his grip. "I did no such thing!"

"Then what else are you going to do with her alone in the woods?"

"Use your imagination."

I was relieved to hear a hint of laughter in his voice.

"I did! Though I have to say, you're the friendliest serial killer I know," I said, leaning into the ridiculous idea. There were other activities I could imagine taking place alone in the woods, but it was probably better I didn't think about doing those activities with Derek right now.

"Do you know many serial killers?" Derek's shoulders relaxed as our banter continued.

"I thought we already covered this. None that I know of, though you didn't deny being one, so I guess that brings the tally up to one." I raised a finger and waved it at him. "With how long I've known you, should I be impressed or disappointed that you haven't tried to murder me already? Though, maybe this bet was all an elaborate ruse to finally do me in." I tapped my finger on my chin as if genuinely pondering the possibility of my best friend being a serial killer.

"I'm not a serial killer. I don't lure women out to the woods to kill them."

"But you've yet to tell me what you *do* lure women out to the woods to do." I tilted my head to the side, watching as Derek did his best to fight down a smile, his dimple evident in his cheek.

"Fine, Chloe! When I lure women out to the woods just the two of us, I'm hoping for a kiss." His voice was filled with exasperation and something else I couldn't name.

"Just one? Hiking several miles seems like an awful lot of work for just one measly peck." I was being difficult, and I knew it, but the ridiculousness of the conversation was finally working to distract Derek, so I leaned in to better hear his answer. Maybe I could get a job as a professional distracter. I was good.

"If I'm lucky it'll be more than one and much longer than a peck." Derek mimicked my motion leaning towards me and, before I knew it, our faces were only inches apart.

All thoughts of murder clowns, serial killers, and deadly heights fled as I thought about Derek and kissing in the woods and I couldn't help but wonder what it would feel like to have his lips pressed against mine. I was sure it would serve as a distraction, pulling both of our focuses away from our fears toward something else. Something much more pleasant.

But this was Derek I was thinking about. Derek, who had seen me eat an entire pizza in one sitting during finals week in college. Derek, who had also watched me throw-up said pizza a few hours later thanks to food poisoning. Derek, who was my best friend, my honorary roommate, my go-to when life got hard. Derek, who I'd firmly placed in the friendzone but who, recently, I'd started seeing as something more. Someone who I could be something more with.

I didn't see Derek this way. I didn't *want* to see Derek this way. Did I?

Derek's gaze flicked from my eyes to my lips and back again and my tongue snaked out, licking my lips and drawing his attention back down. All it would take was leaning a little further forward and our lips would meet. I'd know for sure if my best friend was a good kisser. Not that I'd ever wondered. Well, maybe on occasion. In a totally best friend appropriate way.

The air between us crackled, the tension between us having nothing to do with heights or monsters. Instead, it dealt with only a few, small inches and whether one of us would be bold enough to close the gap. My breath stuck in my throat, my heart pounding as Derek tilted his head hesitating just a moment, as if waiting for my invitation.

Before I could decide what to do, the lift started moving again. The motion was gentle, but going from a standstill to climbing up the mountain again sent Derek back into a place of fear. He leaned away, his hand releasing mine and returning to grip the safety bar as he sank into his seat as far as he could go.

My stomach dipped and I told myself it was from the sudden motion and was not from disappointment over the space Derek had created between us. He was my best friend. Best friends didn't kiss, especially not in the mountains on haunted lifts as a method of distraction.

So what did that mean for me and Derek and our relationship? Was I really as content with our "just friends" definition as I'd always claimed?

"Thank goodness we're moving again. Hopefully it means we'll be off this death trap soon," he said, the strain back in his voice.

"Hopefully," I agreed, though a part of me wanted to go back to the moment before the lift started moving again. If I had closed those couple of inches between me and Derek, would everything really be different? And, if they were, would that be as bad as I'd always feared? Or could it have been the start of something unexpectedly good?

Chapter Twelve

THE REST OF THE ride passed in a blur. I was too busy thinking about the almost kiss to pay attention at the last station where a group of vampires threatened to drink our blood and hold us captive. They definitely were not of the *Twilight*, sparkly, vegetarian variety. However, their shrieking and threats did little to capture my attention. Instead, I replayed the moment before the ride started moving so many times it was burned into my brain. What had I been thinking? And why did I want to go back and take the "almost" out of the situation?

Derek's stress had significantly eased once the lift started back down the mountain, tension no longer rolling off him in waves. His grip on the safety bar had slowly loosened until we reached the bottom of the mountain and it was time to get off.

"You okay? You were quiet the last half of the ride." Derek asked, placing his hand on the small of my back to guide me as we climbed off the lift and made our way to a nearby bonfire where our group was gathered, laughing and chatting about their experiences.

"I'm fine," I promised, wishing I could just get off the mountain and back home to my apartment where things made sense and I didn't consider kissing Derek. Maybe I'd read one too many friends-to-lovers books recently. Or watched a few too many rom-coms.

Or maybe I was finally giving myself permission to consider something that, due to past relationships for both of us, had never truly been an option until now.

It wasn't that I *suddenly* found Derek attractive. He had always been attractive. Back in college when I'd first met him, I'd thought about dating him. But he quickly became my friend, and I had found other guys to date. And that was that. I'd questioned our "just friends" status a handful of times when people asked me why I wasn't dating him or when friends pointed out that Derek was clearly interested in me. But in the end, I'd pretended it all away, not allowing myself to see it as a real option because I was too afraid to let Derek be anything more than my friend. If things went wrong, I was too afraid to lose him forever.

What about tonight had been different? And why did I have a feeling I'd opened a box of possibilities I wasn't going to be able to easily close again?

"Dudes! You totally missed out," one of Nate's friends called as we approached the group, pulling me from my thoughts and twisting emotions. "One of the vampires asked Diane if she wanted to join their coven and you know what she said?" He pitched his voice high, no doubt mimicking Diane, who I had yet to meet. "'Only if you sparkle in the sunshine.'"

I mustered a smile as the group burst into laughter, a couple of the guys slinging their arms around the shoulders of a dark-skinned woman who I could only assume was Diane.

The woman spoke up, ducking out from under their arms with a laugh. "All I'm saying is that if they'd had Edward Cullen hiding in one of the coffins, I would have stayed up on that mountain. Hot, rich, and eternal youth? Sign me up!"

Nate and his friends continued to joke and banter, and I watched the exchange. Normally, this was exactly the type of social interaction I loved joining: lots of flirting and no pressure. But right now, I felt unsettled and uncertain how to fit into the group dynamic. Especially when my thoughts were so jumbled over Derek.

"What did you think of the ride, Chloe?" Nate asked, coming to stand behind me. He leaned in closer toward the fire, invading my space and distracting me from thoughts of Derek and what-ifs. "I was sad we didn't get to sit next to each other."

My lips tipped into a smile as I read the clear, uncomplicated interest on Nate's face, something he underscored as he rested a hand on my arm.

"It was an experience." I hedged, trying to find something positive to say that would impress Nate. "The witches were my favorite." I bit back a grin as I remembered our banter with the group on the way up the mountain.

"Yes! Did you get them to talk with you?" We chatted for a moment, blocking out everyone else and comparing experiences from our rides. I left out a few key details, like how often my eyes were closed, focusing instead on the beauty of the mountains and moments of humor.

If all else failed, laughter made a great flirtation tool.

The group started to get restless, drawing our attention to where a couple of Nate's friends were roughhousing off to the side while everyone else soaked in the heat from the fire. I'd lost track of Derek. I'd been too busy ignoring my churning emotions and trying to salvage my evening with Nate to realize Derek had wandered to the far side of the group, watching the exchange between Nate and I with a furrow in his brow.

"You guys hungry?" Nate asked.

Everyone else shook their heads, mentioning other plans for the evening or a desire to get home. When Nate turned his gaze to me, I gave into the hope I saw in his eyes. Spending time with Nate, not Derek, was why I'd come in the first place. I needed to take advantage of any opportunities I could. Maybe reminding myself why I was on this haunted mountain in the first place would help me find my equilibrium again, free from thoughts about kissing Derek and wondering if his lips were as soft and full as they looked.

"I could eat," I hedged. "Maybe we could find a dessert place or something open on the way home."

"I've heard great things about the restaurant up here," Nate offered, gesturing to a rustic-looking building down the hill from where we stood.

His response had me seeing dollar signs. I was no expert, but restaurants located at ski resorts were hardly known for their frugal menu. Especially not this particular ski resort which was known for its celebrity sightings.

While under normal, employed circumstances I could probably stretch my budget to make a single meal at this restaurant work, I couldn't right now. Only a few days ago, I'd been running the numbers and found I could last until Mallory's wedding before I either had to have a job or move back in with my parents. Those calculations had not included eating at perhaps one of the most expensive restaurants in the county.

I turned panicked eyes to Derek who seemed to pick up on my hesitation from across the circle and stepped in to rescue me.

"Actually, I was Chloe's ride and need to get home. I have to help my dad with a few things in the morning." Derek offered me a lifeline and I took it without hesitation.

"Right! And I left my purse in your car." I hadn't brought a purse with me, but Nate didn't need to know that. "Maybe we can get dinner another time, Nate," I said, trying to leave the door open for a date while firmly slamming the door closed on spending money on a meal that would likely cost more than my monthly utility bill.

"Okay, but I'm holding you to that, Chloe." Nate gave me a wink before waving goodbye and turning back to the few members of the group who were interested in staying for dinner.

I waited for disappointment to hit at not getting to spend more time with Nate, but I just felt relief. It had been an off night. I'd probably feel differently tomorrow, in the light of day and away from all the surprising emotions of the evening.

Derek and I picked our way down to the parking lot, careful not to trip in the dark. While the ski resort had some lights lining the path, it was still too dim to see clearly. I could all too easily picture one of us tripping over a root and rolling down the slope.

A breeze stole across the mountain, and I shivered, burrowing deeper into my coat and wishing we were already at the car. When I got home, I was making a giant mug of hot chocolate and wrapping up in my thickest blanket. Now that my adrenaline from earlier had fully worn off, I was exhausted and more aware of the mountain chill surrounding us.

Derek draped his blanket around my shoulders, and I gratefully accepted it, pulling it tighter around me.

"Thank you for coming to my rescue with the whole restaurant thing. Maybe someday, when I have a job again, I can afford dinner at ski resorts," I said to Derek as we reached the parking lot and headed towards his car. He'd had to park near the back of the lot and we still had a bit of a trek ahead of us. At least we hadn't had to park in one of the upper lots and ride the shuttle.

"No problem," Derek said with a shrug, reaching up to rub the back of his neck. "I should probably be thanking—"

"Derek, Chloe, wait up!"

I looked over my shoulder to find Nate running towards us, a giant grin splitting his face.

"I almost forgot! A group of us are going up to the amusement park for their Halloween thing Thursday night. Want to come?" He fairly vibrated with energy, reminding me of an overeager puppy.

I internally cringed as I forced a giant smile at Nate's invitation. The haunted displays at the amusement park were legendary, and I'd successfully avoided them my entire life despite growing up only 15 minutes away from the park. Before I could say no, I caught the look of disappointment that Derek quickly disguised into mischief at the interruption. He waggled his eyebrows at me as if daring me to back out of our bet. There was no way for me to get out of this outing and still win. My budget didn't include paying for a ticket to the amusement park, but I'd been given a free ticket to the park as a graduation present from some friends, and Derek knew it, so I couldn't use that excuse to get out of the invitation either.

"Sounds great." I forced excitement into my voice as Derek silently laughed behind Nate's shoulder. Two could play this game. "Derek loves rollercoasters, the taller the better. He especially loves those tall towers that shoot you into the sky and drop you without warning."

If I had to suffer through another haunted attraction, so did Derek. And, of course, my desire to have Derek there had nothing to do with my newfound interest in possibly kissing him, right?

Chapter Thirteen

THE DRIVE DOWN THE mountain was quiet, the terror of the night leaving us both exhausted. At least, that's what I told myself as I stared out the car window, watching the shadows of trees and cliffs pass in dark blurs. An odd tension had settled between us, and I couldn't decide if it was because Derek was mad I'd forced him to accept an invitation to the amusement park or if it had to do with our almost kiss and the attraction I could still feel sparking between us. Derek kept tapping his fingers on the steering wheel and I wanted to reach over and cover his hand with mine, force him to relax, maybe even lace my fingers with his.

Which was a terrible idea. I was moving soon. I needed something temporary and fun.

This time the mantra felt more like I was trying to convince myself, as opposed to truths I believed.

Derek's phone ringing broke the silence, and he pressed a button on his dashboard to answer it. I gave a sigh of relief, grateful for anything that could ease the tension of the moment.

"Hi Dad. You're on speaker. Cee's in the car," Derek said. His brow pinched in concern, as if wondering why his dad would possibly be calling well past 9:30 at night when he usually went to bed.

His dad's voice filled the car and I smiled at the familiar, welcoming sound. "Chloe! When are you going to visit me again? It's already been too long. I keep telling Derek he needs to bring his girl around more often."

My lips tipped up in humor, curious how he'd react if he knew Derek and I had nearly kissed. I could only imagine his excitement and the number of I-told-you-so's he'd throw Derek's way if we ever started dating.

"I was just there yesterday," I said with a laugh. "Besides, I don't want to wear you out with too many visits."

I remembered all too clearly Meg's illness and how visitors, while welcome, came with extra complications. The need for constant sanitizing and hand washing. The joy and exhaustion that would etch themselves into Meg's features in equal measure as she sat, propped up in the recliner in our living room, and talked with people.

"You could never wear me out. Visitors help break up the day! Besides, it's nice having someone else to look at besides Derek and Axle. They're good-looking boys, don't get me wrong. Take after their dad. But they don't hold a candle to a pretty girl like you."

"Flattery will get you everywhere. You tell me when, and I'll be there." I watched Derek as I responded, trying to read in his expression if I'd been out of line to promise such a thing. Chris would never admit if a visit was a hassle.

Derek simply smiled, mouthing a silent thank you before rejoining the conversation. "As great as it is to listen to the two of you make plans,

I'm guessing you didn't call at almost 10:00 at night to shoot the breeze. What's up, Dad?"

"Just wanted to see what time you're picking me up tomorrow for my appointment."

"I'll be home in about 20 minutes, you couldn't wait to ask?" Humor laced Derek's voice as he gave a show of rolling his eyes. Apparently, he would be staying at his dad's house again. At this point, Derek really should just give up his lease, save some money and move back home.

"I'm heading to bed and wanted to make sure I set my alarm for the right time."

"Your appointment isn't until the afternoon. Since when do you sleep past noon?"

"You can never be too careful!" Chris persisted, sounding like a stubborn child instead of the father in this relationship. Chris had been a high school teacher before cancer forced him to take a leave of absence. I doubted he'd slept past 8:00 a.m. once in the last thirty years or more.

"Your call has nothing to do with the fact that you knew I'd be with Chloe and that this would be the perfect opportunity to embarrass me in front of her?" Derek arched an eyebrow, suspicion filling his tone.

"Absolutely not! I would never try to tease, prank, or embarrass you in front of your girl." Chris's tone of mock seriousness was more than I could take, and I had to bite my lip to keep from laughing.

"Just like you would never hide all of my clean shirts right before you knew she was picking me up to go hiking?" Derek rolled his eyes, exasperation filling his voice as he recalled one of his dad's pranks from last summer, before the cancer diagnosis had slowed Chris's mobility and limited his pranking ability.

"I would never!" Chris's tone of outrage was Oscar worthy. Maybe he should take up acting at a haunted lift ride. He could probably teach the murder clowns a thing or two.

"Of course not. I promise if by some miracle you're still asleep after noon I'll wake you up. We won't miss your appointment," Derek said with a shake of his head.

"That's all a man can ask for. Have a good night you two! Don't do anything I wouldn't do."

"That leaves a lot of activities on the table," Derek said. "Some of which may or may not be legal."

"Exactly!"

With that, Chris hung up the phone, plunging me and Derek back into the tense silence of earlier. At this point, we had reached the mouth of the canyon and were passing businesses and homes, the streets far less crowded than when we'd driven up only a few hours earlier.

"He sounds like he's in good spirits," I observed, keeping my voice neutral and inviting Derek to share more if he felt like it. After our conversation earlier today, I wasn't quite sure what to expect. He and Chris and Axle were likely still processing the latest news from the doctors and figuring out how best to move forward.

Derek rubbed his forehead as if trying to relieve building pressure. "You know Dad, always looking on the bright side. The other day he told Axle and me he would have gotten sick sooner if he knew it meant his kids would visit so often. He's stoked to have Gemma's family visiting right after Halloween and then again for Christmas, even though it's their year to be with her in-laws."

"That'll be nice to have everyone together." I said, aware of the words left unspoken. When cancer got thrown around, you never knew which holiday, which moment, would be your last with the people you loved.

"When he's having another good day, let me know and I'll come for a visit."

"You don't have to go out of your way to visit," Derek said as he turned onto my street.

"What else do I have going on?" I asked, my stomach clenched as I thought about my abysmal job prospects. "Besides, I need to ask Chris if he knows about your fear of heights. I feel like that's something that could come in very handy with his pranks."

Derek snorted a laugh, the sound finally dispelling the tension of unanswered questions from earlier as he parked the car in front of my building. I breathed a sigh of relief, grateful to be back on familiar footing, the spark of attraction from the lift ride fading into the background as I climbed from the car.

Chapter Fourteen

THE NEXT NIGHT FOUND me in the living room with my roommates, once again wearing our matching lounge sets. I was ignoring my phone on the off chance any messages that came through were Nate inviting me to another Halloween activity or Max complaining about his latest spat with Mom.

When it came to the current battle between Max and Mom, I sided with Mom this time around. Max had skipped class and gotten caught. Mom had revoked her permission for him to drive to the football game. It seemed pretty fair to me, though she'd threatened to ground him from all football games for the rest of the season—which seemed a bit extreme—but I was staying out of it for now, giving them a chance to work things out on their own. If I was lucky, Dad might even step in, finally pay attention to something besides his job.

In regard to my bet with Derek, if I didn't see an invite to a Halloween activity before it happened, I was never really invited, right? I felt like Derek couldn't fault that logic. At this point, the only other vampires I wanted to see were of the sparkly variety while I had a giant tub of popcorn in my lap.

The day had brought one bright spot in my job hunt. A tech company in California had reached out requesting to meet with me. I quickly scheduled the video interview for the next day, my nerves jumping and dancing in my stomach every time I thought about it. It had been weeks since my last interview, and I was trying not to get my hopes up too far. Still, I felt antsy, a mix of nerves and excitement that left me at loose ends as I waited for the morning.

I desperately needed a distraction, preferably one that did not involve monsters or murderers, so when both of my roommates were home, I quickly suggested we finish watching *Pride and Prejudice*. I hadn't told them about my interview, not wanting the pressure of other people knowing. But Mallory and Audrey both seemed to notice something was off tonight and had quickly agreed.

"Pumpkin spice candles and pedicures! Finally, a fall themed activity I can get behind. Do you know how many haunted activities are in the world?" I asked from my spot on the floor where I contorted myself to reach my toenails. I'd picked a soft peach color with sparkles, telling myself it was close enough to orange to count as a fall pedicure. Never mind that it was also my go-to spring pedicure color.

Ruby lifted her head from Audrey's lap to blink at me in what I took as agreement before she settled back down in a tight ball. Audrey mindlessly petted her dog as she finished something on her laptop, her dark hair in a lopsided bun on top of her head.

"Too many?" Mallory asked, reaching for a bag of chips from her spot on the couch. Ridge had caught a cold and, while I wouldn't wish illness on anyone, I would take full advantage of the opportunity to spend some quality, uninterrupted time with my roommates.

"Way too many! Who even knew haunted chairlift rides were a thing?" I cringed, thinking of the night before and the murder clown that had made it his mission to scare me to death. Though not everything from the night before had been negative. There had been that moment with Derek when his lips had been mere inches from mine, something I'd thought about way too often today.

"I did a haunted train ride as a kid. Zero stars. Would not recommend." Audrey shuddered, closing her laptop and sitting deeper into the couch. "A zombie stole my hat. Who does that?"

"Maybe he was cold." Mallory offered Audrey the bag of chips and she grabbed the bag before securing a handful.

"Do zombies get cold?" I asked, biting my lip as I concentrated on my toes and only getting nail polish on my nails and not my skin. I wasn't exactly the best at coloring in the lines, which might explain my English degree and lack of career plan. "I mean, they're dead."

"That's not the point! I was a traumatized eight-year-old who did get cold because a teenager dressed as a zombie pilfered my beanie." Audrey gave a huff of exasperation, emphasized by the crunch of a chip.

Mallory laughed, stealing the bag of chips back from Audrey before leaning back into her seat on the couch.

"Just more proof that haunted activities are a bad idea and should be avoided at all costs." I persisted, finishing my last toenail. I closed the nail polish and placed it on the coffee table before awkwardly pushing to my feet and carefully walking over to join my roommates on the couch, making sure to lift my toes so they didn't brush the rug.

Mallory shifted to the middle couch cushion, making room for me on the end.

"Even when an attractive man invites you?" Mallory waggled her eyebrows, a mischievous grin stealing across her lips.

"Maybe not at all costs," I said, ducking my head. "Though trying to impress a man with my cowardice was not my best idea. I doubt I've impressed Nate at all. Not to mention, Derek can attest I'm doing my best to block out the scary bits. He's had to rescue me from my fears more often than I care to count." Of course, Derek hadn't been the only one doing the rescuing yesterday, and I hadn't minded being his protector.

"How do you block out the scary bits of a slasher movie? Isn't the whole thing supposed to be terrifying?" Audrey asked, her forehead scrunched in confusion.

"I may or may not have closed my eyes at the beginning and then . . . fallen asleep." I felt heat steal into my cheeks as I thought about my lacking survival skills and the sensation of waking up on Derek's shoulder.

"On Nate? Please tell me you got some unplanned snuggling in!" This came from Mallory, who was the queen of unplanned snuggle sessions with her soon-to-be husband. The number of times I'd come home to find a movie playing and the two of them asleep on the couch, Mallory's head on Ridge's shoulder, was impressive.

"Unplanned snuggling is a good move. Definitely recommend!" Audrey said with a glint in her eyes that made me think she had a story I wanted to hear later.

"Unfortunately, Nate sat on the other couch." My disappointment over that still smarted some, but now I was even more disappointed about the kiss that didn't happen with Derek last night.

"Dang! What's the point of falling asleep during a movie if you don't have a perfectly good shoulder to rest on?" Mallory's outrage at the inconvenience was clear as she crossed her arms across her chest with a huff.

Audrey nodded her assent, making me wonder if there was an unofficial rule about snuggling and dating. If it was up to these two, the beginning of *Pride and Prejudice* would sound something like, "It is a truth universally acknowledged that a man with an available shoulder is in want of a woman to sleep on it."

"I didn't say I didn't have a shoulder to sleep on." The words spilled out before I could second-guess them, and I immediately wanted to call them back. Instead, I covered my mouth with my hand, as if that wouldn't draw more attention to the comment.

Both Audrey and Mallory straightened, looking at me with interest, their eyes wide and far too observant.

"Explain!" Mallory demanded, grabbing my arm in her excitement.

"And don't leave any details out," Audrey added, shifting so she could face me fully.

I reached forward to touch my toenails, making sure they were dry and trying to avoid the inevitable. When my fingers came back clean, I curled my legs under me, settling cross-legged on the couch, taking a few extra moments to situate myself as I gathered my thoughts.

"There's not much to explain. Nate sat on the other couch, so I settled in the only seat available—next to Derek. The movie started, I closed my eyes and kind of ducked my head behind him to block out the first murder. Based on the sounds I was hearing, I decided it was best to keep my eyes closed." I shrugged, trying to communicate how unexceptional the moment had been. "Next thing I knew, the credits were rolling and Derek was gently nudging me awake. Though he probably should have done it sooner. I think I drooled on his shirt."

Heat filled my cheeks as I remembered the not unpleasant feeling of waking up on my best friend's shoulder. If I had known Derek had such nice shoulders, I would have taken advantage of the opportunity sooner.

"Your words are saying it was nothing, but your cheeks and goofy grin tell a different story!" Mallory pointed an accusatory finger at my face. I shook my head vehemently, as if denying it would do me any good. My roommates knew me better than most.

"I swear, it was nothing! Derek and I are just friends." I insisted. The argument I'd been using for the last several years sounded forced to even my ears. Did just friends think about kissing each other or wish they could snuggle again?

"Have you told your heart that?" Audrey asked quietly, as she reached around Mallory to place a reassuring hand on my arm.

I leaned forward, breaking the contact, and buried my face in my hands, groaning as I thought through all the complications dating Derek would bring. In addition to my usual logic about moving, there was also the worry of what would happen if it all went wrong. I couldn't lose Derek. He'd been my source of sanity and comfort on more occasions than I cared to count, particularly when Max and Mom were at it. And even though I was leaving, I was determined to maintain the friendship, no matter how far I moved.

Not to mention everything going on with his dad added a layer of emotional complication I wasn't sure I could navigate. Not after Meg.

If I pushed my feelings for Derek down and avoided them, they would go away, right?

"I don't think I can risk it," I whispered, hating the words even as I spoke them. I continued hiding my face, not wanting to read my roommates' expressions as I spoke. "If I lose Derek, I don't think I could survive. My family's a mess. My job hunt's a bust. He's the one steady thing in my life."

Mallory's hand rubbed soothing circles on my back as she listened to me speak.

"He's not the only steady thing in your life." Audrey added, her voice filled with quiet comfort.

I exhaled, looking up to see the worry etched into the lines of my roommates' faces. "That came out harsher than I meant it. It's more, the two of you are dating and getting married, starting new phases in your lives. I'm just stuck here. Stagnant. Nothing changing, not going anywhere."

I paused, choosing my next words carefully. "If I were to date Derek and things went wrong . . . I don't know if I could handle that."

"But what if dating him gave you something even more? What if it led to the life you've always dreamed of?" Mallory asked, clear concern in her voice. For Mallory, the risk had been worth it. She was about to marry her high school sweetheart. But I doubted life would be as kind to me if I took a chance with Derek. I had the track record to prove it.

Sitting up, I brushed my hair back from my face and took a steadying breath.

"I don't think it matters. I'm pursuing something short-term with Nate. I'm going to freaking Halloween at the amusement park for Nate. That has to mean something." My words came out with a forced confidence that I hoped my roommates wouldn't question.

They watched me for a moment, reading something in my face that convinced them to drop it for now.

As the three of us settled back into the couch, we watched Elizabeth Bennett and Fitzwillian Darcy's happy ending play across the screen, and I felt a pang of longing deep in my chest. If only the path to my own happily ever after was so easily found. Like making a wish on the pumpkin spice candle that sat burning on the counter.

Chapter Fifteen

"TELL US ABOUT A time when you used teamwork to solve a problem in the workplace?" The interviewer asked, her boredom coming through loud and clear on the video call. She had a white, carefully styled bob that framed her face and contrasted sharply with her rich, dark skin tone. Either she'd aged well or some cosmetic work was doing a fabulous job at masking her age, which I estimated was between 45 and 60. She personified professionalism in a way that made me want to run to the store and swap my collared shirt and slacks for a pantsuit and heels.

"Teamwork has been essential in all my work environments," I said, the practiced response slipping from my lips with ease. At this point, I'd lost track on the number of times I'd been asked an iteration of this particular question. Most of my work experience included moments when teams caused more of the problems than they solved, but I spun the story, trying to paint myself and my work experience in a positive light. This was the first interview call I'd gotten in weeks, and I refused to blow it, even if the interviewer clearly did not want to be meeting with me.

Unfortunately, I also felt less than ideal physically and mentally. I'd tossed and turned most of the night, unable to get comfortable. My mind had refused to settle, and I'd felt strangely warm, despite the near freezing temperatures of fall outside my window. At one point I even turned on my bedroom fan, hoping that would help.

I'd finally drifted off only to wake up with a cold that left my brain foggy. Karma must have picked up on my excitement over Ridge having a cold and how it made a redo of roommate movie night possible. Prior to the call, I'd used every home remedy I could think of to erase all signs of congestion. Unfortunately, while the remedies had cleared my sinuses, they hadn't cleared my muddled brain. All I wanted to do was lay my head down on the desk and sleep for hours, possibly days.

"Tell me about a time you navigated a stressful situation with success." The interviewer continued, not even pausing to ask follow-up questions or really process my answer.

"When I worked as a sales associate, we often had moments where the store was full and we needed all hands on deck to meet customer needs." I started, pulling from my most recent job: a retail position at the campus bookstore. A job that had ended the minute I graduated, thus my current desperate job hunt.

My phone buzzed on the desk next to me, making me wish I'd turned it off or stashed it somewhere I couldn't see or hear it. A text from Max filled the screen, followed almost immediately by a phone call from my mom. I prayed the faint buzzing of my phone wouldn't come through on the video call as I finished my response and listened to the next question.

My phone stopped ringing, but my relief was short lived as Mom immediately called me again.

"Do you need to take that?" The interviewer asked, arching a perfectly styled eyebrow.

"No, it can wait. I thought I'd put my phone on silent, not just vibrate. Must have hit the wrong button," I lied, knowing full well I'd left the device on vibrate because usually it wasn't a problem. I should have known better. I snagged my phone from the desk and stashed it under my thigh, hoping to stifle any noise it might make.

An awkward silence followed my pronouncement, and I forced a smile, hoping it came across as friendly and not desperate. Chances were good my expression looked more crazed than happy. This was proving to be my worst job interview to date, and that included the one over a month ago when my period unexpectedly started on my drive to their office. My fingers itched to reach up and fiddle with a necklace that I wasn't wearing as my nerves danced in my stomach. Though I'd stopped wearing the necklace months ago, the habit honed over several years still shone through when I was at my most anxious.

"Can I be honest, Miss Green?" The interviewer's expression shifted into something earnest that I didn't want to examine too closely. It was the most energy I'd seen on the woman's face since we'd started this conversation.

"Please do," I said, knowing this couldn't bode well for me.

"This was a courtesy interview. We already have an ideal internal candidate for this position, but we had to complete a certain number of interviews to align with company policy. You seem like a nice enough girl, but I really don't think this is the right fit. Maybe apply again when you have a few more years of experience under your belt."

It was the same feedback I'd received countless times since starting this job, and I fought to keep my professional smile from slipping.

"Thank you for the insight. I appreciate you taking the time to meet." The words felt like chalk on my tongue. This had been my most promising job lead in weeks and it was already slipping through my fingers.

The fogginess in my brain seemed to settle in further, adding a level of detachment to the conversation.

We ended the call and I leaned my forehead on the desk with a groan, the solidness of my desk grounding me in the moment. If I sat up and opened my eyes, I'd have to acknowledge that my life really was as terrible as it seemed at the moment.

My phone continued to vibrate, ringing for the third or fourth time in so many minutes. Sighing, I sat up, pulled it out from under my thigh, and answered, hoping that this time my mom might actually have good news instead of another fight between her and Max.

"I was starting to worry you wouldn't answer," Mom said as soon as I answered the call with a tired hello.

"I was in a job interview," I said, my head pounding too hard for me to care if I sounded as hopeless as I felt.

"Really?" The hope in Mom's voice was painful.

"I'm not getting the job, Mom. It wasn't the right fit."

"Oh." The disappointment in that single syllable could be bottled and used to guilt children for generations.

"I'm not feeling well, Mom. Do you need something?" I pinched the bridge of my nose, trying to relieve the pressure in my sinuses and behind my eyes. Maybe if I took a nap, I'd feel better. Maybe I'd wake up to find that disaster of an interview was just a dream and that I still had my whole day ahead, full of possibility, rather than my current waking nightmare filled with yet another disappointment.

"It's Max. I'm sure he's texted you already, but I need you to know, I'm not the villain here! He's the one that keeps missing curfew, and don't get me started on his grades. I know he can do better." Her voice came out in a rush, almost as if she thought the faster she spoke, the more likely I was to believe her and choose her side. I heard a cabinet slam closed on her side of the phone, and I could picture her grabbing her favorite cleaners and picking an unsuspecting area of clutter to take out her frustrations on.

"Okay . . ." I trailed off, waiting for more details. When it came to Mom and Max, nothing was ever that simple. I waited, even though accepting the conflict at face value meant I'd get off the call faster and would be able to lay down.

"I know it's homecoming and all, but that's just another reason he shouldn't be on the road. You'd be amazed at the number of accidents that happen when kids go to these big school events. Really, it's a miracle any parents let their kids go." Mom continued, trying to win me to her side before I knew the full story.

"Max is going to homecoming?" I asked, trying to follow her explanation, but the pressure in my head made it next to impossible. I just wanted to close my eyes and try this conversation again after a long nap.

"Yes! He's already asked a date, but I really don't feel good about him being out driving that late. Not to mention he's grounded, again. Like I said, his grades need some work, and he was five minutes late getting home after the football game earlier this week. So I told him he can't go, not unless he lets me drive him, which of course he thinks is overkill, but you can never be too cautious. You never know what could happen and—"

"Mom, I'm going to stop you there. What does Dad think?" I rarely used Dad to resolve these arguments, but I couldn't stop wishing my parents would be parents, plural, and stop pulling me into the middle of these squabbles.

Didn't becoming an adult and moving out entitle me to space from all the drama?

"You know your father. He's too busy working." That was Mom's code for she hadn't actually asked him.

"I think you should talk to Dad."

She scoffed. "He won't understand. He doesn't have all the facts."

"Then explain them to him," I said, trying for patience in my tone that I really didn't feel.

"I don't want to interrupt him when he's busy." A thudding sound in the background told me she'd acquired a target and was cleaning something while we talked.

But you have no qualms interrupting me?

I shook my head, trying to erase the thought, though it seemed to snag on the fogginess I couldn't quite clear from my mind. "Mom, I currently feel like garbage. I just got another rejection and have no idea what comes next in my job hunt. Forgive me for not wanting to be a surrogate parent or voice of reason when it comes to raising my *little* brother."

"He's taller than you are," Mom pointed out, taking issue with the word "little" like Max did every time I used it. How the two of them could be united on this front, but nothing else would never make sense to me.

"Great. If he's tall enough not to fall under the 'little brother' category anymore, he's tall enough to drive himself to a school dance," I said, pushing up from my desk and settling onto my bed. I lay across the covers, a sudden chill making me want to bundle up in the blankets and ignore the world.

"Height has nothing to do with it! It's about responsibility. When Meg was in high school—"

"When Meg was in high school you didn't hesitate to let her go to dances and stay out late with friends, even if she missed curfew by five minutes. You encouraged *both* of us to go and make memories, to live our lives." The words were tired, worn from years of repeating them to my mom every time we had one of these discussions.

"And look where Meg is now." Pain filled Mom's voice, and I flinched, recognizing in it an echoing pain that I tried hard to keep buried deep, but that I was too tired to push away right now.

"Meg had cancer, Mom. She wasn't killed in a car accident. She had an incurable disease that our family spent a year battling. Meg lived her life. Don't you think it's time you let Max do the same?" My voice was soft, as gentle as it could be when being wielded like a knife.

Silence greeted me, telling me she'd paused her cleaning, likely shocked I'd gone there. I typically tried to avoid the word "cancer," knowing the punch it packed, but I didn't have the mental capacity at the moment to find a softer way to have this conversation. I waited a full minute before continuing.

"I love you. Max loves you. But if you expect him to ever come home again once he's graduated high school, you have to loosen the reins. Otherwise, you're going to be left with Dad and a house full of regrets." While I was certain the words were the result of feeling sick, there was a certain mix of relief and regret as I registered what I'd said. I'd finally spoken the words I'd thought countless times but never found the courage to say.

I didn't wait for Mom to respond. Instead, I hung up my phone and turned it off, stashing it in my nightstand drawer and refusing to care about who else might want to talk to me.

Normally, after a blow up with my mom involving conversations about Meg, I'd text my friends. Find something fun and distracting to do. But I didn't have the energy. Right now, I needed sleep and to wake up in a new world where my parents actually spoke to each other, and my brother left me out of their disagreements. And since I was dreaming, maybe it could also be a world where I found a well-paying job and had a rom-com-worthy boyfriend who would come take care of me when I was sick.

Gathering all of my energy, I stood and walked to my closet. I stripped out of my interview outfit and slipped on an oversized hoodie, sweatpants, and fuzzy socks before sinking into my bed and pulling the covers up to my chin.

Reaching into my nightstand, I fumbled for a moment until I found the familiar, scratched frame. The family photo greeted me with its smiling faces, expressions forever frozen in this moment of forced happiness and fading hope. My eyes locked on one face, a face I'd give just about anything to see one more time alive, happy, and smiling. A face I'd made a promise to and felt like I was failing every day I stayed in Utah, not progressing, not chasing the adventures I told her I'd take for the both of us.

"Miss you, Meg. Every single day," I said as I ran my finger over her image.

It was the most I ever admitted to out loud. Missing her, acknowledging the never-ending ache in my heart just led to pitying looks and stilted conversations with people who never knew what to say. As if there was anything you could say to make the loss of a sister and friend hurt less.

I placed the photo on my nightstand, needing her close and watching over me. My own guardian angel as I allowed sleep to settle in my bones and erase the day.

Chapter Sixteen

"CHLOE."

A gentle hand shaking me pulled me from slumber, and I cracked an eye open to find Derek standing above me, concern crinkling his forehead. I wanted to reach up and smooth the wrinkles away. I hated seeing worry written on his face. It was an expression I'd seen way too often since his dad's diagnosis. I much preferred his smile and the dimple it made appear in his cheek.

"You ready to go? We're supposed to leave for the amusement park." His voice was soft and filled with worry.

I groaned, rolling away from him and pulling my blanket over my head, hiding the halo of spikes I was sure my hair had devolved into. There was no way I was getting out of this bed, let alone braving another haunted attraction. I felt like death and probably looked like it too.

"Come on, sleepy head. We've got a bet." Derek tugged on my blanket, but I refused to let it go, needing the warmth as I fought back another chill.

"Go away," I muttered, snuggling deeper into the soft, welcoming warmth of my bed. "You win the bet. Now leave me here to die."

Derek wrestled the blanket from my grasp and pressed the back of his hand to my forehead. His touch felt good, and I leaned into the cool contact.

"You're burning up," he said, withdrawing his hand.

"Come back." I protested, trying to follow his hand, but unwilling to sit up. "You feel good."

"Have you taken anything?" He asked. At some point, he'd let go of my blanket and it settled back over my shoulders.

"Just cold medicine," I mumbled.

"How long ago?"

"I don't know," I said, yawning. I was frustrated my nap was being interrupted. My eyelids felt heavy, and I just wanted to close them, shut out the world and rest. Instead, Derek was here interrupting my dreams.

It was only then it occurred to me that I should be questioning how Derek got into my room. As if reading my mind, he spoke up.

"Mallory let me in on her way to meet Ridge," he said, his hand returning to my forehead. I gave a contented sigh at the soothing contact. "She said she hadn't seen you all day. How long have you been sick?"

Instead of answering, I wiggled deeper under my covers. I really just wanted to go back to sleep, but I knew it would be rude to fall asleep with Derek watching. Though I wouldn't mind falling asleep on his shoulder again. He had nice, comfortable shoulders, not to mention he'd be cozy to snuggle with.

I must have dozed off again because the next thing I became aware of was another voice in the room. Based on the worry I could hear in their voices, it must have been a significant amount of time since I'd grumbled at Derek and settled back under my covers, thoughts of sleeping on his shoulder playing through my mind.

"I tried waking her up, but she just rolled over and fell back asleep." The deep, male voice could only belong to Derek.

"I don't think it's just a cold." A female voice joined Derek's, her whisper doing little to disguise her clear concern. "I wish I had a thermometer."

"I've tried getting her to drink water a couple of times, but she just mumbles and pushes me away. Even sick, Cee might be the most stubborn person I know," Derek said, and I cracked my eyes open, trying to read his expression. His forehead was furrowed, no dimple in sight as he looked toward someone I couldn't see.

My room was dim, lit by my bedside lamp but nothing else, the lack of light outside my window telling me more time had passed than I'd realized.

"Do you think she needs a doctor?" Audrey asked, stepping into my field of vision wearing her usual yoga clothes and messy bun.

"No doctors," I grumbled, shaking my head for emphasis when my voice didn't carry beyond the barest whisper. "Don't like doctors." This last sentence was said with all the poutiness of an inconvenienced four-year-old. A four-year-old who just wanted to be left alone to nap.

I didn't have insurance, not to mention doctors brought back too many memories. Memories of hospitals and IVs and sterile rooms that smelled like hand sanitizer and cleaner. Memories of Meg's infectious smile that slowly faded in brilliance, but never fully disappeared from her face, even in her last moments.

The mumbled voices continued talking, but I couldn't make out their words. It took too much focus to separate the voices and words into coherent sentences. Instead, I let the sound comfort me as it settled around me, lulling me back to sleep.

The next thing I remembered was Derek sitting by my bed in my desk chair that he must have dragged over, holding a glass of water and attempting to get me to swallow a couple of pills.

"Come on, sleepy head." His voice was soft, as if he was afraid to spook me.

"No," I groaned, feeling like I'd been hit by a truck. My head pounded, my senses were foggy, my throat sore and parched.

"I promise this will help." Derek coaxed, trying to get me to sit up.

"Don't want to." I shook my head, knowing I was being stubborn.

"Just two pills and then you can go back to sleep." Derek persisted, holding out the medicine again.

"Fine." I opened my mouth but couldn't muster the energy to sit up.

"Can you take this?" Derek asked. He must have handed the glass to someone behind him, because the next thing I knew his arm was wrapping around me, gently lifting me up into a seated position. I welcomed the contact, wishing I wasn't so congested that I couldn't enjoy his familiar scent.

"You need to swallow these." Audrey moved to Derek's side, offering me the pills and water he had been holding earlier.

I obediently opened my mouth, allowing Audrey to put the pills on my tongue and then press a straw to my lips. I swallowed carefully, the motion causing my throat to throb with pain. After a couple of swallows, I shook my head, refusing to consume more.

"You need water," Derek insisted as he lowered me back to the bed. I instantly missed his embrace. He really had great arms. How had I not taken better advantage of those arms during all our years of friendship?

"No water. Just sleep." My eyes were already drifting closed, giving into the siren's call of rest and the mountain of soft blankets surrounding me.

"Okay, but Audrey's coming back to check on you in a couple of hours."

Derek adjusted my covers, pulling them back up to my chin. I snagged his fingers as he pulled away.

"Don't leave." I wasn't sure if I actually spoke the words, but I felt a certain desperation at the thought of being left alone with the pain and loneliness that had nothing to do with illness. The conversation with my mom had stirred up emotions and memories I normally pushed aside, but now I didn't have the energy to keep them at bay.

I felt a hand smooth my hair back before soft lips pressed a light kiss to my forehead, lingering for a moment. The gentle pressure made something inside me ache for more.

"I'm not going anywhere. Sleep good, Cee. I'll be right here when you need me." Derek's familiar voice lulled me to sleep, its deep timbre full of promises of caring and safety. And for just a moment, I felt like my life wasn't spiraling out of control.

Later, in a moment that I wasn't sure was dream or reality, I peeked my eyes open to find Derek, Audrey, and Mallory all standing to the side of my bed. They appeared to be studying something silver in Derek's hands. When it finally registered what they were looking at, my stomach dipped as I realized it was my family photo. But that didn't make sense. It was always in my nightstand drawer. Aware this must be a dream, I waited to awaken or for the dream to fade.

"I don't have her mom's number, so I'm not sure who to call if Chloe's not feeling better in the morning," Audrey said, pausing for a moment as she looked at the frame. "Not that I know her mom well. I think I met her the day Chloe moved in."

"She never talks about her family," Mallory said, her voice quiet. "Maybe we're not supposed to see this."

"Maybe. She's always so open about everything else, but not her family. I wonder if this is why. I've heard her talk about her brother and parents but never . . ." Derek paused, his voice full of hesitation.

"Should we ask her, you know, when she's feeling better?" Audrey asked, biting her lip.

Mallory shook her head. "If she wanted us to know, she'd tell us. I think we wait until she's ready."

"I can't believe she's never said anything." Derek's voice was soft, a hint of pain and disappointment in his voice.

"She must have a good reason," Mallory said, resting her hand on Derek's arm. Audrey nodded, grabbing the frame and placing it on my nightstand.

"I vote we leave it to Chloe to tell us about it when she's ready," Audrey said.

"Agreed." Mallory's voice was soft enough I almost missed it.

"Okay, but this feels like something too large for her to carry by herself," Derek said, his voice hesitant.

"True, but she has to be the one to ask us to help her carry it," Mallory said, her face pinched in clear sadness and concern.

I allowed the moment to fade, trying not to think too much about the strange dream and what it could possibly mean as deeper waves of sleep welcomed me into their depths.

Chapter Seventeen

SUNLIGHT SLANTING IN THROUGH the blinds of my room was the first indication a significant amount of time had passed. I swallowed and, while my throat was dry, the sharp, painful soreness from earlier had faded to a dull ache.

Stretching, I flinched slightly at the stiffness in my muscles as I pushed to sitting. I was going to have to ask Audrey which yoga moves stretched everything because all of me was sore.

"There she is." Derek's voice, rough with sleep, startled me, and I looked over to find him in the desk chair by my bed, scruff shadowing his chin and his hair mussed as if he'd been running his fingers through it. He had bags under his eyes with uncertainty and worry written all over his features.

"You stayed." The words escaped with a rasp before I could think better of them. Heat suffused my cheeks as I waited for his reaction.

A small smile teased his lips, his dimple flashing in his cheek. "Of course, I stayed."

I let the warmth of his words settle around me before a thought registered, making me reach for his arm.

"What about your dad? Doesn't he need your help? And what if he gets sick with whatever I have?" Guilt tugged at the pit of my stomach, robbing me of the warm fuzzy feeling that had accompanied waking up to find him here.

He waved away my concerns, snagging my hand and giving my fingers a squeeze of reassurance. "It was Axle's turn to stay with Dad and get him his medicine. And I'll be extra careful around Dad: wash my hands, wear a mask, limit contact for a few days. It'll be okay."

I nodded, not sure if I believed him, but unwilling to examine his words and my emotions too closely.

"What happened? I remember my interview and deciding to take a nap, but after that. . ." I trailed off, not sure how to explain the bits and pieces playing through my head, a mix of dreams and reality that made no sense. All I remembered for sure was Derek's comforting presence, and that I had wanted him to stay.

"Best I can tell, you caught some kind of 24-hour bug. You slept most of the night, though Audrey did have to help you to the bathroom a couple of times." Derek rubbed his hand down his face in clear exhaustion, the dark circles under his eyes seeming even deeper than before. "We did our best to keep you hydrated, but I have to say, you're a terrible patient." His lips tipped into a small, mischievous smile. "Perhaps the worst patient I've ever worked with, and that includes my dad. He's a stubborn old man in his fifties with a propensity for pranks and a tendency to shoot me with hidden squirt guns. Yet, you somehow beat him for the title."

"Sorry," I whispered, feeling heat steal into my cheeks. "I've never been a big fan of being sick and letting others take care of me."

Sickness brought with it too many memories of Meg and hours spent in the hospital, watching her get poked and prodded. I preferred to avoid the whole experience, pretending health even when I felt like garbage.

"Well, that's too bad, because I'm here for the foreseeable future to do just that."

Derek reached for a large blue tumbler sitting on my nightstand, handing it to me. The tumbler definitely hadn't been there yesterday, and I vaguely recognized it as belonging to one of my roommates. I owed them both apologies, recalling snippets of both of them helping Derek over the last day.

Those memories brought with them the strange dream of the three of them studying my family photo, which still didn't make any sense. The only reassurance I had that it was a dream was that Derek hadn't asked me about it yet. I knew him well enough that I was certain that topic would have been one of his first questions as soon as he was sure I was feeling better.

I ducked my head, taking the cup and gratefully drinking the cool liquid, letting it soothe my sore throat.

"Thanks," I said, handing the tumbler back to Derek and settling against my pillow. I didn't want to think about what I must look like, my hair a matted mess, lines from my pillow creasing my face, makeup from my interview smudged under my eyes. "But you don't have to stay. I should be okay now." My congestion and sore throat made the words sound funny, contradicting my statement.

Derek returned the cup to my nightstand, placing it inches away from my family photo which I only now realized was still out instead of stashed in my nightstand. Maybe that's what had triggered that dream: a subconscious worry my friends would see it and ask me questions. I froze, staring at the photo a moment too long as I processed what I was seeing. I quickly looked away, hoping Derek hadn't noticed what had snagged my attention.

Sensing my hesitation, Derek followed where my gaze had been and spotted the photo, curiosity pinching his forehead and giving no indication of whether he'd already seen it during the night while caring for me. I wanted to reach out and smooth away the furrow in his forehead, tell him not to worry. Even more than that, I wanted to snatch the photo, stashing it back in the drawer where it belonged, my secrets safe.

"Is this your family?" He reached for the frame, as if to study the picture closer. "I noticed—"

"Applesauce," I all but shouted, desperate to distract him from the photo, my stomach churning for reasons not related to my illness.

I knew one day I'd have to tell people about Meg and my loss, but I'd gone so many years without talking about it. I didn't need today to be the day that changed. I didn't know if I could handle it on top of being sick. Not to mention there was no natural way to tell Derek about Meg, too much time had passed. Telling him now would feel unnatural and insincere.

"What?" Derek froze, his fingers an inch away from closing around the frame.

My heart thundered as I thought about how close he was to learning about my history. How would I explain to him that I had a sister who'd died from cancer, but that I had never mentioned it, even in the wake of his own father's diagnosis? The words seemed to stick in my throat, and I prayed he'd accept my change of topic without question, at least for now. At least until I found a better time. Not that there was a good time for that conversation as my seven years of never telling him indicated.

"Applesauce sounds amazing. Can you get me some?" I turned wide eyes on Derek, begging him to ignore the picture and the questions it would trigger.

"Of course. I think Mallory picked some up on her way home from her date with Ridge when she heard how sick you were."

Derek left the room, leaving me alone for only a moment, my bedroom door cracked. Moving as quickly as my sick body would allow, I snagged the photo, tucking it safely in the drawer and settling back in my bed before he returned.

It wasn't that I was ashamed of my family and my past. But I had learned from experience that hearing about Meg led to questions and pitying looks and statements like "I'm so sorry" and awkward pauses and so many other things that I preferred to avoid. Often those exchanges, stilted attempts at providing comfort, led to me comforting the other person, apologizing for having a complicated life story that wasn't all sunshine and rainbows and happy endings.

In the first few years after Meg passed, I'd lost count of the number of times I was left trying to console and reassure someone who had never met my sister. Most people really didn't want to know the pain and hurt that I'd endured or that the pain continued every day. They didn't want to hear that I still had a Meg sized hole in my heart that would always be there. I'd learned that it was easier to avoid the topic altogether. People wanted the surface level, so that's what I gave them. I stopped telling people I had two siblings, doing my best to avoid questions about my family, where they were, what they were doing. Instead, I jumped into social situations with both feet because if I was having fun and leading the conversation, no one questioned me too deeply. Though even that had become exhausting of late as my job hunt and my worry about failing to keep my promise to Meg took their toll.

I hadn't intentionally hidden Meg's existence from my friends the way I did with acquaintances, I just hadn't brought it up either. She was the one part of me that I refused to share. It hurt too much otherwise.

One of these days, I'd find the courage to let someone see all of my broken, hidden places. Today was not that day.

Derek returned with the applesauce, his eyes taking in the empty space on my nightstand, curiosity written in every line of his face.

I thanked him for the food and immediately began eating, hoping having a full mouth would be enough to avoid answering any questions he might ask.

Derek opened his mouth, starting to say something, but hesitated before closing it. He gave a small shake of his head, indecision in his eyes before he spoke again. "You know, you'll have to give me your mom's number for emergency purposes. None of us knew who to call when you got sick."

I swallowed my mouthful of applesauce before responding, enjoying the sweetness on my tongue.

"Oh, I can get that to you. Just in case, though hopefully this is the only emergency illness situation in the cards for us," I said, attempting a lighter tone. I studied Derek's face, certain he'd ask about the picture and where it had gone.

His eyes drifted to the empty spot on my nightstand but then he gave a definitive shake of his head before pushing to his feet, his expression unreadable.

"You know, I'm going to let your roommates know you're awake. They'll want to talk to you, see for themselves you're doing better."

Derek slipped from the room, leaving me alone with my applesauce and a mixture of churning thoughts that I wasn't sure how to process. Why hadn't Derek asked about the picture? The only explanation I could think of was that my dream hadn't been a dream, but I was almost positive that it hadn't been real. And why was a tiny piece of me disappointed he hadn't asked, opening the door on a conversation I'd spent so many years avoiding?

Chapter Eighteen

A FEW DAYS LATER, I finally felt well enough to get back to job hunting. After reassuring my roommates and Derek that I really was fine, I'd showered, dressed in leggings and a sweatshirt, and settled at my desk, a diet Coke with lime at the ready.

I'd received the official rejection email following my interview but hadn't bothered responding. It didn't matter if more opportunities opened at that company. That interview confirmed for me it wasn't a good fit. I had no idea what the right fit would be, but I knew it wasn't that.

But what if the right fit is closer than you think? A voice in my head asked, but I pushed it aside.

I was starting to feel more and more resistance at the thought of moving away from Derek and his support. He'd been amazing the last few days as I'd focused on getting better. He might have checked on me more than my roommates, only leaving me alone when he was sure either Audrey or Mallory was home to see to my needs. Though he hadn't spent the night after that first night, he'd texted me before bed each evening, checking on me even when he'd only just left and leaving me feeling warm and fuzzy with every text.

Needing a distraction from my thoughts of Derek and his sweetness, I glanced at my phone to find a text from Max.

MAX: *You feeling better?*

ME: *I no longer feel like I'm going to pass out every time I stand, so yes.*

MAX: *Is now a good time to ask you to talk to Mom about homecoming again?*

I snorted a laugh, shaking my head as I pressed the Call button. If my brother was going to ask me for more favors, the least he could do was actually talk to me.

"You know teenagers hate talking on the phone, right?" Max didn't bother with a greeting. His voice was teasing, and I knew he wasn't actually put out by my call.

"False. According to the internet, which is never wrong, teenagers of your generation like phone calls. Something about not experiencing the same level of anxiety as those of us who didn't grow up with cell phones constantly at our fingertips." Humor laced my tone as I leaned back into my desk chair, my feet curled up underneath me.

Max sighed, a verbal eye roll if ever I'd heard one. "Fine, I don't hate talking on the phone with the right person, though I prefer video calls."

Implying I wasn't the "right" person, but I wasn't offended at that reality. In fact, it gave me perfect ammo.

"What's her name?" I asked in a sing-song voice guaranteed to get his hackles up.

"What's whose name?" Max's voice became instantly wary, telling me I'd hit on the right line of questioning.

"The girl you're taking to homecoming who you don't mind talking to on the phone." I swiveled my chair back and forth, waiting for Max's reply. One perk of being a big sister: getting to tease your younger brother whenever you wanted. Particularly when said younger brother wanted something from you.

"What makes you think there's a specific girl?" He hedged, clearly trying to throw me off the scent.

"The fact that you've asked me to go toe-to-toe with Mom even more frequently lately. It's either a girl or you've developed significantly more school spirit now that you're a senior," I said, sitting up and uncrossing my legs, pointing my toes so they brushed the floor as I continued to swivel my chair.

"Danica," he huffed in clear exasperation. If I was a better person, I'd drop it and promise to talk to our mom about the dance. Unfortunately for Max, I was a meddling big sister who, despite living hours away, still wanted to have her fun.

"Danica? Sounds nice. Is she blonde? Brunette? Red head? Tall? Short? Freckled? Tan? I'm trying to get a visual so I know who I'm fighting for when I call Mom after this." My lips tipped up in a wicked grin. I was having far too much fun.

"You're so weird." I could hear humor in Max's voice, proving he wasn't as annoyed with his older sister as he liked to pretend.

"It's part of the job description of big sister. The day you were born, the hospital actually gave me an instruction manual with tips on how to be the most obnoxious, annoying sister I could possibly be."

Max snorted, before his voice softened, hesitant. "Did Meg get one too?"

The unexpected question cut to my core and I froze, leaning forward in the desk chair and sliding to the edge of my seat so that my feet could actually reach the floor. Max didn't often talk about Meg unless it was to use her as ammo in a fight with Mom. I was fairly certain it was his way of coping. Mom overshared about Meg, making her sound like a saint or mythical creature. Dad didn't talk about her. And Max only mentioned her if he had something to gain. Not that I was one to judge. I doubted anyone would call my coping strategy of never talking about her "healthy."

I reached up to clasp my necklace, my fingers brushing my throat when I remembered I still wasn't wearing it. Someday I would break the habit. Maybe.

"I can't really remember her. There are bits and pieces, but mostly it's her being sick." Max's words came out slow and hesitant. He spoke as if he'd been holding the words in for so long, he wasn't sure what would happen when he finally let them out.

I bit down my knee-jerk reaction to make a joke and dodge the question. Instead, I took a deep breath, letting the memories wash over me. Memories of bickering with my sister, driving together to school, painting toenails, reading books and swapping recommendations, cheering her on at basketball games, singing along to our favorite musical as we got ready in the morning. Hundreds of memories that had faded around the edges as time continued to pass. But at least I had them.

"She definitely got an instruction manual on how to be an irritating big sister." A smile hovered at my lips, even as each word I spoke seemed to make my heart ache more. People said time healed all wounds, but I'd decided people lied. "She knew how to push all of my buttons and then some. Yet, she would fight for me without hesitation."

Countless nights spent fighting over the bathroom and bickering over silly things played through my mind, making me wish I could go back. I'd even repeat one of our worst fights, if it meant I got to see her again.

"I was a little jealous because I'm pretty sure you were her favorite person in the whole world." My voice tightened with each word, tears burning the backs of my eyes. I'd lost count of the number of times Meg had talked Max into pulling a prank on me.

"I can almost remember, almost picture her, but I never know what's from a photo I saw and what's my actual memory." Max's words were stilted and quiet. "I feel like I can't ask Mom. She'll just sing Meg's praises, paint this rosy impossible picture and then get sad. Dad just dodges my questions."

My heart broke as I realized for the first time that after Meg's death, I only had a couple of years at home before I left. Within a short time, I was gone, jumping at every opportunity for escape that came my way: college, study abroad, parties, on-campus jobs. Max had to stay, dealing with the fallout of Meg's death every day, even a decade later.

"You can always ask me about her, you know," I said, promising myself I would be better about being there for my brother. "I can't promise I won't get emotional, but you can always ask me."

"Thanks, Chloe." His soft words came through the phone, a slight catch in his voice indicating his emotions were closer to the surface than my strong, seventeen-year-old brother typically liked to acknowledge. It made me wish I was there to give him a hug, show him that he wasn't alone in the hurting and missing and aching. Even if we hadn't talked about it much before now.

My conversation with Max lasted another hour as he asked questions about Meg I hadn't thought about in years. Questions I'd always assumed he knew the answers to. By the end, there were tears for both of us and yet, I somehow felt lighter.

"Don't forget to talk to Mom about homecoming," Max tacked on as we were wrapping up the conversation, a clear tactic to move us back to safer, less emotional ground.

"Fine, but you know my job is much easier when you *aren't* late for curfew," I said, my tone teasing but needing him to understand that I couldn't fight Mom on everything.

"I know," he rushed to add. "It was one time by five minutes, and I helped clean the garage to make up for it."

"What about your grades?" I asked, remembering Mom's other argument for saying no to Max going.

"I have a B. It's not like I'm failing," he said, his voice stubborn.

"But is a B the best you can do?" I persisted, knowing he was a smart kid, especially in science and math.

"No," he said on a sigh.

"I'll talk to Mom if you stop intentionally pushing her buttons. Actually do your best in school and please stick to curfew. I know she can overreact to things, but you're not helping by riling her up."

"Fine," he said in a huff, and I gave a sigh of relief. Playing referee between the two of them was much easier when Max at least tried to follow Mom's rules, no matter how suffocating he thought they were.

We ended the call, and I slumped into my chair for a moment, taking a deep breath to try to process all my feelings. While I'd made some much-needed progress with Max, I was still recovering from being sick and the exchange had left me emotionally exhausted and ready for a nap. Recognizing that sleeping now would likely cause my roommates undue concern after I'd finally convinced them I was feeling better, I opted instead to venture into the living room and turn on a show.

I stepped out of my room to find my roommates clustered around the kitchen island chatting, a fall-scented candle burning on the counter. Audrey had a rubber scraper in hand, a bowl of chocolate chip cookie dough sitting in front of her ready to be scooped for homemade cookies.

Mallory was waving her hands, talking animatedly about something wedding related.

I walked over, settling onto the stool next to Mallory, swiping my finger through the bowl of cookie dough and snagging a good-sized chunk before Audrey could swat my hand away. Her lips pressed into an exaggerated pout, and I winked at her, feeling no remorse. Audrey made the best chocolate chip cookies, which meant the dough was incredible. If asked, I might even say it was better than the baked cookies.

"She lives!" Mallory cheered, swiveling on her stool to face me. "How are you feeling?"

"Much better, thanks," I said, wishing I was past the lingering congestion that made my voice come out nasally. Crying with Max hadn't helped anything.

"Good! We were all worried, especially Derek," Audrey said as she measured balls of dough onto a cookie sheet. Mallory took advantage of Audrey's distraction, sneaking a scoop of cookie dough of her own.

"Are you sure that man is meant for the friendzone? Because I don't think he's gotten the memo." Mallory watched me carefully, gauging my reaction as she ate the contraband, swallowing quickly before Audrey caught her.

When Audrey looked up, we both pasted on innocent expressions, pretending like we weren't enjoying the cookie dough every time she turned away—-though her eyebrows still pinched in suspicion as she eyed us whenever she glanced up from her task.

My eyes dipped down to stare at the black-speckled countertop as I processed Mallory's question. I'd been so absorbed in the conversation with Max that I had entirely forgotten about my knight in sweatshirt-armor and how he'd come to my rescue. And just how much I'd enjoyed it. How long had he been sitting in that chair, watching out for me?

I simultaneously wanted to call him and invite him over right now, while I also wanted to keep my distance until I understood the feelings swirling inside of me.

"I don't know. All I know is that I'd be lost without him," I said, deciding for complete honesty.

My roommates both squealed at my answer and warmth filled my cheeks. Thankfully, my phone buzzed twice on the counter, providing a much-needed escape.

I reached for it, my heart pounding at the possibility that it was Derek. I could feel my roommates' eyes on me as I unlocked my phone. Two texts popped up on my screen. The first was from Nate, inviting me to a haunted corn maze tonight. My stomach tightened, realizing that my reprieve from Halloween activities had officially come to an end. While I still had some congestion, it wasn't enough to keep me home. If I could smell the candle burning and the cookies baking in the oven, I was feeling well enough to be social. Probably.

The second text was from Derek, checking to make sure I was okay and asking if I would be at the corn maze. This time my stomach flipped for an entirely different reason.

"Oo, someone got a text from Derek," Mallory's voice was teasing.

"Or was it Nate?" Audrey asked, pointing her cookie scoop at me. "Because if it was Nate, I vote you ignore it and wait for a text from Derek."

My roommates had clearly picked a side, not that there were sides to pick. But still.

I bit my lip, trying to decide how to respond to either text message.

"If you must know, I got texts from both of them," I said, trying to sound imperious and like it didn't phase me to have two attractive guys texting me at this exact moment.

My roommates both begged for details, talking over each other in their excitement. Mallory planted her elbows on the counter and rested her chin in her hands, fully invested in my response. Audrey paused her cookie scooping to listen.

"It's nothing. I guess a group of people is going to a haunted corn maze." I shrugged, trying to play it cool while my insides danced with bottled up anticipation. I might not be game for a haunted maze, but I was more than happy to see Derek again. And Nate, I hurried to tack on, recognizing that it was my interest in him that had led to this ridiculous Halloween bet in the first place. Not to mention everything would be so much cleaner and easier if I just stayed interested in Nate and let these growing feelings for Derek fade.

Unfortunately, "cleaner" and "easier" rarely factored into decisions of the heart.

Chapter Nineteen

I TRIED TO IGNORE the flutter of nerves cartwheeling in my stomach as I climbed out of my car and walked towards the corn maze's entrance, the gravel of the parking lot crunching under my feet. Cold wind whipped through the night, making me gasp and pull my hoodie closer. I immediately regretted not grabbing my gloves and scarf. If it wasn't for our bet and the chance to see Derek, I meant Nate, I would have stayed home, safely wrapped in a blanket watching *Sleepless in Seattle* or something equally cozy. Really any romance would do, just as long as it didn't involve monsters, blood, or gore.

Derek had given me a pass on the trip to the amusement park and he probably would have done the same tonight, but I didn't think I could handle another evening at home alone with my thoughts. So I told him I was feeling up to it, trash talking in our texts, bragging about the movies I'd make him watch once I won the bet.

How scary could a corn maze really be? It couldn't be that bad, right? I'd survived the haunted lift, murder clowns and all. This maze would be a piece of cake.

I stopped just outside the entrance, searching the crowd for familiar faces as families pushed past me to enter the park. The fall air nipped at my cheeks, smelling of cinnamon and fried food and making my stomach growl. Maybe I could convince the group to skip the maze and just sample the carnival food. A funnel cake and a big mug of hot chocolate sounded amazing right now.

Finally, I caught sight of Derek's familiar brown waves, and my stomach dipped. He wore a faded royal blue sweatshirt that I immediately wanted to wrap up in, breathing in his scent and soaking in his warmth.

I'd just seen him yesterday, but things had changed during my illness, and I wasn't quite sure what to expect. I had so many questions running through my mind when it came to Derek and where we stood. Was I interested in him as more than a friend? Yes. Was he interested in me? I hoped so, though there was always a chance I'd read all of his signals wrong. On top of that, I was fairly certain he'd seen my last family photo with Meg, making me wonder what he thought. If I told him about Meg and my family, how would he react? Would he be hurt I hadn't told him?

I'd spent so much time hiding my past, I hadn't spent much time considering the ramifications for when I finally told someone close to me, like Derek.

I tucked my hands into my jacket pockets, suddenly nervous as I watched Derek for a moment. He was laughing and joking with a tall redheaded woman I hadn't met yet, and a feeling I struggled to identify twisted in my stomach. It felt an awful lot like jealousy, and I wasn't quite sure how to handle the sensation. This was Derek we were talking about. Mallory's question from earlier in the day rang through my mind: *Are you sure that man is meant for the friendzone?* I was fairly certain I knew the answer to that question now and it changed everything.

"Chloe! You made it." Nate stopped beside me, slinging an arm around my shoulders, a giant smile stretching across his face. "We missed you at the amusement park. There was this one zombie whose makeup was insane. Like, I thought he was real for a minute there."

"Sorry I missed that..." I trailed off, not fully able to hide my sarcasm. I watched Nate for a moment, taking in his infectious, dimple-less grin and artfully mussed hair. He was wearing a blue flannel that hugged his arms and shoulders and made his eyes pop. And yet, I felt nothing. It was so different from my emotions at our initial meeting, making me wonder if I imagined it all.

"I think that's everybody. Guys, let's go!" Nate called, waving the group over to buy tickets.

He kept his arm draped over my shoulders, pivoting us towards the ticket booth. I followed his lead, not sure how to react to my complete lack of reaction. I'd watched a horror movie and rode a haunted lift ride for this man. Now that I had his attention, I wanted him to turn it elsewhere. In fact, the redhead who'd been talking to Derek seemed like the perfect option.

I looked up and caught Derek watching us, his forehead pinched and tension clearly visible in his shoulders. He looked jealous, and I felt warmth steal into my chest at the realization. Just as I had the thought, Derek turned to the redhead he'd been talking to, his grin stretching to reveal his dimple and my stomach clenched. Then again, maybe I was wrong.

We reached the ticket window and Nate withdrew his arm as he paid for his ticket and then waved me forward. I only hesitated a moment before requesting a ticket for the haunted corn maze. The teenager working the booth must have heard the reservation in my voice, because he quirked his eyebrow at me before telling me the total. I tried not to flinch as I ran my credit card and accepted the black wristband that would give me access to my own personal purgatory.

The group met on the other side of the ticket booth where food stalls held a variety of fall-themed, deep fried confections including apple cider donuts that sounded divine. Families with kids were everywhere I turned, climbing on tractors, riding the giant slide, and petting barnyard animals. This was the part of the corn maze I'd visited before. I'd even done the non-haunted maze with my roommates last year, managing to get lost in the twists and turns that, according to a map, had made up the Scooby Doo gang and Mystery Machine.

I followed our group to the one part of the park I'd done my best to avoid over the years. It seemed to radiate darkness and terror, though that was probably in my mind. A foreboding black arch stretched across the entrance, a sign proclaiming "Haunted Corn Maze" hung from the arch written in a font that made each letter look like it had been written in blood. With each step we took, the cheerful sounds and smells of cinnamon faded, replaced by eerie music and the smells of metal and sweat.

I had never wanted to turn around and run toward a churro so much in my life.

Nate stuck to my side, talking nonstop about how excited he was and how epic he'd heard the haunted maze was this year. For a guy who'd just moved to the area, he'd done a remarkable job at finding all the scary activities. There couldn't be that many more to participate in, could there? Halloween was only a few days away. Surely, we were reaching the end of his list.

"I've been told it's their scariest year ever. The new owner loves horror and made some updates." Nate practically glowed with excitement.

I swallowed hard, trying to bite down the instant anxiety clawing its way up my throat. If I survived tonight, I would never leave my couch again. I was staying where it was safe and warm without zombies, serial killers, clowns, or sock monkeys. And if Derek asked, I had plans to dog-sit Ruby while Audrey worked on her yoga certification or to arrange flowers for Mallory's wedding. Surely, I could find something to fill every night from now until Halloween. Because if Nate invited me to go paintballing with zombies or something equally terrifying, I was likely to lose my marbles.

After showing our wristbands to the gate attendant, we got in line. I'd hung back, trying to gather my courage, which was how I ended up at the back of our group with Derek and his new redheaded bestie.

"Chloe, have you met Natalie?" Derek waved to the woman at his side, and I instantly disliked her.

She had long red hair that flowed down her back in waves. She was tall and trim with vibrant green eyes and a dusting of freckles across the bridge of her nose. She looked too beautiful, too put together, too . . . not me.

"Nice to meet you!" Natalie held out her hand and sent me a bright white smile, her teeth perfectly straight and contrasting prettily with her lipstick. "Derek was telling me all about you. I'm so glad you're feeling better. Whatever bug you caught sounds terrible."

Just how everyone wanted to be introduced, as an invalid who'd just barely mustered the strength to leave her bed. I felt like I was back in junior high with a face full of acne and braces trying to make friends with a cheerleader.

I gave her hand a shake before returning my hand to the warmth of my hoodie pocket. I instantly regretted drawing attention to the old, too-big black sweatshirt I'd opted to wear. It contrasted sharply with the emerald green of her own jacket, which hugged her curves and emphasized her assets. Assets I was sadly lacking.

"I'm glad I'm better too. Wouldn't want to miss the haunted corn maze." I forced a smile, hoping she couldn't see the fear lurking in my eyes. I felt the color leaving my face with each step we took closer to the entrance.

Derek turned concerned eyes on me, straightening from where he was leaning against the metal stanchions guiding the line. "Are you sure you're fully better? I don't think anyone would blame you for taking another day or two to get back on your feet."

His words were spoken with a gentle kindness that would have melted me on the spot if it wasn't for our surroundings. Instead, I was using all my mental focus trying to ignore the rowdy teenagers in line ahead of us and the grown men wearing masks and carrying chainsaws nearby. If I tried hard enough, I could pretend we weren't listening to ominous music while we waited to enter a building that looked like it should have been condemned. Apparently, haunted corn mazes, or at least this one, didn't actually start in the corn. Instead, it started in the sketchiest building possible in case you'd missed the memo that it was supposed to be scary.

"But then she would have missed both the amusement park *and* the haunted corn maze! And where would the fun be in that?" Nate had walked back to join us, nudging me with his elbow as he spoke.

I forced a smile, pretending excitement at what lay ahead. As we approached the main entrance to the haunted corn maze, I began to reevaluate every decision that had brought me to this point. The next time I wanted to impress a man, I was *not* pretending to love Halloween, and I definitely wasn't going to let a bet with Derek dictate my actions. In fact, I was probably going to swear off all betting for the rest of my life.

But I couldn't back down from *this* bet. At this point it was a matter of pride. Derek had to know he'd owe me one epic favor when all was said and done. Forget about watching *Pride and Prejudice*, he was taking me to a regency ball or something equally extravagant.

Our group reached the front of the line and the worker, a teenager dressed like a skeleton, divided us into groups of four. Natalie, Derek, Nate, and I made up the last group to go through. We stood outside the main door, a strobe light and fog machine lending to the creepy atmosphere as we waited to enter.

"You know, it's not too late to skip this part and go straight for the apple cider donuts." I joked, hoping no one could hear the nerves in my voice as the seconds counted down to our turn. A cackling witch noise followed by a crash of thunder made me jump. I whipped around to make sure no one was trying to sneak up on me and turn me into witchy-stew ingredients.

"Then we'd miss the best part! Besides, donuts taste better after an adrenaline rush," Nate said as the door swung open and a worker dressed as the grim reaper beckoned us through the door with a crook of his finger.

I took a deep breath and stepped into the room, my opportunity for escape evaporating as the door closed behind us with a loud, distinct click. My heart was already pounding, and the maze had just started. It was going to be a long night.

We stood in a dark cement room. A single bare bulb hung from the ceiling, providing the only light. The grim reaper stood by a door opposite the one we'd entered through, standing guard as a girl wearing ratty jeans and a t-shirt with the corn maze logo on it, shared the rules.

After we'd each verbally agreed to the rules, my agreement was much quieter and more begrudging than the others, the girl waved us towards the grim reaper. The boredom in her voice was almost insulting, considering the amount of fear already pulsing through my veins.

"Best of luck in the haunted maze. We hope you all make it out . . . alive." This came from the grim reaper who took way too much pleasure in the statement, his voice deep and filled with glee.

With that final word, the second door swung open, and the room plunged into darkness, the only light a trail of LED lights directing us into the maze. Shrieks, screams, and wails filtered through the door along with a buzzing sound I refused to identify.

My hand wrapped around Nate's arm of its own volition, squeezing tight. I was too busy fearing for my life to even notice the muscles in his arm. Instead, I held on, needing some reassurance that I wasn't facing this nightmare alone.

"Ouch! Watch it with the death grip," Nate said, jumping away from me as he led the way into the maze. "Come on guys, we don't want to finish too far behind the rest of the group. If we catch up to them, we might even be able to scare them!"

My breaths came in quick short gasps as I considered everything that could be waiting for us past this door. I stood frozen, unable to move, feeling alarmingly faint.

"You've got this." Derek's calming voice sounded next to my ear, reassuring in a way only he could be. "I'm here with you every step of the way. Just think of it as an adventure."

Somehow, I didn't think this was what Meg had had in mind when she'd made me promise to live life to its fullest, seeking adventure for both of us. Though, if this Halloween bet had taught me anything, there were many more adventures to be had close to home than I'd ever anticipated.

He grabbed my hand and tucked it into his elbow before leading me into the maze and one of the worst ideas I'd had in nearly three decades of life.

Chapter Twenty

We stepped into a nondescript room that immediately put me on edge. It looked like a normal, if somewhat dark, classroom with desks arranged in rows facing a TV screen playing static. The florescent lights above flickered, adding to the sense of foreboding building in my chest. There appeared to be a handful of students occupying a smattering of desks. They faced forward, not even turning to see who had entered. Quiet, suspenseful music played through hidden speakers, interrupted occasionally by a cackle or scream from somewhere deep in the building.

"What do we have here?" A gravely gruff voice asked right behind me.

I screamed, letting go of Derek and running to the far side of the room, as far from the voice as possible. I realized my mistake almost immediately as the students turned grinning faces covered in blood toward me. In my panic, I'd failed to notice the door nestled in the corner on the opposite side of the room from where I stood. Now I was trapped with a terrifying room of nightmarish-pupils between me and escape.

It's not real. It's part of the maze. They're just teenagers who need better hobbies. I chanted the words to myself, trying to calm my racing pulse and find the courage to move. Instead, I stood there, afraid to draw even more attention to myself as the weak link in our group.

"Are you our teacher?" Three of the students said in unison, titling their heads at odd angles, their faces splitting into morbid grins. They must have taken lessons from the murder clowns at the lift ride.

"Keep moving," the gravelly voice from earlier shouted. A guy with a giant stitched-up cut on his neck was attempting to herd the rest of our group out of the room with the ax he was carrying, cutting me off from friends and safety.

"Not without her," Derek said, his voice ringing with a level of confidence I'd only heard from him on rare occasions. He stood his ground, his hands planted on his hips, drawing attention to every inch of his over six-foot-tall frame and those secret muscles I was very much a fan of.

The teenager, whose clothes were bloody and torn, leaned into Derek's face stopping just short of touching him.

"She'll be along, just as soon as she's been disciplined." He raised the ax and pointed it towards me.

I huddled further into the corner, my legs refusing to move as my heart pounded in my chest. If it pounded any harder, it would escape. What happened if my body produced too much adrenaline? Was it possible to tense up so much my muscles would never move again? I was not a medical professional, and I doubted I wanted to learn the answers to the questions currently filling my mind.

"Then I guess we're getting disciplined together." Derek pushed past the worker, beelining it for me.

"No, she must stay. She must learn her lesson." One of the students hissed.

"Don't look at them, look at me," Derek said, standing in front of me and using his body to block the scene in front of me. He titled my face up, forcing me to look at him. I wanted to lean into the warmth of his touch and allow it to drown out everything else. "Don't look around and don't let go. We're getting out of here."

Forget about men in period clothing, I was all for men in oversized sweatshirts coming to my rescue.

Derek grabbed my hand and pulled gently. I took two stumbling steps before my legs steadied and I could easily keep up with his clipped pace.

We pushed out of the room, past plastic sheeting that lined the door. Nate and Natalie were nowhere in sight, apparently forgetting us in their rush to find the rest of our group. The next room we entered was lined in blood-covered plastic. A hint of motion out of the corner of my eye had me freezing and slamming my eyes closed.

"I can't. I can't do this," I gasped out through gritted teeth, dropping Derek's hand and wrapping my arms around myself. This had been an epically bad idea. I knew I was a scaredy-cat, but I'd figured my survival instincts would turn on like they had when I'd been surrounded by monsters while waiting for the lift ride, causing me to bolt into the middle of our group of friends for protection. Instead, when faced with overwhelming obstacles, I found myself freezing. Maybe I was more like a fainting goat than I'd realized.

"Yes, you can. You're strong and I've got you." Derek placed his hands on my shoulders, gently shaking me, trying to coax me to continue.

I shook my head furiously, hiding my face in my hands. The smell of fear and sweat filled my nostrils.

"I have an idea," he said.

The pressure of Derek's hands disappeared from my shoulders, and I felt instant regret. If he abandoned me too, I really would die in this corn maze. They'd prop my body up in one of the corners and I could become part of the décor, add an unexpected element of authenticity to everything.

I could feel Derek shifting in front of me before he spoke again. "Wrap your arms around me."

I cracked an eye open just enough to make out his back.

"What are you doing?" Curiosity filled my tone as I opened both eyes, focusing on his sweatshirt. Royal blue was fast becoming my new favorite color as I stared intently at the knit texture and not the horrors around us.

"Just trust me." He stood straight and tall, as if all the terrifying things encircling us didn't even phase him.

I snaked my arms around his waist, holding tight. I would worry about the implications of this moment later, after we'd both survived.

"Easy, I still have to breathe." Derek huffed out a laugh, one of his hands resting on my arms that were currently squeezing the breath out of him.

I loosened my grip slightly, resting my cheek against the worn, soft fabric of his sweatshirt. I took a deep breath, inhaling his aftershave and allowing the familiar scent to chase away some of the fear gnawing at my gut.

"Not that I'm complaining, but how is this going to get us out of here?" I asked, relaxing into the embrace and allowing his warmth to chase away some of my tension.

"I'm going to lead you out of here," Derek said, as if it was the most obvious thing in the world. "Keep your arms around me and your eyes closed. Whatever you do, don't let go."

I nodded, burying my face into his back.

The rest of the building passed in a blur of flashing lights, sounds, and smells as I followed Derek from one room to another, my face pressed into his back. The flexing and bunching of his muscles became familiar and comforting, guiding me until we reached a chute that we had to ride down separately.

"I'm right behind you," Derek said as I let go and took in the small, square opening.

"Promise?" I knew it was silly, but I needed the reassurance.

"I'll never leave you behind, Chloe." He hadn't abandoned me like the rest of our group, and our years of friendship told me he wouldn't, but having him say it out loud did more for my frayed nerves than I anticipated. Derek brushed his fingers gently down my cheek, gazing into my eyes for just a moment before stepping back and gesturing to the chute. "Ladies first!"

I climbed into the chute, pausing for just a moment to bolster my courage. I took a deep breath, closed my eyes, and let go, sliding down and landing on a blow-up pad in a patch of dirt lined by corn stalks. The rush of fresh air that filled my lungs was a welcome change from the stuffy, humid air that had enveloped us in the haunted rooms we'd been navigating. I stepped away from the landing area, taking in my surroundings. There was only one direction to go. I just hoped it led quickly to the exit as I shivered in the night, wishing I'd grabbed my coat. As soon as we escaped this nightmare, I was buying the biggest mug of hot chocolate available.

A quiet thud and huff let me know Derek had landed behind me. I turned in time to see him straighten, brushing his hands on his pants as he also took in the corn maze. His lips pulled to the side with a grimace.

"I don't think we're done quite yet," Derek said, reading my mind. "Ready to get out of this place?"

He offered me his hand and I took it, interlacing my fingers with his and holding tight.

"I was ready before we even started."

Compared to the gore and noise of the indoor portion of the maze, the actual corn maze part was quiet, a somewhat welcome change from the horrors we'd left behind. Though it did bring its own type of terror, an eerie uncertainty whether something was watching us, waiting to grab us and drag us back into the building we'd vacated. As we turned blind corners, workers in masks jumped out at us, startling screams from me that I was too exhausted to be embarrassed about. Thankfully, the corn maze portion was short, the path leading directly to the exit without any misguiding turns.

By the time we found ourselves outside the maze, our entire group was standing there waiting. I paused just outside the maze, needing a moment to process the experience before jumping back into the group. I watched as some of the guys rough-housed, laughter tingeing the air as they discussed their experience.

My eyes found Nate, his hair tousled from the adventure, and I felt nothing but objective appreciation for an attractive man and perhaps disgust at how quickly he'd left a friend behind. Natalie was leaning in to better hear what he said, clear interest written on her face. In that moment I realized I would leave tonight not caring if Nate ever invited me to another activity. In fact, if the activities continued in this vein, I'd be relieved never to see his name light up my phone again. I might even block his number to protect myself from the possibility of additional haunted invitations.

I looked to my right, where Derek stood, patiently waiting for me to regain my breath and approach the group. I wanted to lean into him, embrace the comfort and protection he'd given me as we navigated the maze. Something had been shifting between us since the lift, something that felt a little like possibility and hope.

"They made it!" Someone from the group exclaimed, calling attention to where Derek and I stood just outside the maze.

The others waved us over and, with a quirk of his eyebrow, Derek led the way. I watched him from behind, not quite sure what to do with the emotions filling me.

I was falling for my best friend, and the thought wasn't nearly as terrifying as I'd always imagined it would be.

Chapter Twenty-One

WE EXITED THE HAUNTED section of the park, and I walked quickly, doing my best to put as much distance between me and my nightmares as possible. Nate loped over to me, resting an arm around my shoulders with a chuckle.

"Wait up, scaredy-cat." He threw me a giant grin and I forced one in return. "Where's the fire?"

"I just don't feel like getting chased by another chainsaw wielding lunatic," I said, doing my best to keep the emotion out of my voice.

"But they're the best part of an attraction like this. They add to the ambiance." Nate waved behind us, his tone serious like he was discussing a five-star French restaurant and not a local haunted corn maze.

I made a noncommittal sound as I shrugged, slipping out from under his arm and making a beeline for a nearby booth selling hot chocolate. I needed warmth and sugar to compensate for the adrenaline crash that was starting to settle over my bones. I glanced over my shoulder, noting Derek wasn't too far behind, chatting with a few other people from the group. He looked up at me, a dimple-inducing smile tugging at his lips as our gazes locked and my stomach dipped, indicating not all of my hormones had crashed after the corn maze.

Nate followed me, clearly not picking up on my signals of disinterest and pulling my attention away from Derek.

"So, a group of us are planning to—"

I held up a hand, cutting him off before he could finish. If he didn't complete the invite, then I technically hadn't been invited to another terror-filled activity. Not that it mattered, if another person used the words "haunted" or "Halloween" when inviting me to hang out, I was going to run screaming for the hills. No bet with Derek was worth this much suffering. If he did force me to run a marathon with him, I'd find a way to get out of it. Maybe sprain my ankle during training . . . or flee the country.

"I'm pretty busy. I don't think I can swing it," I said, focusing on the menu and hoping Nate would pick up on my clear lack of enthusiasm.

"You don't even know what I was about to say! Halloween's only a few days away. We've got to squeeze in the fun while we can. Natalie was talking about this haunted train ride involving the headless horseman that sounds a little childish, but I'm sure it'll still be fun." He nudged my shoulder with a laugh. "You'll probably get a good scare out of it."

It was my turn to order, so instead of responding I stepped up to the cashier, ordering a large hot chocolate and a churro. I probably should be more mindful of my budget, given my current employment status, but I couldn't bring myself to really care in this moment. I was exhausted mentally, emotionally, and physically. At the very least, I'd earned guilt-free carnival food to help me navigate this conversation with Nate.

I could feel Derek's eyes on the back of my neck, and I had a sinking suspicion he could hear our exchange and was finding it highly entertaining. It was the power of being friends this long, I once again could feel him smirking without even looking.

"What do you think?" Nate asked after placing his order. We both moved to the side to wait for our food.

"What do I think of what?" I asked, my eyebrows pinching together as I tried to remember what he'd been talking about. I'd been too busy counting down the moments until I could wrap my cold hands around a warm cup.

"The haunted train ride!" He said, surprised I had to ask.

"Can I be honest?" I was tired and done putting on a show for this guy who had dropped in my estimation with each of our interactions until tonight, when he'd hit rock bottom with a spectacular thud.

Nate smiled and nodded, clearly not realizing that the words I was about to speak weren't flattering by any stretch of the imagination.

"I'd rather get a root canal without health insurance than participate in another haunted activity," I said, my face deadpan. I had no more emotions left in me for this man. They had spilled out of me in the maze, and I only regretted that it had taken me this long to realize he wasn't worth the effort. "I hate haunted things. I get scared watching Disney movies when they get a little too intense. These last few days, doing haunted activities to impress you, have been my actual definition of Hell. Please don't invite me to anymore. I'm done, and frankly I'm a little concerned for a guy who's so focused on the next scare that he doesn't notice when someone legitimately needs his help."

Nate gaped at me, clearly shocked at my words and uncertain about how to respond. Finally, he shook his head, an incredulous smirk tilting his lips.

"Look, if this is about walking away from you and Derek in the maze—"

I held up a hand, cutting him off. "That's part of it, but not the whole thing. I hope you love Utah and that you find a group of friends who love all the scary things. I'm not one of those people. Have a great night."

The workers called my name, and I grabbed my food, walking away from the concession stand and not bothering to wait for Nate to receive his order. Instead, I walked over to a picnic table and sank down onto the bench with an appreciative groan, certain Derek would come find me. I hoped he was entertained by my exchange with Nate because at this point, I found it sad that I could have been so wrong about pursuing someone, even for just a fling. I sipped at my hot chocolate, not even caring when the too-hot drink burned the tip of my tongue. I took a bite of my churro and groaned with pleasure, the sugar and cinnamon helping revive me some.

"Long night?" A familiar voice asked.

I looked up as Derek settled onto the bench next to me. The metal gave a slight creaking sound at the added weight.

"You could say that," I said with a small laugh, brushing at a strand of hair that had caught in the breeze and blown across my forehead. "I hate Halloween."

He nodded sagely. "I could have told you that."

"Also, I'm done with guys who think scaring the living-daylights out of somebody makes for a good friend activity. I can only imagine what he would have come up with for a first date."

"Probably dinner at Dracula's castle," Derek said without missing a beat.

"Or watching a slasher movie at a cabin in the woods while splitting a bucket of popcorn. And, as you know, I have to really like someone before sharing my popcorn."

"Because that's the problematic part of that date scenario," he said, laughter tingeing his tone.

"Obviously. I love scary things. It's the sharing I don't do," I said with a snort before shaking my head. "You tried to warn me."

"I'm not here to tell you 'I told you so,' Cee." His voice softened with the words, warmth filling his face, which I could just see thanks to the soft glow of string lights hanging above our heads.

"You should be," I said, waving my churro at him to underscore my point. "I was so stupid! I should know better now than to chase after a guy who's clearly all wrong for me. I got lost in my daydreams again. When will I learn?"

"I hope you never do," Derek said, reaching over and breaking off a piece of my churro to pop into his mouth. "Daydreaming makes you who you are, and I wouldn't change that for the world."

Warmth settled over me, and I didn't bother questioning it. Tomorrow I had a list of questions to answer, most of them having to do with Derek and this growing realization that I didn't want to stay only friends. But for now, I was going to sit here grateful to have survived perhaps the most terrifying night of my life with this man by my side. A man who saw me at my worst and still believed the best of me.

Chapter Twenty-Two

THE NEXT MORNING, I woke slowly, remembering the night before as I stretched and settled into my freshly laundered sheets. The mix of terror while still feeling entirely safe had been something new, making the night not entirely unpleasant. Though the haunted maze definitely wasn't an experience I was looking to repeat any time soon. After I'd finished my hot chocolate and churro, Derek had walked me to my car, neither of us bothering to tell our group goodbye. We hadn't spoken much outside of commentary on the activities around us, but I'd enjoyed the comfort of just being in his presence. There was so much left unsaid, but I hadn't known how to start. Instead, I'd stuck to safe topics until we'd reached my car at which point I'd ducked my head, given him a hug, and driven home. Though I had glanced back in my rearview mirror and noticed he'd watched me drive away before walking to his own car.

Regret curled in my belly as I thought about the many other ways the night could have ended. Each possibility more enticing than the last.

"Would I have kissed him?" I asked the question aloud, trying to make sense of this new possibility.

I hadn't even bothered telling Nate goodbye last night after our conversation at the concession stand. He'd disappeared with friends, Natalie among the number, and I had no regrets about that fact. He'd shown me his loyalty when he'd left me behind in the first room of the maze. Now a different man had snagged my attention, a man who knew me better than any guy I'd ever dated.

I got ready quickly, hoping Derek would call, but also nervous about what to say, how to react the next time I saw him.

Breakfast and lunch passed without a word, and I did my best not to worry about the shift in our relationship. Friendship? Whatever I should call this *ship* of ours. I knew I could call or text him, but that somehow felt too vulnerable, so instead I did my best to keep myself busy and to not check my phone every ten seconds.

I half-heartedly searched job listings, skipping over what felt like the same listings I'd seen repeatedly these last several weeks. Only one held any promise. It was a local job, something I'd been adamantly avoiding

But would staying be so bad if something happened between me and Derek?

Going against my instincts, I applied, continuing to watch my phone and pray for a call. Or a text. I'd even accept an email. Just something to indicate that he was thinking about me as much, or even half as much, as I was thinking about him.

"You know, that thing works both ways, right?" Mallory asked when she caught me staring at my phone hours later in the living room while a rom-com played in the background. "Unless it's broken?"

I groaned, flopping back onto the couch and pulling my blanket up over my head. "I know, but what do I even say to him? The guy came to my rescue last night, and I can't even come up with an opening line of conversation."

I'd told my roommates all about the corn maze when I'd gotten home. Their excited squeals and exclamations at *something* finally happening between me and Derek could have woken the dead.

"I've found 'hi' to work really well when communicating with others. Following it up with, 'How are you?' also works nicely," Mallory said, nudging my feet out of the way and sitting on the couch next to me.

"Yes, but what do I say after that?" I was never this uncertain when it came to talking to guys. And yet, somehow it felt different with Derek in this moment.

"You could ask what he's doing tonight and make plans to hang out," Audrey commented from her place on the loveseat. She'd been watching something related to her yoga certification on her computer with headphones on, and I hadn't realized she was listening.

"Or you could just offer to make out with him as a show of appreciation for him saving you from all the teenage serial killers at the corn maze," Mallory offered, giving me a sly look.

"That one! I like that one," Audrey said, sitting up and setting her laptop and headphones on the coffee table. "Just make sure you brush your teeth first."

I snatched the throw pillows from behind me, chucking one at Mallory and the other at Audrey and somehow managing to miss them both despite our close proximity. Ruby, who'd been snuggled next to Audrey on the loveseat lifted her head long enough to give me a disapproving look before returning to her curled-up position.

"You guys are the worst."

Our laughter was cut short as my phone started ringing and I sat bolt upright, snagging it from the end table.

Derek's photo filled the screen, the same shot from our early college days greeting me, even as the emotions I felt were far from familiar.

"It's him!" I said, my voice coming out oddly squeaky, filled with both excitement and nerves.

My roommates squealed and I shushed them as I answered the call and pressed the phone to my ear.

"Just remember the plan," Audrey stage whispered, picking up her laptop and following Mallory out of the room, the pair of them making kissing noises the entire way.

I covered my face, mortified. Thankfully it was a phone call, not a video, so Derek could not see the resemblance between my face and a tomato. Nor was he privy to Audrey's and Mallory's expressions as they walked away.

"Is this a bad time? Those sounds aren't normal," Derek said in lieu of a greeting.

I groaned, my embarrassment complete. "Now's a great time. I just have the world's worst roommates."

"And here I'd thought they were so nice," he said, his voice full of humor.

"They're world class actors and deceivers," I said without missing a beat. A disgruntled huff from the hallway told me my roommates may have disappeared out of sight, but they were definitely still close by, ready to get the play-by-play once this conversation was over.

Derek and I sat in awkward silence for a moment, neither of us knowing where to go from here. The events of the night before continued to play through my head—the moments with my face buried in his shirt would be burned into my memory for the rest of my life. Especially the combination of his steady presence and familiar scent that had provided a comforting balm during my moments of complete terror.

"I've been meaning to call all day," he said, finally breaking the silence.

"Oh?" I asked, praying my hope and excitement didn't come through on the phone. I was still attempting, and failing, at playing it cool. I didn't want to show my interest too soon, scaring him away and ruining our friendship.

"I wanted to make sure you were okay after last night. I know it was kind of traumatizing." He hesitated on the last word, as if unsure how to describe our experience. There was so much good and bad all rolled into one that it was hard to distill down into a single word.

"Parts of it were, but other parts . . ." I trailed off, at a loss for words.

"Other parts?"

Was that hope I heard in his voice?

"Were really nice." The statement felt inadequate, but it was as much as I could give him right now. I'd never felt so vulnerable and exposed, as if I was asking Derek to see all of me in this moment. Even the parts I was just discovering.

"I felt that way too," he said quietly, and my heart gave a giddy skip of joy.

A more comfortable quiet settled between us and I held my breath, waiting to see what he'd say next.

"I don't suppose you want to come over to my dad's place?" It wasn't the invitation I'd been expecting, but there was a certain rawness to the question that spoke to my heart.

"You know I love visiting your dad. Can I bring anything?" I stood from the couch and walked into my room, already mentally reviewing my wardrobe and picking something to change into. What outfit did one wear when seeing one's best-friend-turned-potential-love interest? I didn't know the answer, but I was fairly certain it wasn't the ratty sweatpants and t-shirt from high school that had a hole in the collar that I was currently wearing.

"Just you."

—*ele*—

Twenty minutes later, I stood outside Derek's house, soaking in details with a new perspective. The house blended in with the rest of the neighborhood: white siding, neat, dormant flower beds, faded pink mailbox. How much of Derek's life had this house witnessed? And what would it witness now? Was everything about to change? Or was I reading too much into a single night full of heightened emotions?

As I looked back on our years of friendship, a part of me felt like this had been building for years. From late night diner dashes in college to countless hours talking in his car, we'd been growing closer until now, when the line between friends and something more had blurred so thoroughly I couldn't point to an exact moment when everything changed. Ever since I'd met Derek, I'd felt like we'd been making our way to this moment. And yet, a part of me was still terrified to make the shift, to allow Derek fully into my life. Yes, I trusted him. It was kind of impossible not to trust him after all of these years. But what happened if I took the leap, changed this relationship, and it all went wrong? Yet, I didn't think I could go backward and pretend like things between us hadn't changed. The only way forward now was out of the friendzone into something completely new, and I was both terrified and excited to discover what that meant for us.

I rang the doorbell, tucking my arms behind my back in an attempt to keep from fidgeting. I wanted to smooth my hands down my sides or fiddle with the necklace I wasn't wearing, as if calming my nerves could be accomplished through a simple movement.

"You're being silly. It's Derek, Axle, and Chris. You've been here countless times. Stop being ridiculous." I muttered just as Derek opened the door looking amazing in jeans and a black t-shirt that seemed to emphasize his chest and shoulders.

"Talking to yourself again, I see. This is starting to become a habit. Or maybe last night knocked something loose?" Derek winked at me before pulling the door wide open and waving me inside. "Dad's in the family room. He was stoked when he heard you were coming over."

"I was just here last week," I said on a laugh as I stepped into the entryway.

Derek shrugged, turning and waving me towards the family room.

"You know Dad. You could have been here yesterday, and he'd still say it had been too long."

The house smelled of lemon with mild undertones of disinfectant. I followed Derek and the sounds of the TV down the tiled hall into the family room where Chris sat in a recliner watching a cooking show in sweatpants and a t-shirt that had seen better days but looked soft and comfy. The scene was just missing Axle, and we could re-create our evening from the week before.

"There she is," Chris called, reaching for the lever to sit up.

"No, stay sitting. Derek said you could use some company so I'm here to say hi." I stopped next to Chris and reached down to give him a hug. His frame somehow felt even smaller after only a week, though that was likely in my head. Every time I saw Chris, I searched his face and body, trying to find evidence that he would be okay or that he was doing worse. As if I could tell from the tiny details what his future held.

"You're always welcome to visit! Come sit." Chris waved me over to the couch, his smile revealing where Derek's dimple came from.

"Mostly, he's excited to have anyone visit so he doesn't have to spend the entire evening talking to me or Axle." Derek joked, settling onto the couch next to me. He lifted his arm to rest along the back of the couch behind me.

It's so he'll be more comfortable. Don't read too much into it. I told myself, even as I leaned back, wishing I was a couple of inches taller so I could feel the warmth of his arm a bit more.

"Gemma and the kids can't get here soon enough," Chris said with a wink, and I snorted a laugh.

"When do they get here?" I asked, excited to see Gemma again. While I didn't know Derek's only sister well, the few times I'd interacted with her had been fun, and I looked forward to the chance to get to know her and her family better.

"In two weeks," Derek said as Chris responded, "Twelve days."

I laughed.

"Not that anyone's counting?" I asked, leaning around Derek to wink at Chris.

"She's bringing the grandkids, of course I'm counting!" Chris said, excitement evident in his voice. "Those kids are growing up too fast and I don't get to see them often enough."

We settled into a comfortable quiet, the cooking show on the TV capturing our attention for the moment. On the screen, a group of celebrities tried their best to cook using an odd assortment of ingredients and no recipe. One country singer in particular was attempting to flavor fried chicken with lavender, and I was very grateful not to be one of the judges for the show. Instead I laughed along with Derek and Chris until a commercial came on.

"Derek said the two of you braved a haunted maze last night," Chris said, his voice raspy like he needed to cough. He turned to watch us, a twinkle in his eye.

Derek stood, grabbing the cup from the end table next to Chris's chair and offering it to him.

"I can pick up a cup! No need to mother me," Chris said, his voice making him sound five instead of somewhere in his fifties. Despite his protests, he took the cup, but waved Derek back to the couch before taking a long drink and returning the cup to the end table.

Derek sat back into his seat, and I felt instant regret that he didn't return his arm to its former position on the back of the couch behind me.

"It was definitely an experience I'm not looking to repeat." At least parts of it. There were some parts I wouldn't mind revisiting at all, like the feeling of Derek's back flexing beneath my cheek. My cheeks flushed at the thought, and I shifted back, further into the couch, trying to distract myself from the conversation I hoped to have with Derek. My toes barely brushed the floor once I was settled, so I crossed my legs under me to get more comfortable. It also meant I took up more space on the couch, moving closer to Derek in the process.

"I never understood the appeal of paying other people to scare you. I'll scare you for free." Chris waggled his nonexistent eyebrows, and I couldn't help but laugh to see how proud he was of his joke.

"I'll keep that in mind next Halloween when my friends are suggesting haunted activities." Derek grumbled with a shake of his head.

I held up my hands in protest. "I've had enough scary activities to last several years."

"Really?" Derek looked at me, his eyebrow quirked in interest. "Does that mean I've won our bet?"

I shook my head as the commercial ended, the cooking show resuming and snagging Chris's attention. "Hardly. I haven't been invited to any other activities, and I'm pretty sure my evenings are booked from now until Halloween."

I gave a delicate shrug, trying to communicate nonchalance at my pronouncement.

"That's too bad. I had a couple of evening activities I was hoping to persuade you to participate in," Derek said in a quiet, low tone that turned my bones to jelly, a mischievous glint in his eyes as he watched me.

My heart pounded at the possibilities his words conjured. What kinds of activities? I could think of more than a few I wouldn't mind participating in. I bit my lip, considering my response.

"I mean, I might be able to reschedule one or two of my plans for the right offer," I said, my voice sounding breathless to my own ears. I prayed Chris was too absorbed in his cooking show to pay attention to our exchange. I'd said bolder things to guys before, but there was something about saying these types of things to Derek that made me feel like a junior high girl talking to her crush for the first time. Having his dad in the room added an extra layer of anxiety that I could do without.

"Is that so? Interesting." Derek turned back to the cooking show, his dimple making an appearance as a self-satisfied smile tipped up one corner of his lips. Lips I knew fairly well as a passive observer, but that I wouldn't mind getting to know in a much more up close and personal kind of way.

We settled in to watch the show, an odd tension sparking between Derek and I as we watched. I felt my nerve endings crackling in anticipation, though of what, I wasn't sure. It wasn't like anything was going to happen with Chris sitting feet away, but my body hadn't gotten that memo. For some reason, now that I'd opened myself to the possibility of seeing Derek as more than a friend, my whole body seemed to take it as a green flag, ready to charge ahead regardless of who else was around. Regardless of what the next steps in my life looked like.

On the next commercial break, Chris asked Derek something about work and he shifted to better see his dad, his thigh brushing mine in the process. A zing of attraction shot up my leg, making me want to lean closer and continue the contact. Not wanting to draw Chris's attention, I leaned away and fished my phone out of my pocket. I tapped at the screen, checking my email and pretending to be busy when in reality I wanted to capture Derek's hand and drag him from the room so we could finally talk. I had so many questions that needed answers only he could give.

We continued watching the show, chatting during commercials with Chris asking about life, while I tried to ignore the tension between me and Derek. It grew to the point that I wanted to flee the room, escape to the bathroom or just drive home and try to talk to Derek another day. Instead, I pasted on a pleasant expression and did my best to stay present with Chris until the episode we were watching ended, and he turned off the TV with a giant yawn and stretch.

"I think I'm going to take a nap. Why don't you take your girl to get some dinner or something?" Chris asked as he leaned further back into his recliner, getting comfortable.

"Dad, she's not . . . Never mind," Derek said with a shake of his head. It was the first time he hadn't fully corrected his dad when it came to our relationship, and I felt my heart give a small leap. "Get some sleep. I'll be back to check on you in a couple hours."

Chris waved the offer away. "It's Axle's night to babysit. You two go have some fun. It's not like I can get into much trouble at the moment."

Derek sighed, pushing to his feet and helping me up.

"Fine, Dad, but call if you need anything. I'll stay close by." Derek leaned down to give his dad a hug, which Chris accepted before shooing us out the door.

"Go! He's worse than a nursing mother, I tell you," Chris said as I bent to give him a hug goodbye. Laughter sparkled in his dark, tired eyes.

I followed Derek out to the car, the crisp fall breeze ruffling my hair and making me shiver.

"So..." Derek trailed off, clearly unsure what to do next. "Are you hungry?"

"I could eat." I gave a noncommittal shrug, shoving my hands into my jeans pockets and scuffing my shoe along the sidewalk. The tension had built to an awkward, almost painful level now that we were alone, and I was worried what would happen if we didn't do something to relieve it soon.

"I can drive." Derek waved to his car, and I followed him to the passenger side, pausing while he unlocked and opened the door, holding it for me as he waited for me to settle into my seat. "What sounds good?"

In that moment, something inside me finally snapped. I'd spent the entire summer and beginning of fall with constant uncertainty as I'd searched for a job. Not to mention the almost daily challenges I'd dealt with for my family, wondering if Mom and Max would ever settle their differences. I wasn't going to stand for uncertainty in my love life.

Before Derek could close the door, I stood from my seat and turned to face him. Channeling all the courage my five-foot two-inch frame possessed, I snagged his hand, forcing him to stop and look at me.

I bit my lip, trying to find the words to share my thoughts and feelings, to take this next step with Derek.

"Cee, what—" Derek broke off, seeming to read the hesitation and desire I was fairly certain was written all over my face.

"You feel this too, right?" I asked, my words quiet.

One corner of his mouth tipped up as he responded, "Feel what?"

"This . . . attraction. This need for more. This . . ." I trailed off with a shake of my head. "Derek, something's shifted, and I'm not really sure how to describe it or what it is or what it means but I . . ." I stopped, the words clogging in my throat. What if I was reading the signs all wrong? What if Derek didn't actually want to change anything, and everything I thought I'd seen in his face was just a result of heightened emotions from last night? Could I really lay it all out there, take this big of a risk?

"You?" He asked, reaching up to tuck a strand of hair behind my ear, his hand lingering a bit longer than necessary, the contact giving me the sign I needed to be brave and continue.

"I've always said we're just friends and up until now, that's been enough. But after the lift ride and then last night, I don't think it's enough anymore. Which is crazy because I'm moving out of state and who knows where life's going to take us, but—"

Derek pressed a gentle finger to my lips, cutting off my rambling.

"What do you want, Chloe? In this moment, right now. Forget about the future and what may or may not happen for just a moment and tell me. What do you want?" His expression was full of heat that shot straight to my toes, telling me exactly what Derek wanted if I would only give the signal.

I knew my answer, I just had to be brave enough to show him.

I hesitated one heartbeat, gathering my courage, and then I pushed up to my toes, wrapping my arms around his neck and using his surprise to pull his face down to mine.

"You," I whispered as I pressed my lips to his, finally accepting everything that had been building between us since the moment we'd made our ridiculous Halloween bet and even before that, all the way back to the day we met.

Chapter Twenty-Three

IF I HAD KNOWN this is what kissing Derek Hansen would feel like, I would have done it years ago. He clearly knew what he was doing as his lips met mine, movement for movement. His initial surprise and shock at my kiss quickly faded as I continued pressing my lips to his. It only took a moment before he wrapped his arms around my back, pulling me in close so that I was finally enveloped in his warmth. His hands traced down my spine as his lips and tongue tangled with mine. This was not the timid, sweet kiss of a first date. This was the type of kiss shared between two people who had known each other for years, who understood each other in ways no one else did. And the sensation was intoxicating.

Derek was the first one to pull back several moments later as he straightened but kept me wrapped in his arms. I accepted the break, needing a moment to catch my breath even as I wanted to pull him back down for more. The man definitely knew his way around a kiss.

"What—" he broke off, shaking his head and taking a deep breath before continuing. "What was that?"

"I believe the word you're looking for is a kiss," I said, my lips tilting into a smirk that I hoped he'd feel the need to kiss away. "And a very good one at that."

Derek somehow resisted the urge to lean in for more, watching me with a level of scrutiny I'd much prefer he directed elsewhere. We'd just shared perhaps the best kiss of my life. No need to question it. We probably just needed to embrace it and give it some competition with a few more incredible kisses.

As if reading my mind, Derek took a shuffling step backwards, breaking contact and putting space between us. His shoulders hitched up towards his ears, as if prepared to fend me off if I came after another kiss.

"I had hoped that maybe, after we talked, we could get to this point." He shook his head again, an adorable half smile on his lips that I'd never seen before. "But I didn't invite you over to watch cooking shows with my dad followed by a make-out session in the front yard like we're in high school."

I held up a finger to stop him. "First of all, I love watching cooking shows with Chris. And second, if I wanted to re-create a moment from high school, I would have waited until we were in the car and it was only five minutes before curfew. Kissing you in broad daylight in front of your childhood home is a level of boldness *I* didn't even realize I possessed."

It was the right thing to say because Derek laughed, easing the tense set of his shoulders and he reached for my hands, pulling me back towards him.

"I think I just learned some critical details about a young Chloe," he raised an eyebrow, as if daring me to contradict him.

"Actually, young Chloe was not nearly this bold, and current Chloe is still shocked with her behavior," I said, rubbing the back of my neck and looking away from Derek. "Though I also wouldn't say no if you were to lean down and go for round two." I bit my lip and gave him a hopeful look, not fully sure how to move forward from here. I'd acted on instinct with that kiss and now the instinct was gone, leaving me second guessing the decision to kiss first and talk later.

He shook his head with a disbelieving laugh, making his dimple pop. "I can't believe I'm about to say this but, as much as I want to kiss again, I've waited too long for this moment to mess it up."

I waited, relieved that I hadn't been out of line but also sensing there was more.

"I think we need to talk. While I very much enjoyed and would like to continue enjoying this, we have some important things to say to each other before we can do *this*," he let go of one of my hands and waved it back and forth between us, "again."

Recognizing his logic and the stubborn set of his shoulders, I nodded and accepted Derek's wisdom. Though, I would much prefer to skip the difficult conversation and keep kissing. Kissing was straightforward. Given a choice between the two, I'd definitely pick kissing. Ten out of ten, would recommend over talking, every single time. Talking came with the risk of saying the wrong thing, of messing things up just as we were getting started. But it also brought some relief because we'd finally resolve my uncertainties from last night.

"Fine, but please note that I would like to resume kissing once we've finished talking. It's a much more preferable way to use my lips as opposed to talking about difficult things." Pretending to feel confident and flirty, I threw a wink over my shoulder and reopened the car door that had closed at some point during our exchange, settling into the passenger seat and closing the door behind me, with Derek watching me wide-eyed the entire time.

The whole effect was only slightly ruined when I attempted to lean back into my seat seductively and instead fell back, thanks to the seat being much farther back than anticipated. Axle had struck again. I gave an unattractive yelp, cursing Derek's brother the entire time as I reached for the lever to adjust the seat.

By the time he reached the driver's side, Derek was shaking with laughter as I grumbled about potential options for making murder look like an accident.

"You know I'm going to kill your brother, right?"

He just nodded as he turned on the car and put it in drive. "And here I was going to ask you to remind me to thank him."

"Why on earth would you want to thank him?" I asked, folding my arms over my chest in righteous indignation.

Derek's voice softened as he looked at me, his dimple flashing as the half smile he'd given me earlier reappeared. "Because he made the most memorable kiss of my life even more so."

When he put it that way, I might just owe Axle a "thank you" of my own. Warmth filled my chest at Derek's pronouncement, and I settled back into my seat, curious to see where Derek was taking us and nervous about the conversation ahead.

Chapter Twenty-Four

AFTER CIRCLING PLEASANT GROVE, Derek finally pulled into a familiar park with a pond and walking trail. Several groups were also at the park with people fishing, riding bikes, and walking dogs, their voices adding a soothing soundtrack to the moment. I climbed from the car, grateful I was wearing tennis shoes as we started down the path. The ride to the park had been quiet, but not in a strained way. More like we were both reliving the kiss and trying to gather our thoughts.

If I had thought yesterday changed everything, it had nothing on today. If you'd told me two weeks ago that I was going to kiss Derek and immediately want to do it again, I would have laughed it off, secure in the knowledge that we would always be friends and nothing more. Now, I was just hoping this conversation led somewhere that included the possibility of more kissing and time with Derek.

We passed a few families as we walked, Derek and I both absorbed in our individual thoughts. He'd shoved his hands into his jeans pockets, the picture of pondering as he walked with his head down, watching the path.

I took the opportunity to take him in, from his tall, lean build to his confident stride. I had spent countless hours with this man and yet, I had no idea what would come next.

"Do you like cheese?" I finally asked, at a loss for words but desperate to start this conversation. Desperate for additional confirmation that my impulsive kiss hadn't been a mistake but a stepping-stone to something great.

Derek's head jerked up, his expression pinched in confusion. "Excuse me?"

"There is a right answer to that question involving a very specific movie quote and if you don't give it, I'm afraid we're going to have to go back to the car and pretend like this evening never happened," I said with faux seriousness.

"And what if I refuse to answer the question because we have more important things to discuss?" He asked, raising an eyebrow. That infuriating eyebrow communicated more in this moment with a single gesture than I felt confident communicating with all the words in my vocabulary. I might need a refund on my English degree.

"Fine, but don't think we won't be revisiting that question at a future date," I said, hoping there would be a future date and that I hadn't just ruined years of friendship with a kiss. It was one reason why I'd insisted Derek and I were just friends. Keeping him in the friendzone was so much cleaner and easier, but also, as that kiss had taught me, much less fun.

"Don't worry, I'll quote *She's the Man* with you later," Derek said, alleviating at least some fears as I braced myself for the conversation ahead. If the man I dated wasn't fluent in movie quotes, we were going to have a serious problem.

Dating. Was that what Derek and I were doing? There was only one way to find out.

"So, last night," I said, hoping that if I took the lead on the conversation, it would help us get to the end faster. Or at least I could give myself the illusion of control. I wished I was wearing my necklace, so my fingers had something to play with right now. Or I wished Derek's hands weren't shoved into his pockets so that I could hold onto one, use it to ground me.

"Last night," Derek responded, nodding sagely.

"You saved me."

"I don't know about saved—"

I grabbed his arm and pulled him to a stop. "You did! I froze in that maze and never would have gotten out. I would have given my best impression of a fainting goat and been trapped in there until I died or wet my pants." Exactly the visual I wanted to give someone when talking about the possibility of a relationship. "You saved me, Derek."

He shrugged and ducked his head, as if trying to downplay the whole thing. "It was the least I could do. I was the reason you were stuck in that place to begin with. All because of a stupid bet."

His words gave me pause, and I realized, for perhaps the first time, that Derek held himself responsible for my stupid decision that had landed me in a haunted corn maze when I knew I was about as brave as Scooby Doo without any Scooby Snacks.

I moved to stand in front of Derek, waiting until he finally met my eyes. I needed him to listen to me and to believe the words I spoke. "It wasn't your fault. I'm the one who took the bet. I knew I couldn't handle the maze, but I went anyway. If anyone's to blame, it's me."

He shook his head, and I wanted to reach up and smooth away the guilt creasing his forehead.

"I was the one who suggested the bet."

"And I was the one who accepted it and wouldn't back down." I persisted. If this more-than-friends thing was going to stand any chance, it had to start here and now with Derek letting go of any misplaced guilt or blame.

"I know, I just can't stop thinking about what would have happened if I hadn't been there. If you'd gotten hurt." He brushed a thumb over my cheek, leaving a trail of heat in its wake.

"But you were there, and you saved me," I said the words softly, needing him to hear them. To hear me.

"Derek," I said after a moment as he continued to stare past me, guilt clear in his features. "Between work and your dad, you have enough on your plate to take responsibility for. I'm not letting you add my actions and choices to the list." I reached up, cupping his cheek and trying to communicate my sincerity with the gesture. "The only thing you get to take responsibility for right now is how you choose to answer one question."

"Oh yeah?" He asked, his lips finally tipping up into that smile I loved.

"Do you want to kiss me again?" I asked, biting my lower lip as I waited for his response.

His eyes tracked the gesture, the heat in his gaze causing my stomach to tighten in anticipation.

"And if my answer is yes?" He hooked his fingers in my belt loops, using them to pull me in slowly.

"Then you're going to let everything about last night go because I'm not wasting my time kissing a guy who doesn't respect my decisions." I said the words with a level of confidence I didn't fully feel. If Derek continued to cling to his guilt, I probably could be persuaded to still kiss him. Though it would be somewhat begrudgingly. Maybe.

"Is that all?" His voice was full of humor as his hands settled on my hips before his arms snaked around my waist, pulling me flush with him.

"That and you have to admit defeat," I said as he ducked down, his lips mere inches from mine. All I'd have to do was push up on my toes and I'd get to kiss him again, a sensation I could see myself becoming quickly addicted to.

He pulled back at my words, and I wanted to groan. I'd had the upper hand for the moment, but if Derek realized how close I was to giving into my desire, guilty consciences and stupid bets be darned, I'd be running a marathon with him or baking a dozen pies or something equally dreadful before the year was over.

"But I haven't lost the bet yet," he said, voice serious and a teasing glint in his eye. "There are still several days between now and Halloween. How do I know you won't be invited on another scary outing?"

"Because," I reached up, pulling his face back down to mine, "you're going to be my plans from now until Halloween and beyond. That is, if you want to be."

I paused, waiting for his answer, waiting for him to choose me and accept this leap from friends to more. We could pretend like the kiss at his dad's house had been nothing, forget about it and stay in our comfortable friendzone. Or we could be brave and choose this moment to start something new. Either way, we both had to make a choice—and we had to make it together.

"Cee, I've never wanted anything more," he said, tracing his fingers along my jawline.

"Promise?" I asked. I'd lost count of the times others had told me this was what Derek wanted. I'd even seen Derek's actions that seemed to confirm that observation. But I needed him to tell me.

He didn't hesitate. "Promise."

With that final word, I pressed my lips to his again, quickly learning that our first kiss, while magical, was just a starting point. We kept this kiss tame, aware of our surroundings, but even with a mild kiss, Derek left me breathless with the gentle pressure of his lips on mine, his arms holding me close.

As we broke apart, my heart danced an elated rhythm that seemed to chant Derek's name with every beat while simultaneously demanding we find a less public place so we could enjoy more than just sweet pecks.

"So, what are you doing tomorrow night?" Derek asked, his voice husky and my new favorite sound.

"Hmm?" I asked, my thoughts still considering alternative locations where we could take this activity.

"If I'm going to be your plans every night from here until Halloween, I've got to start planning now."

It took a moment for my kiss-addled brain to process what he was saying, and when it did, a blinding smile stole across my face, making my cheeks ache with the sheer joy of it all.

"In that case, we better get to work making plans," I said, lacing my fingers with his and leading him back to the car. "We're going to be very busy tomorrow night. And the night after that and the night after that."

Chapter Twenty-Five

THE NEXT EVENING FOUND me wrapped in Derek's arms on the couch in my apartment. Both Mallory and Audrey were out with their men and, when I realized Derek and I could have the entire space to ourselves, I'd immediately invited him over. We'd have plenty of time to plan fancy dates out. For now, I wanted to relish the sensation of just being together as more than friends.

"Why are we watching this again?" Derek asked for perhaps the hundredth time as I burrowed into his side, a blanket draped over my legs and a bowl of popcorn in my lap.

When Derek had arrived, I'd gleefully told him my plans: watching the 2005 version of *Pride and Prejudice*. I'd sweetly told him I was saving the five-hour version for a future date, when we had time to fully appreciate its artistry. He'd groaned but good-naturedly settled in to watch. No doubt he'd been expecting the movie watching to quickly devolve into our activities from the night before. Those activities would come eventually, but I was not giving up this opportunity to show him the magical, though abbreviated, love story that was Elizabeth Bennet and Fitzwilliam Darcy.

Derek pulled me closer into his side. "I could think of several other activities that would be a better use of time. Getting a colonoscopy, cleaning the gutters, taking my dad to the doctor, making out." He trailed off for a moment pretending to ponder. "Really, just about anything would be better than watching two people with too much time on their hands fall in love."

"Shhh," I hushed with a laugh, reaching up and popping a piece of popcorn in his mouth to make him stop talking. "If you keep talking, we're going to miss something important and then we'll have to start the movie over and," I paused for effect, watching his expression over my shoulder, "that would cut into our time to complete at least one of the activities on your list. I'll even let you choose which one," I said with a flirtatious wink.

Derek straightened, making an exaggerated show of zipping his lips, pressing them into a thin straight line that only lasted for a moment before his secret little half smile, the one I was starting to think of as mine, broke through.

"I wonder how I'll possibly pick which activity to do. It has been a long time since Dad cleaned the gutters, so they're probably pretty full. Though I've never gotten a colonoscopy, so maybe that's the better choice." He nodded his head, as if genuinely considering his options as he tapped a finger on his chin.

I scoffed, setting the popcorn bowl on the coffee table and turning to face him fully.

"Sounds like a tough call. I'll just end the movie now so you can get to it. You have a busy evening." I pretended to stand, and Derek looped his arm around my waist, pulling me back down next to him.

"Kidding, kidding!" Laughter rang through his voice. I'd seen more joy in Derek's face the last few days than I'd seen since his dad was diagnosed, and I was addicted to it. To making him smile and laugh and embrace this happy side of himself that had disappeared for far too long. Another casualty of cancer. "What I'm really hoping to do is dust and paint all the baseboards at home. They need it, especially before Gemma comes to visit."

With a put-out shout, I started tickling him, forgetting about my determination to force him to watch the whole movie without distraction. Instead, I skated my fingers over his ribs, making him laugh and squirm as he attempted to duck away from me. Unfortunately for him, he was firmly wedged between me and the arm of the couch, and I was using his position to my fullest advantage. After a couple of minutes of tickle warfare, Derek was finally able to capture both of my hands, holding them firmly against his chest as we both panted, trying to catch our breaths.

I loved the feel of his chest beneath my hands, the beating of his heart a comforting sensation. If I listened close enough, would I hear my name in every beat?

I shook my head at my ridiculousness and tried to sit up, but Derek refused to release my hands.

"I promise no more tickling," I said. If I could have, I would have raised my hands in a placating gesture, but he kept them pressed firmly to his chest.

"I'm not sure I believe you." He quirked an eyebrow at me, suspicion written in every line of his face.

"Scouts honor?"

He shook his head. "You weren't a scout."

I gave a huff of laughter. "Fine! I swear on Mr. Darcy's hand-flex then."

"I don't know if that's much of a promise."

"You clearly weren't watching closely enough if you don't think that's a serious promise," I said, thinking back to the iconic moment and how I'd sighed with pure joy as we watched. The internet was not wrong about the attractiveness level of that single, involuntary hand gesture.

"I said it earlier and I'll say it again. I don't understand the appeal of a hand spasm. Mr. Darcy probably has arthritis from all the letters he has to write and simply needed to work out the tension." As he teased me, Derek released my hands, and I curled back into my comfortable cocoon at his side.

"If that's all you got out of that scene, we really do need to watch it again," I said, only partially joking. If I had my way, this would not be the only time I watched *Pride and Prejudice* with this man. In fact, I wouldn't mind finding a way to make Derek's hand flex involuntarily.

"All I'm saying is that it seems like a lot of hype for—"

I held up a hand, stopping him before he could distract me again from the movie on the TV screen. "I'm serious about restarting this movie if you keep talking."

He watched my face, reading the sincerity in my expression before nodding and reaching for the bowl of popcorn on the coffee table in front of us.

"Fine. I'll stop talking, but don't think I'll forget your promise about letting me pick our next activity." He waggled his eyebrows, and I couldn't help but laugh. Images of what that next activity could possibly consist of filled my mind and a blush stole into my cheeks. I wouldn't mind some of those activities. Not one bit.

Was this how dating was supposed to be? With Derek, it felt so easy, so natural. He already knew me so well. I felt like we'd skipped right past the awkward small-talk stage straight to the deep conversations and enjoying favorite hobbies together, and I didn't mind one bit. I'd never been a big fan of the friends-to-lovers trope, but now I fully understood the hype, and I was here for it.

When the movie ended, I grabbed the remote and turned off the TV, more than ready for our next activity. While Derek had kept his word and hadn't spoken once the rest of the movie, it hadn't stopped him from occupying himself in other ways. He'd traced patterns on my bare arms with his finger, toyed with the hair at the nape of my neck, and bumped my thigh with his every few minutes. It was almost as if he wanted to remind me that what I had here, in real life, was so much better than the love story I was watching play out on the screen.

I turned to Derek, already tilting my head to press my lips to his, when a mischievous look flashed across his face.

"So how do you feel about..." he trailed off, leaning in close, his lips only inches away from mine.

"About?" I asked, breathless at the possibilities ahead. My stomach danced like I'd downed an entire two liter of diet Coke, and I knew I was in trouble.

"Playing two truths and a lie?"

"What?" I jerked back, bumping my head into the back of the couch and nearly toppling over sideways in surprise.

He shrugged. "I feel like I know everything about you, but also not at the same time. I thought we could play a game, something that would answer questions but not in an awkward first date kind of way."

"Or we could skip the questions and go straight to the fun part."

"I thought watching *Pride and Prejudice* was the fun part." Derek lifted his chin, as if daring me to contradict him.

"I mean, it's a fun activity. I'm just guessing there's one or two other activities we could participate in that would be more fun." My voice came out husky and enticing.

"Like playing get to know you games. I couldn't agree more."

"Nothing says fun like get to know you games," I said, my voice petulant. I crossed my arms and shifted to put some space between me and Derek. "Should I be offended you don't want to kiss me right now?"

I tried to fill my voice with sarcasm, but some of my genuine concern must have come through because Derek's face softened and he reached over, brushing a lock of hair from my forehead.

"I very much want to kiss you," he said, tracing his fingers along my cheek before trailing them along my jaw.

"But?" I asked, sensing there was more, even as I wanted to lean into his touch, wrap my arms around his neck, and make us both forget this conversation.

"But I also don't want to mess this up. I like you, Cee! I have for a long time."

The familiar observation that I'd heard from my roommates on more than one occasion, played through my mind, and I opened my mouth to respond though I wasn't quite sure what to say. I was still getting used to this feeling of allowing myself to be something more than friends with Derek, of accepting and acting on his interest.

He pressed a finger to my lips, halting any words for a moment.

"Let me finish. I've liked you since the moment we met, but you just wanted to be friends, and I accepted that. I would have accepted almost any type of relationship if it meant I got to be in your life." He paused, an expression of sadness and hope playing across his face as he dropped his hands into his lap. "Now that I have the chance to really, truly pursue something more with you, I don't want to ruin it. You've been one of the few steady, dependable things in my life since Dad's diagnosis and the fact that I could mess that up terrifies me."

"You could never mess this up." I reassured, cupping his cheek with my hand as I tried to communicate just how sincere I was through my touch.

"Maybe not, but I also know getting too physical too fast has spelled disaster for more than one of my relationships, and I care about you too much for that to happen." He gave a self-conscious shrug, rubbing the back of his neck.

I felt warmth steal into my chest at his words. Recognizing the level of vulnerability those words would have required, I scooted to the opposite side of the couch and turned so I was facing him, my legs crossed underneath me. It was my attempt to put space between us and respect his wishes. If I sat too close, I'd give into the attraction between us faster than you could say "Mr. Darcy's hand flex."

"Okay, no touching, but also no cheesy games. Let's just talk," I said with a decisive nod. "Though if this night ends without a kiss, I might reconsider joining Nate's gang for more Halloween activities. Maybe he could introduce me to a single friend who moonlights as a murder clown at night." I waggled my eyebrows, doing my best to keep a straight face at the absurd suggestion.

Derek just shook his head before asking the first question. "If you could live anywhere, where would it be?"

I titled my head, considering. This question hinted at one of the unanswered questions that lay between us and our relationship: my out of state job hunt. But so far, we'd steered clear of that conversation and, until I had a good job offer, I wanted to keep it that way.

"I mean, I'm a sucker for British accents so probably London. Especially if the men there can hand flex like Darcy."

Our conversation went from there and, while I'd never admit it to Derek, I enjoyed the opportunity to ask him questions I'd never thought of before this moment. We learned we both preferred beaches to mountains and that our dream trips involved exploring Europe, though he wanted to visit Iceland while I was more interested in the United Kingdom. We talked for what felt like only minutes when it had really been hours. I realized I wasn't checking the time or wishing to be somewhere else. Instead, I eagerly awaited his next answer or question. Until he asked the question I'd been avoiding our entire friendship.

"I don't think I know much about your family. You never talk about them. What are they like?" Derek asked. Over the course of the conversation, we'd slowly scooted closer together. The back of my hand currently rested in one of his palms while he played with my fingers with his other hand.

I took a deep breath, knowing now was as good a moment as any to finally share my biggest secrets. I just hoped my emotions would hold. I hated crying. I'd much rather shove my emotions down and ignore them.

"My mom is a neat freak. She's always cleaning and decluttering. My dad does something in business. He's explained it to me more times than I can count, and I still don't understand." I gave a self-deprecating laugh. "All I know for sure is that he's working all the time and goes on the occasional business trip to the Midwest."

Derek had stopped playing with my hand, interlacing his fingers with mine and watching my face as I talked.

"You have a brother, right? Max?"

"Good memory," I said. Derek had met Max once at my college graduation, and I rarely talked about anything connected to my family. It was easier to keep that door firmly closed, so I was impressed that Derek remembered.

"Max is a senior in high school and counting down the days until he graduates and can move away to college. He's very good at testing his boundaries and my mom is very good at," I searched for the right word, "smothering him."

"Oof. That's hard. I remember being a teenager and not wanting to answer a single question my dad asked. I was a bit of a punk," he said with a laugh, and I tried to picture it.

I'd been in Derek's childhood home enough times that I'd seen his high school photos. He'd looked like a nice guy, though his hair was maybe a bit long for my liking. Of course, my high school self probably would have loved it. Assuming I could have looked beyond my grief long enough to notice him. Those years were a bit of a blur for me.

Derek continued talking, lost in decades old memories. "I was at my worst after Mom left, but I calmed down when I moved to college. I met this girl who introduced me to her friends and helped me look on the bright side of life." He nudged my shoulder with his and warmth filled my chest at the contact.

"She sounds pretty incredible."

"She is." He gave me a warm smile. "But I'm talking too much about me," he said, and I wanted to protest, to ask questions that would keep him talking, wandering memory lane. Anything to avoid what I knew was inevitably coming next: Meg. He paused, seeming to select his words carefully.

"You only ever talk about Max, but I saw the photo on your nightstand when you were sick, Cee. Do you have a sister?"

"I wondered if you'd noticed that," I said, shaking my head and trying to decide what to say. "I actually thought I had a dream about you, Mallory, and Audrey looking at the picture and asking questions. Guess it wasn't a dream."

He shook his head, looking sheepish and a bit hurt. "We wondered why you'd never said anything about having a sister. But we also decided you needed to be the one to tell us. That you had to have a reason for keeping her a secret."

My muscles bunched and I curled in on myself as he spoke, feeling a combination of worry and guilt at his statement. I knew I should have said something, but it had been so long since I'd talked to anyone outside of my family about Meg that I'd forgotten how. Sensing my tension, he rubbed soothing circles on the back of my hand and wrist as he waited for my response, not pushing but clearly needing me to explain.

I took a deep breath, swallowing down my instinct to run and hide, to avoid the hard. There was a reason I only liked happy endings. It was because my own life was sorely lacking in them. Between Meg's passing and my parent's lackluster relationship, it was a miracle I still had hope for the future. Watching happy endings gave me hope that someday, maybe, I could find my own.

"As you saw in the picture, I have a sister," I said, sticking with the present tense. I never knew which tense to refer to Meg in. Yes, she was dead, but she was still my sister. Cancer had stolen more than enough from me. It didn't get to take that reality away from me too. Living or waiting for me in the next life, Meg was my sister and that would never change. Even if it made conversations like this even more difficult.

"Tell me about her." Derek released my hand and leaned forward, resting his chin in his hands. I both missed the contact and was grateful for the space. It somehow made it easier to keep going.

I swallowed, my mouth feeling like it was full of sawdust. I could really use a diet Coke with lime right about now. Forget about caffeine making it impossible to sleep tonight. But I resisted the urge to jump up and mix up the drink. Instead, I pulled my legs up to my chest, wrapping my arms around them, needing the comfort.

"Her name is Meg. She's older than me by two years." I trailed off, my voice soft as I tried to gather my courage to say the words I hated most about Meg's story. Not that it was a detail I could or would hide. It just still hit hard when I went from being the girl with an older sister to the girl with a sister who died.

"She died from cancer when I was in high school."

Chapter Twenty-Six

I'm NOT SURE HOW I expected Derek to react. Since Meg's passing, it felt like I had experienced every possible reaction. The overly sympathetic response with wide eyes and the insistence that the other person was "*so* sorry for my loss." Or the sensitive soul who I ended up comforting because Meg's death was such a sad reality. There were also the friends who avoided me or ignored any details I shared about Meg because it made them uncomfortable to think about death and loss, especially at such a young age.

It was those reactions that had made me stop talking about Meg. My emotions could only handle so much, walking the halls of high school being the girl whose sister died. So, once I moved away from home, I became someone different. Miss Happy-Go-Lucky. It was just easier that way. I didn't have to deal with other people's emotions on top of my own. And that way Meg was mine to remember and hold close.

But here in this moment, I regretted not telling Derek sooner, not letting him into that quiet corner of my heart before now because he reacted in a way I hadn't experienced.

There was no forced sympathy. Instead, he pulled me in for a hug, holding me close.

"I'm sorry, Chloe. I had no idea," he whispered into my hair.

The wall I'd built around my heart where I kept my deepest, hardest emotions about Meg started to crumble.

"If something like that happened to Gemma or Axle . . ." He trailed off, clearing his throat and pulling back to look at me. "But why have you never said anything? Especially with everything going on with my dad. You never said a word."

He kept his arms around me, but I could still hear the hurt in his question.

I looked down into my lap, not wanting to read his expression as I tried to explain.

"I never know how to tell people. It's just easier to keep that part of me hidden from everybody."

"But I'm not everybody," he said, releasing me and tipping my chin up to read my face. "At least, I like to think that's not how you see me."

"No, it's not." I rushed to reassure. "It's just . . . no one teaches you how to move forward with life after loss, not really. There's no one-size-fits-all user manual. And for me," I paused, needing to get this right, "it was easier to hide behind a mask of smiles and happy endings. If I didn't tell anyone about Meg, I didn't have to share her with people who didn't . . . couldn't understand. And eventually, it just became easier to keep that piece of me hidden."

Derek's hand dropped from my face, and he stood, walking over to one of the windows we hadn't closed the blinds on yet, looking out into the night. I wanted to go to him, to wrap him in a hug, to beg him to understand. I was messing this up, but I wasn't sure what else to do to make it right, to help him see how sorry I was but also that my actions had been out of survival.

"It also means you never gave others . . . me a chance to get to know Meg, a chance to help you when the days got hard. You keep telling me you want to help me with my dad, but you never gave me the same chance with you mourning Meg." He turned to face me, his expression one of pain. My heart ached at the sight.

"I can't imagine . . ." He trailed off, shaking his head. "Actually, I can because right now it's my worst nightmare. It's what I fear most with Dad, and here you are, dealing with it every day, with me and Audrey and Mallory and everyone else in your life none the wiser."

I walked to him then, grabbing his hand and praying I could get this next part right.

"I'm sorry. I know I should have told you, all of you, so much sooner. Can you forgive me?" I searched his face, terrified of his response but knowing we couldn't move forward if we didn't settle this now.

He studied me for a moment longer before his face softened and he framed my face with his hands. "Of course I forgive you. But with one condition."

"Anything." My voice was a desperate plea.

"No more secrets. When you hurt, I want—no *need*—to know. Promise?"

I leaned into his touch, my heart filling with relief. "I promise."

Chapter Twenty-Seven

WE SETTLED BACK ON the couch, a tender, sensitive truce between us. I wasn't sure what to say next as I settled against Derek, the silence loaded with emotion and memories. His hand rubbed my arm in a reassuring gesture I could easily get used to. I breathed him in, the familiar smell of his aftershave providing comfort in this moment of vulnerability.

"I'd like to hear more about Meg, if you want to tell me," Derek said, his voice soft and filled with invitation. His chest rumbled under my ear, and I could get used to the sensation of talking to Derek while snuggled up close.

I was tempted to leave the conversation there. To take Derek's offer at face value, to continue to hide this part of me and my story. But I knew doing so wasn't fair to Derek—or to Meg. And for the first time in my life, I didn't *want* to leave the conversation there when talking to someone outside of my family. I wanted him to see Meg the way I did, not as a victim of cancer, but as a vibrant, living human being who played basketball and loved musicals and pushed my buttons while being one of the people I loved most in the world.

"Meg was stability and calm to my energy," I said with a laugh, remembering so many small moments. "We fought, you know, like siblings do. All the time. But we also fought for each other without hesitation. I was never afraid to go to school or to participate in something because I always knew she'd be there. At least, until she got sick." My words were soft, trailing off as I tried to think through what I wanted to say.

"She was athletic and kind and sassy. She was the voice of reason when I wanted to do something crazy like ice blocking down a giant hill or dyeing my hair hot pink." A sad smile lifted my lips as I allowed myself to remember so many things I'd tried to bury for so long.

"Can I see a picture?" Derek asked, bringing me back to the present.

I stood from the couch and walked into my room, grabbing the frame from my nightstand along with the silver box. I handed him the picture and he sat up, leaning over to examine the photo.

"You've seen this one before," I said, not sure why I felt the need to explain as he studied the image.

"I didn't look at it too closely that night you were sick, just close enough to realize you had secrets you hadn't told me. You look like your mom. You and Meg both do." He handed the frame back to me and I set it on the coffee table, propping it up where we could both see as we continued this conversation.

I settled back on the couch, placing the silver box in my lap as I bit my lip and debated what to say next.

"It's been a long time since anyone's told me that," I said, fiddling with the box lid, my hands needing somewhere to channel my anxious energy now that I had decided to have this conversation. "People used to ask if we were twins. I once told someone we were but that my mom was in labor for two years."

"That would be quite the birth story," Derek said, reaching over and placing a hand on mine, stilling my fidgeting for the moment. "Meg was a forward on the high school basketball team. That's how we knew something was wrong. She took herself out of a game because she was in pain, something she'd never do unless it was really bad. My parents took her to the doctor the next day and, by the end of the week, we had a diagnosis." It was such a clinical word for something that had the ability to completely turn your world upside down.

"Ewing's sarcoma," I continued. "I didn't know what it meant back then, just that my parents said the prognosis was good and that our family would fight this thing with everything we had. And we did, for an entire year." Even though I'd been a teenager, that year was hazy in my memory. I knew it was filled with a mix of chemotherapy and radiation treatments. I'd spent countless hours in the hospital visiting Meg as she underwent different treatments and received blood and platelet transfusions. But I couldn't recall details about the conversations we had, the things we did, the other people who visited.

"I started keeping this box," I held it up as if there were any question about which box I was talking about, "that last year. I filled it with things to help me remember." I opened the lid, revealing a mix of items from photos to movie ticket stubs to an eraser I'd won at a local arcade when Meg had been feeling up to an outing. I shuffled through each item, holding things up for Derek to see. It felt like the world's saddest version of show-and-tell as I shared each memory and deposited the corresponding item on the coffee table next to the picture. My own mini memorial for my sister.

My fingers stilled when I reached the last two items in the box: a necklace that consisted of a ring on a chain and Meg's funeral program.

I held up the necklace, showing Derek where the word "sisters" had been engraved into the silver in a swirling script. It was simple. A trinket picked up at a store randomly on one of Meg's good days.

"I was out shopping with Meg when she saw these rings." I smiled, thinking back to that unassuming day and moment. "There had been two rings, both too small for our fingers, but Meg said it was a sign, so we bought them and chains to put them on. I wore it every day until I left for college. After that, I shifted to wearing it under my shirt and then only occasionally because I got tired of answering questions when people asked me what the ring meant. I finally stopped wearing it all together and slipped it in the box a couple of months ago."

I'd gotten the gamut of possible explanations for the ring. One person asked me if I had a secret fiancé. Someone else asked if it was the ring from *The Lord of the Rings*. No one ever guessed the real reason, that it was a reminder of someone who was no longer here, but who I missed every single day. I still reached to fiddle with the necklace when I was anxious, even though I hadn't worn it daily in years. Now I only pulled it out when I felt especially alone or overwhelmed.

"I think it's a beautiful reminder," Derek said softly, holding out his hand for the necklace. I carefully placed it in his palm, and he studied it for a moment before undoing the clasp. "Turn around."

I did, knowing what he was about to do but unsure why.

He draped the necklace around my neck, securing the clasp before placing a kiss on it where it rested at the base of my neck. Emotions burned the backs of my eyes at the sweet gesture, and I blinked rapidly to hold back the tears. Resting a hand on the ring where it sat at the base of my throat, I paused, wanting to hold the moment close and never let it go.

"Gemma used to have a pair of earrings that belonged to my mom," he said, cautiously, giving me a glimpse into a piece of his story that he rarely shared with me. I knew little about his mom, just that she'd left, shattering their family in the process, and that it was never a good day when she reached out and tried to contact him. "I got mad at her for it once. I couldn't understand why she'd keep something that reminded her of someone who abandoned us." He paused, gathering his thoughts. "But then Dad pulled me aside and told me I owed my sister an apology. We all had different ways of handling our hard, and if wearing those earrings made my sister feel better able to face the world without a mom, it wasn't my place to question her."

I waited, sensing there was more.

"You shouldn't be afraid to show people all of yourself. Even if it's not a picture-perfect happy ending." He whispered the words into my hair, making goosebumps erupt down my spine. "Don't let fear steal this from you."

A lump lodged in my throat at his words and the simple, unassuming gesture. When it came to life, I liked to think I wasn't a fearful person, despite my aversion to haunted activities. I went zip-lining and cliff jumping. I'd even gone skydiving once on a dare. But when it came to owning my story and letting the world see me as anything other than the happy-go-lucky, down-for-anything girl they expected, I tended to shy away. It was easier to let the world see what they expected. They couldn't reject you completely if they never saw the full picture.

So I pushed on, needing Derek to see my full picture and understand exactly who he was in a relationship with.

"Meg passed away at home shortly after we found out her chemo wasn't working anymore. It was almost exactly a year after her diagnosis. Before she died, I promised her I'd live my life for both of us, seeking adventure, doing the things she never could." My voice cracked with these last words. Up until now, I'd been able to stay detached, keep my full emotions at bay, but the dam broke as I finally put into words the way Meg's story ended. Tears cascaded down my cheeks and I tried furiously to wipe them away. "Sorry, I hate crying. It's part of why I never talk about Meg."

"Hey, it's okay." Derek reached for me, turning me around, pulling me into his side, and using one hand to wipe away the tears. "Let it out."

So I did. I don't know how long we sat there, tears coursing down my face as I cried for me, for Meg, for all the lost years and forgotten memories. My grief was a pain that faded but never really went away, though some days I wasn't even sure it faded. It was more like it hid, waiting for the perfect moment to jump out and surprise me, sucker-punching me with all the hurt, regret, and loss once more.

When my tears finally stopped, I lay there exhausted, snuggled into Derek's side as we held each other on the worn couch. I felt a certain level of amazement at the man who'd sat with me as I talked and cried. I couldn't picture Nate sitting here in this moment. In fact, I couldn't picture any of the guys I'd dated in the past doing that. They'd been there for me during the fun and happy moments, but they definitely weren't the kind of guys to lean on when life got hard. Which was why I'd never told them about Meg and why our relationships hadn't lasted more than a couple of months at most.

"You still with me?" Derek asked after I'd been quiet for a while.

"Yes, just thinking."

"About?"

I sat up so I could see his face.

"How incredible you are, and how lucky I am to finally have someone to share all of this with. Other guys I dated would have run for the hills the second I started crying." My voice was scratchy, and I was certain I looked like a hot mess, mascara trailing down my cheeks, my eyes puffy and red from crying.

Derek gently cupped my face with his hand. "Those other guys were idiots."

"You can say that again. I'm just sorry I didn't tell you sooner." I settled back into Derek's side, enjoying the comfort of simply being with him, his chest rising in steady breaths. The sound and motion soothed me, and I realized I felt relief at finally being fully seen by someone. There wasn't pressure to entertain, to put on a brave face. I could just be here, present, and for Derek that was enough.

Chapter Twenty-Eight

THE NEXT MORNING, I stumbled out of my bedroom into the kitchen wearing an oversized sweatshirt and leggings, my hair sticking up and whatever makeup I hadn't cried off the night before still on my face. It was late morning, late enough that I was genuinely pondering skipping breakfast and going straight for lunch. Which definitely had more to do with the time and nothing to do with the fact that I was completely out of milk to go with my cereal. I rubbed my face as I pondered my food options in the freezer, knowing I needed to make a grocery store run, but also wanting to make my last trip stretch just a little bit longer.

I should spend the day searching for more jobs, but all I really wanted to do was call Derek and convince him to skip work.

Deciding 10:45 a.m. was close enough to lunch time, I pulled out a freezer meal and popped it into the microwave, closing the door a bit more forcefully than necessary. I probably could use another hour to fully wake up, but my stomach had been growling, telling me it was long past time to start my day.

Derek had stayed late, holding me close, listening to me and letting me cry. I somehow missed my roommates coming home, lost in the haze of emotions and the feeling of relief that came with finally being seen. It was like a weight had lifted, and I no longer needed to hide pieces of myself because I knew Derek could handle me and all my baggage.

"I wondered when you'd surface," Audrey said from behind me, making me jump. I'd been so lost in my thoughts that I hadn't heard her walk into the kitchen.

She was dressed for work, wearing yoga gear with her hair braided back from her face. She'd recently gotten a part-time job teaching yoga at the rec center and loved every minute of it.

"It was a late night," I said, trying to keep my tone neutral as I pulled my food from the microwave, giving it a quick stir before putting it in for another minute.

"I can imagine." She waggled her eyebrows and stepped around me to pull a reusable water bottle from one of the cupboards. "You and Derek looked awfully cozy. It seems letting him out of the friendzone agrees with both of you."

I couldn't help the goofy grin that filled my face.

"I have no complaints." In fact, I had the opposite of complaints.

"Does this mean you're going to switch to a local job search? Stick around to see where this thing goes?"

Audrey's question was perfectly natural and normal, but it was something I wasn't quite ready to answer. I'd thought about shifting my focus to jobs in the area, but I held back because of the promise I'd made Meg. While it hadn't specifically included a job out of state, I knew Meg had dreamed of becoming a physical therapist for a major sports team, living in and traveling to cool locations as part of her job. I'd always assumed keeping my promise to her meant fulfilling her dreams as much as possible, though I drew the line at a career related to the medical field. I didn't handle injuries and gore well.

Where did that leave me and my promise if I settled for a job in Utah, staying close to home and the man I was falling for?

I pulled my food from the microwave, sitting at the counter to eat as I considered my response.

"We haven't really talked about it." I hedged.

Audrey raised a knowing eyebrow, but didn't comment on my clear reticence. Instead, she started talking about her upcoming yoga class, trying to convince me to come with her. I bowed out of the opportunity, claiming I needed to get back to the job hunt. Which was true. Even if the job hunt would still be there in an hour, after the class.

As Audrey was opening the door to leave, I realized I had one more thing I had to do in the wake of my conversation with Derek.

"Hey, Audrey," I called out and she paused, turning to face me, her expression curious.

"What's up?"

"Next time you and Mallory are home, I have something I need to tell you guys about my family," I said, the words not feeling nearly as awkward as I'd feared. "I should have told you a long time ago, but I was always too afraid."

"Okay," she trailed off. "Should I be worried?"

"No. I'm just learning that I need to be better about letting people in to see all of me, not just the pretty, happy parts."

"I think that's a very important thing to learn," Audrey said with a smile as she slipped out the door.

Once Audrey left, I opened my laptop and pulled up the job sites I knew all too well. I clicked through any new out-of-state listings, applying for a couple that looked promising. Then I did something I'd been avoiding since graduation. I changed my search criteria to jobs in Utah.

Maybe Audrey was right, and I should give a local job—beyond the one I'd already applied for—a shot. Though Derek and I had been friends for years, long enough that we could probably make long distance work, a part of me questioned if that was what I really wanted. I liked having him close, being able to burrow into his side when I was scared, holding hands and kissing and all of the amazing things that came with living close. If I moved out of state, those experiences would be fewer and farther between.

Taking a deep breath, I clicked on the first listing and began the application.

The next couple of weeks passed in a happy blur as I got lost in my new reality as Derek's girlfriend. During the day, I applied for jobs. I even managed to snag a few interviews, though most were dead ends. I hadn't narrowed my job search exclusively to local listings, but I was applying for more and more opportunities in Utah. I just couldn't quite bring myself to give up on my promise to Meg, feeling like I needed to do more to live life for the both of us beyond living a happy, settled life in Utah.

Since my savings were dwindling and I didn't want to move in with my parents, I'd finally caved and started substitute teaching. While it didn't pay much, it was enough to keep me independent for now. Though it had confirmed that not pursuing an English teaching degree had been the right move for me. I was not built for the classroom long-term.

In the evenings, I spent my time with Derek. We watched cooking shows with his dad on Derek's nights with him. When Axle was with Chris, Derek and I would go out to the movies, dinner, hiking. Derek even convinced me to join him at the gym a time or two, though I drew the line at running. We'd called a truce when it came to the scary things bet, deciding we'd much rather spend our time together participating in activities we both enjoyed instead of torturing ourselves with haunted attractions neither of us found fun.

We even celebrated Halloween, watching *Young Frankenstein* with Chris, while Derek and I took turns distributing candy. We had a cooking competition of our own, building Halloween-inspired graham cracker houses, with Chris acting as judge. I won, though Derek definitely attempted to sabotage me, stealing my candy and bumping the table to try to make my house collapse.

It had been an evening full of laughter, making me reevaluate my opinion on Halloween, especially when Derek kissed me goodnight after walking me to my car. I could definitely get behind the holiday if every time it looked like this: laughter, candy, and kisses.

Gemma and her family flew out for a visit between Halloween and Thanksgiving, and I loved watching Derek in his role as uncle, playing with the kids in the fall leaves and enlisting their help in hiding miniature plastic ducks throughout his dad's house. I was more than happy to help, though I'd also slipped a few into Derek's car as payback for when he'd played the same prank on me. The visit was good for everyone, especially Chris, who seemed to have more color in his cheeks and pep in his step after they left. He was already counting down the days until they'd come back to celebrate Christmas.

My own family was doing alright. My parents had planned a vacation, just the two of them, and Max seemed to be following all of my mom's rules, even if he found them excessive and smothering. He'd had a great time at homecoming and was looking forward to having the house to himself while my parents went on a cruise, their first vacation just the two of them since before Meg's diagnosis.

It felt like everything was falling into place, and I was cautiously optimistic for the future.

After some coaxing from Derek, I had even invited him to my family's house for pie next week to celebrate the day after Thanksgiving, introducing him to the whole family as not just my best friend, but also my boyfriend. I had never taken a boyfriend home, and the step felt significant. If I thought about it too much, my stomach gurgled with nerves. While I'd promised no more secrets from Derek, showing him my family with all their flaws and broken pieces was intimidating, especially when I thought about the other place I wanted to take him: Meg's grave. If he genuinely wanted to see and know all of me, I was going to give it to him. Even if it was almost as scary as facing down the sock monkey on the Halloween lift ride.

Today I was slouched at the kitchen table, submitting a writing assignment for a content writing position with a company down the street. I'd interviewed with them the week before and they'd expressed additional interest, asking me to submit a writing sample. If they liked it, I'd be invited back for a second interview. The role sounded almost too good to be true, and I tried not to get my hopes up as I hit Submit.

I leaned back in my chair, wishing someone was here with me to celebrate. The only option was Ruby, who was curled up, dozing on the back of the couch.

As if summoned by my musings, my phone lit up with a call. A picture of Derek holding me close filled the screen. I'd finally retired our old college photo, but only after he'd helped me capture the perfect replacement image at his dad's house on Halloween. It still made my heart skip when I saw the pure joy on our faces as we smiled into the camera in our matching jack-o-lantern sweatshirts.

Curious why Derek would be calling me from work, I answered with a smile.

"Hi, handsome. I was just thinking about you."

The delay in his response told me immediately something was wrong. The choked gasp on the other side as he tried to gather his composure had me on guard, and I leaned forward onto the table, bracing myself for bad news.

"Cee, I'm at the hospital. It's Dad. He—" Derek broke off and I waited in anticipation, registering the sounds of beeping and voices over the intercom sounding in the background. "He has a fever, and we can't seem to get it under control. His platelets are low, so his doctor said to bring him in."

My heart stopped at the news, but I did everything in my power to stay calm and to keep breathing. I refused to think about what this reminded me of, a similar situation with Meg.

I cleared my throat, gathering my emotions as I realized Derek needed me. I couldn't afford to fall apart just yet.

"What can I do?" I asked, my voice sounding brittle to my own ears. I hoped he didn't hear the fear and caution in my tone.

"Can you come, please? I need you here."

It only took a moment for me to decide, even as my stomach tightened at the thought of going to the hospital. I hadn't ventured into one since Meg's death, doing everything in my power to avoid doctors' offices and all the memories they conjured. But for Derek, I could do this. I could be brave. At least, I hoped so.

Chapter Twenty-Nine

I PULLED INTO THE hospital parking lot a few minutes later, my heart pounding and my palms sweating. I told myself I was being ridiculous as I forced myself out of the car, coaching myself through every step from my car to the hospital entrance. I'd survived murder clowns on a ski lift and telling my best friend I wanted to be more than friends. I could handle a hospital room. Especially if it was for Derek and Chris.

I stepped into the lobby, a blast of cool air making me shiver and pull Derek's hoodie closer around me. I'd stolen the hoodie after one of our movie nights when I hadn't had a jacket but needed something to keep me warm on the walk to my car. Now, I needed it even more, using his scent to block out the smells of hand sanitizer and heavy-duty cleaner that I knew would permeate the air of the hospital.

Derek stood in front of the reception desk, relief instantly filling his features when he saw me. He reached for my hand, pulling me in for a tight embrace. I clung to him, needing his presence as much as he seemed to need mine.

"I'm so glad you're here," he said into my hair. I heard the quiver in his voice and held on tighter, trying to convey to him all the love and support I felt.

"Of course I'm here." I hoped he couldn't hear the crack in my voice. I could do this. I could be here, be present with Derek as he faced this demon.

Even as I had the thought, I fought a wave of memories. Meg, lethargic and sick, my dad having to carry her out of the house to the car so my parents could rush her to the ER. Me and Max left at home without answers. Her staying in the hospital for a week, our entire family constantly on edge as my parents alternated between who was staying with her. All the underlying doubts and fears none of us wanted to acknowledge as we waited for news. Holding our breaths with each phone call and text message, until finally she turned the corner and was able to come home.

It had been the worst week of my life up until that point, only overshadowed now by the week she passed away. Yet here I stood on the edge of repeating that experience with Chris, a man I deeply loved and respected. I wasn't sure how I would get through, but I knew I had to. Derek needed me, and I refused to let fear stand in the way of me being here for him.

I blinked back my tears, holding on to Derek a moment longer, making sure I had my emotions under control before straightening.

"Let's go see Chris," I said, trying to sound confident when I felt anything but.

When we entered the hospital room, my heart broke just a little seeing Chris in the hospital bed, Axle sitting in the chair beside him. It was a far cry from his comfortable recliner, though he had managed to find a cooking show to watch.

He gave me a halfhearted smile as I walked in, his eyes tired but laughing.

"There's Derek's girl. You didn't have to rush down to see an old man. The two of you should be out on the town, grabbing dinner, living it up." His words were underscored by a coughing fit. Axle jumped up, snagging a cup from the side table and offering it to him. Derek released my hand and rushed over to help, leaving me alone in the doorway. I felt like an animal caught in the headlights of a car. But this time, instead of fainting like a goat, I wanted to run like a cheetah, putting as much distance between me and this situation as possible.

Instead, I forced myself to take one step forward and then another until I stopped at Chris's bedside. By then, his coughing was under control, and both of his sons stepped away, Axle settling back into the chair by the hospital bed and Derek moving to lean against the wall next to the window. Chris offered me a wan smile and I grabbed his hand, his fingers cold in mine. He gave my hand a soft, reassuring squeeze.

"Can't imagine I look too good right now, but trust me, my boys and the doctor are being overprotective. It's a cold. I'll be back to myself in no time, just you watch." He winked at me and the tight knot in my chest loosened a little bit.

"Axle, why don't you run out and get yourself something to eat? Derek and Chloe can keep me company for a while." Chris waved Axle toward the door.

I could see the protest in Axle's eyes. He looked like he was about to comment, but seemed to think better of it when he caught the look on Chris's face.

"Fine, but I'll just be downstairs in the cafeteria." He unfolded his lanky frame from the less-than-comfortable looking maroon chair and headed for the door.

"Go get something good and maybe run home for a shower and change of clothes." Chris insisted. "Derek will call you if I so much as breathe wrong."

Axle paused in the doorway, indecision written all over his face.

"We'll both be here," I said, sitting down in the chair Axle had vacated. It really was as uncomfortable as it looked. "I promise."

The rest of the day passed in a blur as I held my breath, waiting for Chris to take a turn for the worse or for his doctor to come by with terrible news. Instead, it felt much like our evenings at Chris's home in front of the TV, except instead of Derek and I snuggled on the couch, we were crammed into stiff hospital chairs watching reruns of cooking shows on a tiny TV mounted to the wall in the hospital room.

When Axle finally returned, the constant anxiety and worry that something else was going to go wrong had finally dissipated, leaving me both exhausted and relieved. Chris's doctors had stopped by and, while they were going to keep Chris overnight for observation, just to be safe, Chris was going to be just fine.

Later, Derek walked me out to my car, apologizing for not following me home. He wasn't quite ready to leave his dad, and I understood. As dusk fell, he swooped down and pressed a kiss to my mouth, promising to call me when he left if it wasn't too late.

I nodded, doing my best to keep my emotions in check until I made it home, though I did stay in his embrace longer than usual, soaking in the familiar comfort and hoping to give him some in return.

As I walked through the door of my apartment, I called for my roommates, checking to see if they were home. I'd texted them before I left for the hospital and again when it became clear that Chris was going to be fine. He just had a compromised immune system and a very cautious doctor.

When it became clear that I was home alone, with not even Ruby coming to greet me, I stumbled into my room and collapsed onto my bed, burying my face in the comforter and finally allowing the tears to fall.

Today was not what I had signed up for. I was not equipped to navigate another sad ending like Meg. I couldn't handle it, couldn't survive the hurt and devastation again. Only happy endings were allowed in my life.

Even as I had the thought, I knew I was being ridiculous. Chris couldn't control getting sick any more than I could control the weather. But sitting in that hospital room with one of my worst fears in front of me, I had started to doubt and have second thoughts.

Was letting Derek in, with all his messy family dynamics, really worth risking my heart? Could I let someone else get close to me, knowing that somewhere down the road something just as hard or harder than today would hit? Could I navigate that and survive?

Doubts and fears circled through my mind until exhaustion finally took over and I dozed off with my face buried in my bedspread, my heart and head battling with the fear I'd fought to keep at bay for so long.

Chapter Thirty

Pounding on the front door pulled me from sleep, and I sat up, completely disoriented. I was in my bedroom with my familiar movie posters greeting me, but something felt off. I glanced down, realizing I was still wearing Derek's hoodie and my jeans, the same outfit I'd worn to the hospital. Glancing at the clock, I was startled to see it was almost 10:00 p.m. Based on the continued thuds on my door, my roommates clearly weren't home, so I cautiously made my way to the front door, knowing whatever waited for me on the other side couldn't be good.

Could Chris have taken a turn for the worst? That didn't make sense. If something had happened, Derek would have called or texted me instead of coming over.

I shuffled to the door and looked through the peephole, startled to see Max on the other side, hand raised to knock again. The sight made no sense, and I was half convinced I was dreaming as I unlocked the door and threw it open, causing him to stumble a bit at the sudden movement.

"Max, what are you doing here?" My voice came out a croak as I took in my brother wearing a high school sweatshirt, basketball shorts, and tennis shoes. He was the epitome of teenage boy, clearly not caring about the cold temperature outside.

I gestured him inside, already worried about his response. Max didn't have a car, so I had no idea how he'd gotten here, standing on my doorstep, several hours away from our parents' house.

"Hello to you too," he said, trying to force a light tone but I could see tension in his eyes and the set of his shoulders.

I waved him over to the couch, taking a moment to turn on some lights to better see him as we talked.

Max sat on the loveseat, grabbing a throw pillow and clutching it to his stomach like a lifeline. I took a seat on the couch diagonal from him, unsure of what to expect from the conversation ahead.

"Surprise?" His voice was hesitant, but also stubborn as if he already knew I'd protest his presence but refusing to apologize for the unexpected visit.

"You can say that again." I crossed my legs and settled into the couch, waiting. I could feel the dried remnants of tears on my face and my hair sticking up in all directions, but I ignored the sensations, determined to get to the bottom of why and how my carless seventeen-year-old brother had ended up on my doorstep. The last I'd heard, he and Mom were doing okay. Clearly, something had changed. "You better have a very good explanation for what is going on here."

"Don't be mad." He held up his hands like he was trying to placate a wild animal, always a good way to start a conversation. "Mom and I had another fight, and when you didn't answer your phone..." He trailed off, giving me a sheepish smile. "I asked one of my friends to drive me here."

I sat there stunned, blinking at him.

"Excuse me? You and mom had a fight, so you decided the proper response was to run away?" I shook my head, trying to process what Max was telling me. Most kids had an argument with their mother and hid in their bedroom until they cooled off. My brother hitched a ride several hours away to escape. He'd never acted this rashly before. What could have been so bad to trigger this extreme of a response?

His mention of my phone had me patting my pockets and coming up empty. Realizing it must have fallen out on my bed, I walked into my room to search for the device, still trying to process what my brother had said. After my phone call with Derek, I'd ignored my phone most of the day, only using it to text my roommates a couple of updates. Finding the phone on my bed, I picked it up and saw several missed texts and calls, most of them from Max and Mom.

Going back to the living room, I held up the device.

"Want to explain why I have over ten missed calls from Mom?" I asked, too tired to put any bite into the words as I slumped back onto the couch and rubbed my temples. "I thought you guys were doing better."

"We were," Max said, hesitating before pushing forward. "But then she found my college brochures and she flipped. You should have seen her, Chloe. She was completely unreasonable, ranting about how there was no way I was moving out of state. She started talking about grounding me for looking at colleges that weren't local, threatening to cancel her and Dad's cruise to stay home and keep an eye on me and I just . . . snapped. I stormed out of the house, called a buddy with a car and asked him to drive me here. He has a brother that lives in the area, so he said it was no big deal." Any guilt Max felt for his actions was quickly disguised by a mask of determination and defiance.

I pinched the bridge of my nose, unsure how to respond. I wanted to grab Max by the shoulders and shake some sense into him. But I also recognized Mom's reaction was disproportionate. The only thing Max had been guilty of was not telling Mom his full plans for college.

While not ideal, it was hardly a grounding offense. Though, to be fair, the argument was also hardly a reason to run away.

Before we could continue this conversation, I had to make a phone call. I selected my mom's number from my contacts and pressed Call, putting the phone on speaker so Max could hear the conversation and the fallout from his actions.

Mom picked up on the first ring, her voice frantic. "Chloe, have you heard from Max? We had a fight and—"

"He's here, Mom." I broke in, wanting to alleviate as much of her worry as possible. "He just showed up on my doorstep."

"He's there? We're on our way! John," I could hear her calling to my dad on the other end of the line, "get in the car. Max is at Chloe's."

I watched as panic stole across Max's face, and I realized that, for whatever reason, he needed to be here, away from the house. Sighing, I spoke up, hoping I wouldn't regret what I was about to say. If he thought his punishment was bad after being five minutes late for curfew, I could only imagine what would be waiting for him when I took him home tomorrow.

"Mom, I think it might be best if he stays here tonight and I talk to him, figure out what's going on." Instant relief spilled across Max's features, which he quickly schooled, doing his best to pretend to be a tough teenager. But I knew underneath it all he was just a kid. I had a feeling he was dealing with bigger hurts and emotions than anyone gave him credit for.

"Are you sure?" The rustling and shuffling sounds of my parents loading up their car stopped as Mom waited for my answer.

"I'm positive. I don't have any interviews tomorrow. I can drive him home first thing." I promised, bracing myself for the drive and the emotions that came with a trip home. I loved my family, but going home brought with it a slew of memories I tried hard to avoid. Though maybe it was long past time I stopped hiding from that part of my past too.

"Okay," she said, though I could tell she didn't like it. "If you change your mind, just call us. We can be down in a couple of hours to pick him up. I don't know what he was thinking, running away like that. He could have been hurt or killed or who knows what else, and I would have had no idea. And after everything with Meg—"

"Mom, he's fine. Let me talk to him. Give him some older sister quality time. I'll call you when we leave in the morning." I ended the call and looked over to see Max, slumped into the couch, the picture of defeat and teenage bad decisions.

"I messed up, didn't I?" He asked, his voice a mumble.

"That's an understatement. I wouldn't be surprised if Mom had called the police already and reported you missing."

He groaned, throwing an arm over his eyes. "I just needed to get away. I couldn't handle the constant lectures, the comparisons to Meg. When Mom found my stash of college pamphlets for schools out of state, she just started spiraling, and nothing I said would get through to her."

I watched him, waiting to see where this would go.

"Things have been better since the last time you talked to Mom, but tonight, after she found the brochures, she started talking about grounding me and how I couldn't go to any more dances or sporting events or any activities this year. And I just figured, if I was going to be grounded anyway, it might as well be for actually doing something wrong. So I left." His voice became small and quiet with the last words, and I stood up, settling on the loveseat next to him and wrapping an arm around him.

"Maybe not your smartest moment, but," I hesitated before pushing forward, "I understand. Mom has a tendency to squeeze tighter when she feels like she's losing control."

Max shifted, resting his head on my shoulder. "What am I supposed to do? She can't control my life forever. I'm almost an adult."

I wanted to protest, say that eighteen really wasn't as adult as he probably thought, but I bit down my initial response, thinking through my words first.

"I wish I had a good answer," I said honestly, remembering back to what it had felt like to be a senior in high school, wanting to assert my independence while also not wanting to push Mom too hard after Meg's loss. "But I do know the answer is not running away. And it probably involves more talking than either you or Mom want to do."

Max gave a defeated chuckle. "If she has her way, I'm going to live in my childhood bedroom for the rest of my life."

"I know it feels that way, and you may be grounded that long, but I promise she just wants the best for you. Even if her definition and your definition of what's best are different."

Max didn't respond, and we sat in comfortable stillness until my phone lit up with a call, this one from Derek. The familiar photo of us together filled the screen, and Max reached for the device before I could grab it, a mischievous look on his face.

He held up the phone for my inspection.

"Since when have you and Derek been a thing?" He waggled the phone just out of my reach, and I dove for it, tackling him to the couch in a move perfected by older sisters for generations.

"Since none of your business," I said, grabbing the phone and answering it, making sure it wasn't on speakerphone this time. Not that it did me any good.

"Hey," I said, a bit breathless from my efforts to answer before the call went to voicemail. "Are you headed home?"

"Derek, how long have you been kissing my sister?" Max yelled toward the phone. I put my hand on his mouth trying to quiet him. Instead, he licked my hand, making me shriek in disgust.

"I'm sorry, is now a bad time?" Derek asked, his tone confused.

"It's not great," I bit into the phone as I reached over to pinch Max, he dodged the effort, tickling me in retaliation. Wrestling matches with my brother were definitely on the list of things I didn't miss as an adult living on my own.

"I was just going to see if you were up. Stop by to chat. But we can talk tomorrow." I could hear the exhaustion and hesitation in his voice and recognized it for what it was: a desperate plea not to be left alone.

If this had been any other guy and any other relationship, I would have accepted the out he was giving me. I felt guilty adding to his worry and concern, especially after everything that had happened with Chris today. But this was Derek. I'd promised to let him help carry my hard, and I wasn't about to break that promise now. I'd already told him about the heaviest pieces of my past. Might as well show him my life in all its messy glory.

"My brother's here and he'd love to meet you as my boyfriend," I said. "He's currently the poster child for bad teenage decisions and grounded to my couch until I can drive him home tomorrow."

Derek paused, clearly unsure how to respond. "Do I want to know what all of that means?"

"It means being a big sister is not for the faint of heart. Come over and I'll explain. Have you eaten dinner yet? Because I think part of Max's penance is going to be making pancakes."

Max groaned at this pronouncement, but didn't protest, seeming to recognize this was minor compared to the punishment he deserved. The punishment that would be waiting for him when I dropped him off at home.

"I'm always down for pancakes, especially if you're there. Be there in ten minutes," Derek said.

Maybe it was all in my head, but his voice sounded just a bit lighter at the prospect of being with me, knowing he didn't have to carry his hard alone either.

Chapter Thirty-One

I HAD AVOIDED INTRODUCING my family to any of the guys I dated over the course of my adult life for a variety of reasons. But introducing Derek to Max as my boyfriend showed me I hadn't needed to worry so much. They'd already met back when Derek was just my friend, so it made the whole thing easier, and having Derek there, helping me navigate the emotional blowup between my brother and mom, made the whole thing more bearable. Yes, I was still holding my family together, but I didn't have to do it alone.

Instead, I got to do it with pancakes as I watched two of the most important guys in my life talk. Max had been sullen at first when I'd made him explain to Derek how he'd ended up on my couch, but he'd warmed up as Derek listened, understanding Max's desire for space and new opportunities while also helping Max see where my mom was coming from in a way that only someone he wasn't related to could.

By the time Derek left for the night, we were all drained, but the anxiety that had pooled in my belly over how to handle things with Max had dissipated when Derek stepped in to help, showing me how it felt to have a true partner in moments when life fell apart.

Derek had even volunteered to drive Max home with me. Chris was doing much better and would be discharged in the morning. Once Derek and Axle got Chris settled, Derek would be ready to go.

I'd volunteered to help with picking up Chris, but Derek promised they had it handled, so instead I stayed home with Max, making him help with chores around the apartment as payment for his night on the couch. Both of my roommates had been fine with the overnight guest, but I still made him clean the kitchen and living room. I told him I was just preparing him for whatever consequences Mom had waiting for him when he got home.

It was while he was working that I got two exciting emails. The first was a job offer from a social media platform based out of Oregon. It was the first job offer I'd received that I actually felt optimistic about and, if it had come in only a month sooner, I would have accepted it without hesitation.

The other email was from the Utah company that I had submitted a writing sample to. While they still wanted to conduct a second interview, they were impressed enough with my skill set that they were fairly optimistic I would be hired.

My stomach twisted as I considered my options. I knew which option I wanted to choose, assuming the second interview went well. But would doing so break my promise to Meg? I pushed the thoughts aside, deciding I'd worry about job offers later when everything with Max was settled and I had a chance to talk to Derek.

The car ride to my parents' house was quiet, my stomach filled with nerves as I considered showing Derek my childhood home, filled with pictures and memories of Meg. I also worried about my parents' reaction to Max and his decision to run away. Hopefully, I could smooth everything over, help my mom express her concerns while shielding Max from any out-of-proportion punishments. As we pulled into the driveaway, the nerves faded, replaced by a sudden unexpected calm. I felt peace as I looked at Derek and caught his reassuring smile before climbing from the car. Yes, there were a lot of unknowns ahead, but Derek was here and would help me through.

Max was more hesitant, hanging back as we approached the front door. Before I could knock, the door flew open, revealing my mom on the other side. Her hair was a mess and she had dark circles underlining her eyes. My dad wasn't far behind, the worry lines in his forehead showing his concern.

"Max!" My mom said, rushing past me to wrap Max in a hug.

Dad stepped forward, pulling me into an embrace. "Thanks for bringing him home safe," he said, his voice a low rumble. "Your mom, actually both of us, were a complete wreck last night."

I squeezed Dad back, welcoming the rare embrace. "Of course. I'm glad he knows I'm always here to help."

My words carried no bite, though a part of me wished Max and Dad's relationship were such that Max could have run to him instead of me.

I stepped out of Dad's hug, looping my arm through Derek's and pulling him forward. It was time I stopped keeping my distance from my family and let them into my life fully.

"Dad, you remember Derek," I said. "I thought it was time you met my boyfriend."

Dad extended his hand, giving Derek's a firm shake. "Nice to see you again. I always wondered if there was something more between the two of you."

Derek released Dad's hand and slipped his arm around my waist, pulling me into his side. "We were just waiting for the right time. Chloe's the kind of girl worth waiting for."

I bit my lip, watching as I let Derek into another part of my life. And just like that, something that had been missing from my life snapped into place. Whatever came next, I could handle it with Derek.

—*ell*—

After reintroducing Derek and my dad, I realized there was more to work through between Max and Mom than I'd anticipated. While Mom had rushed out to give him a hug, Max had insisted on keeping his distance, arms crossed over his chest, his shoulders tense.

"Maybe we should take this inside," I said, waving everyone into my childhood home.

We settled in my parents' living room, Derek sitting next to me on the couch, our hands intertwined. Max sat on my other side, his face set in a sullen expression. My parents sat kitty corner to us on the loveseat, my mom the picture of frustration and hurt, my dad looking at a loss for how to handle things. The room smelled of furniture polish, making me wish for one of my fall-scented candles to help brighten the space.

Pictures from my childhood stared back at us from the walls. There were dozens of photos, the most recent one a print of the family photo I kept in my nightstand drawer. My mom hadn't updated much in the house since Meg's passing, which was particularly evident when I looked at pictures of Max as a child, but nothing that showed how he was almost an adult now.

I fiddled with the necklace at my throat, not sure how to get the conversation started but recognizing that someone needed to say something. A clock ticked on the wall, the only indication that time was moving forward, and we weren't frozen in this moment, waiting for the fallout.

"Well, are you going to apologize?" Mom finally asked, getting the conversation started in perhaps the worst possible way. Her voice was curt and demanding, her posture stiff and unyielding.

Max had been remorseful last night, but something about being in Mom's presence had rekindled his resentment, bringing out the stubborn teenager in full force. Instead of responding, he slouched further into the couch.

"Mom, maybe let's ease into this," I said, trying to play peacemaker, even as I questioned why this was always my job. When did I get to just be the daughter instead of the referee?

"Ease into what? How do you ease into the fact that Max ran away?" Mom asked, each word distinct and filled with righteous indignation.

"It's not that simple—" Max started before Mom broke in.

"Really? Because that's exactly what it looks like. You didn't like my rules and ran away to your sister to try to fix things, as usual."

Mom's words stung, but I ignored the dig at me, trying to find a resolution that would actually help my family instead of perpetuating the hurt we were all floundering to navigate. Derek squeezed my hand, a comforting, steady presence at my side. He'd said he wanted to see all my broken, painful, hidden parts, and now he was getting a front row seat to the reason I rarely came home, choosing to intervene from afar.

"Mom, throwing out accusations isn't going to fix anything," I said, keeping my voice calm. "Did Max overreact? Absolutely." Max spluttered in protest, but I pushed forward, ignoring his reaction, needing to get the words out before this could escalate further. "But you overreacted too. Grounding him because he's considering out-of-state colleges? That's hardly something to punish him for."

"It wasn't quite that simple," Mom said, leaning back into the couch, her arms crossed over her chest.

"Then please tell me what I'm missing."

My statement was met with silence. My dad pulled his phone from his pocket, mumbling something about needing to take a work call, and ducked out of the room, avoiding the problem as usual.

"Mom, why did you react that way when you found the college brochures?" I asked, my voice gentle.

"Because I don't want Max to move," she said, her voice quiet.

"Why not?" I persisted, knowing Max needed to hear this, to understand this side of Mom.

She closed her eyes, fighting down emotions. I wasn't the only one who had a tendency to bottle things up. I'd learned from the best.

"Because I don't want him to leave. He's my baby. I want him to stay local, where I can watch out for him. Protect him."

My heart hurt for my mom, but I resisted the urge to go to her, ending the conversation there. If this was going to get better, Max needed to say his piece too and she needed to listen.

"Max," I reached over and placed a reassuring hand on his knee, encouraging him in my own silent way to share his true thoughts and feelings, "why do you want to go to school out of state?"

He bit his lip, seeming to debate for a moment before the words spilled out in a rush. "Because I need to get away. I want to go somewhere where no one knows me, where I'm not the baby brother of the girl who died from cancer."

Mom gave a strangled gasp, tears immediately running down her face.

"How can you even think that?!" She exclaimed, pushing to her feet.

"Because it's true!"

Max shot to his feet as well, the two stalking to each other, hands on hips, talking over each other. The calm, strained silence of earlier was long gone as their voices gained volume, throwing accusations that neither was actually listening to.

I sat back, pondering Max's pronouncement, unable to fully process the scene around me. His words sounded so similar to things I'd told myself, the reasons why I'd never talked about Meg in college. Only now was I recognizing how unfair it was to myself, to my friends, and, in a way, to Meg's memory. It was in sharing about her that I was finding the strength to move forward with my life, despite the pain, but it was a lesson I'd had to learn for myself. Max would need to do the same.

"Can I say something?" Derek asked, surprising us all with the quiet, calm question that somehow carried over the chaos that was my mom and brother.

"Of course," I said, curious what he'd say next.

He squeezed my hand, as if sensing my unspoken question.

"I've known Chloe for seven years, but I only learned about Meg recently. She must have been an incredible person," he said, turning to face my mom with a sad smile on his face. "While I didn't know Meg personally, based on what Chloe's told me about her, I don't think she'd want this. She didn't sound like someone who hesitated, who lived trapped in the past. She sounded adventurous and brave and like she'd want everyone in this family to chase their dreams." He turned to look at me, his expression earnest, as if he was no longer talking to my mom and brother, but that this last part was specifically for me. "Like she'd want you to chase your dreams no matter how close or far they took you."

Somehow, even though he'd never met Meg, I realized Derek was right. She'd want Max to chase his dream of school out of state. She'd want my parents to figure out what happy looked like in this new stage of life. And she'd want me to choose the person and place that made me happiest, even if it meant I never lived out of state or did the many epic, brave things she had planned for her life. Because she'd want us each to live our own lives to the fullest, chasing our happy endings.

Chapter Thirty-Two

I WISH I COULD say Derek's heartfelt words had changed things for my family and that everything miraculously fell into place, but that was far from reality. Max and Mom reached a begrudging truce with Mom only grounding Max for a month because he'd run away. She'd agreed to keep an open mind to the possibility of Max moving out of state for school, though Max still had quite the road ahead of him to win Mom over to his plan. In exchange, Max had agreed to genuinely consider some in-state schools. As for Dad, he stayed on his work call, missing the whole exchange and making me wonder how on earth he and mom would survive their upcoming cruise with just the two of them.

My parents had invited Derek and me to stay for dinner, but we'd deferred, claiming we needed to get home to check on Chris. In reality, I was emotionally drained and needed out of my childhood home as soon as possible. They could get to know my boyfriend better next week, when we came back for pie and stilted small talk the day after Thanksgiving.

Though I did have one more family member for Derek to meet before we drove back to Pleasant Grove.

As we climbed into the car, I asked him to take a detour, driving along one of the main roads until we reached the cemetery. I directed him to park next to a familiar tree and grabbed his hand once we were both out of the car, leading the way past several headstones, not even looking at the names as we walked. I knew where we were going.

Derek didn't question me, seeming to sense the significance of this moment. When we reached the last headstone in the row, I stopped, taking in the familiar words engraved on a white stone nestled in the green, slightly overgrown grass. "Megan Margene Green. Beloved daughter, sister, and friend. Forever in our hearts." Beneath that were her birth and death dates, encompassing a time far too short for the size of the hole she'd left in our lives and hearts. I wished I had flowers to put in the vase at the top of the headstone, but I'd been worried that if we stopped, I'd lose my nerve. I needed to do this now, to show Derek just how much he meant to me.

"It's long past time the two of you met," I said, watching Derek's face as I gestured between him and the headstone. "Derek, meet my big sister Meg. Meg, meet the man of my dreams."

Derek gave a surprised gasp, reaching for my hand and pulling me to face him.

"Do you mean that? I'm the man of your dreams?" Derek asked, a smile teasing the corners of his lips, even as exhaustion rimmed his eyes. It had been a long, emotional 48 hours.

"Absolutely," I said, pulling him into my side and looping my arm around his waist so I could lean my head on his arm. "You were right that night I told you about Meg. I was holding part of myself back, hiding pieces of me. It was part of why I was looking for a job outside of Utah. I was running from who I am and this messy life of mine, using my promise to Meg as an excuse. But I'm done hiding now." I took a deep breath, knowing I needed to speak the words in my heart just as much as Derek needed to hear them. I turned to face him, needing to see his reaction as I spoke. "I got a job offer today for a position in Oregon."

I watched Derek, feeling him tense at the news. I squeezed his hand, trying to reassure him even as I shared the full story.

"That's great." The words sounded halfhearted at best, and I loved him all the more for trying to show enthusiasm for my accomplishments. "Looks like all your candle wishes are coming true."

"They are," I said, biting my lip and playing up the suspense a moment longer. "I told them no."

I waited, watching him as the words sank in. He shook his head, trying to process my words.

"You told them no?" Hope lingered in his eyes, and I nodded.

"I couldn't leave you, not now when we're discovering what this," I squeezed his hand, "thing is between us. I need a job, but I need you in life even more, which is why," I paused for effect, "I've been applying for local jobs. I have a second interview for a content writer position at a company two blocks away from my apartment."

Derek blinked at me, clearly trying to process my words. Then he gave an excited whoop, pulling me into his arms and swinging me around in a circle. I laughed, lost in the sheer joy of the moment. Once he deposited me back on the ground, he bent down, kissing me with all the love and passion I'd come to expect from this man. Though he pulled away too quickly for my liking, seeming to realize where we were.

"Am I allowed to kiss you in front of your sister? I mean, kissing in the cemetery feels a bit weird," he said, pink stealing into his cheeks as he rubbed the back of his neck.

I laughed, looping my arms around his neck and pulling his face back toward mine. "I think she'd be more upset if you didn't kiss me."

"I love you," Derek said, leaning in until his lips were inches away from mine.

"I love you too," I said, meaning the words with my whole soul and so grateful I'd taken the risk to let this man out of the friendzone.

Needing no more invitation, Derek closed the gap between us and pressed his lips to mine once more. It was far from the movie-perfect setting for a declaration of love and yet, it somehow fit. In this moment, I stood with Derek, showing him all of me, and he wasn't running—and neither was I. I was broken in many ways, and my life was filled with less than perfect pieces, filled with heartache and loss. Yet, somehow, those pieces had come together, giving me a happily ever after for now. And I wouldn't trade it for all the candle wishes in the world.

Epilogue

The smells of cinnamon and fried food filled the air, and I shivered as I hurried through the corn maze. With Halloween only a week away, Derek and I had decided to embrace the fall fun, though we'd opted out of the haunted maze. This time, we decided to do the maze shaped like friendly cartoon characters. We'd also come early enough in the evening that there was plenty of light to navigate the twists and turns of the maze, which was good since Derek had opted to turn our time in the maze into a race. First one out got to pick our next movie, and I was not losing this time. Derek had picked our last three movies and if I had to watch one more heist film, I was going to scream.

Praying I wasn't lost, I turned corner after corner, trying to find the bridge in the middle of the maze that I could climb up to get a view from above. A group of teenage girls ran past me from the opposite direction, giggling as they went. I hoped it wasn't a sign that I was going the wrong way.

I turned the corner and froze, not fully processing what I saw. There, in the middle of the corn maze, knelt Derek, a giant grin on his face. In one hand he held a bouquet of roses and in the other was a jewelry box. Surrounding him were both of our families along with Mallory, Ridge, Audrey, and Grey, all of them wearing gigantic matching grins on their faces.

I walked forward until I stood directly in front of Derek, my heart racing with anticipation, knowing exactly what was coming next and yet still not fully believing this was my life, my reality.

"Chloe, our journey together has taken so many twists and turns. From the moment we met, I knew you were the girl for me, and I'm so glad you were willing to give me a chance to prove it a year ago."

I was smiling so hard my cheeks hurt and I didn't even care. I drank in every word he spoke, determined to remember this moment for as long as I lived.

"Every day with you has been better than the last, and I can't wait to write our own happy ending together. Will you marry me?"

I didn't even bother looking at the ring, knowing it would be perfect because it came from Derek, the man who'd shown me how to love and let someone fully into my heart.

"Yes," I said, leaning down to kiss him with all the longing and excitement in my heart. Cheering followed my declaration, but I barely registered it. I was too focused on this man in front of me who I was going to spend the rest of my life with.

Pausing our kisses just long enough to stand, Derek wrapped me in his arms, pulling me close. It was my favorite place to be, holding onto the man I loved. I'd lost count of the number of times I'd blown out candles, wishing for my own happy ending and here it was, far better than anything I could have ever dreamed of.

Love Chloe and Derek? For a bonus epilogue visit authorhillaryslaughter.com

Also by Hillary Slaughter

Author's Note

DEAR READER,

I hope you enjoyed Chloe and Derek's story. Lost Daydreaming is the most vulnerable book I have ever written, but I've known for years that this was a book I needed to write. This book is a work of fiction, but many parts are inspired by my life, thoughts, and experiences. I am not an expert on cancer or loss, but I do know what it's like to lose a sister to cancer. It's hard and ugly and, more than a decade later, it still hurts.

There's no perfect formula for healing. To anyone who has lost a loved one to cancer, know that I see you. Know that you are not alone.

I hope this book touched at least one person's heart and helped them find the courage to own their story, even if the ending isn't a perfect happily ever after quite yet.

Thank you for reading.

Hillary

Acknowledgements

To Mom, Dad, Lindy, and Landon, thank you for supporting me on this author journey. It's been quite the journey and you've cheered me on, especially when things got hard. I could not have done it without you and your incredible love and encouragement.

To Madey, thank you for helping me on this book. I'm convinced you were with me every step of this way on this one. I miss you every single day and will always be grateful for my guardian angel.

Thank you to my extended family for your love and support. Grandpa, thank you for helping with the business side of things and for your patience with all of my random questions.

To Dana LeCheminant, none of my books would be possible without your friendship, advice, and pep talks. Thank you for being my emotional support author friend!

To Annie Peterson, thank you for helping me make this story shine with your incredible editing insights.

To Cassy and Jessica, thank you for being such amazing beta readers.

To Raneé Clark thank you for designing all of the covers for this series and for you fantastic development edits.

To Lindzee Merrill Photography, thank you for the incredible headshots.

To my book club and bookstagram friends, thank you for giving me a space to nerd out about books and for all the book recommendations.

To my arc readers, coworkers, friends, and everyone else who has had a hand in this book, thank you. Your support is felt and so greatly appreciated.

Finally, thank you, my readers, for reading Chloe's story! You make what I do possible, and I will forever be grateful for every person who decides to take a chance on one of my books.

About the Author

Hillary Slaughter is a crafting addict, avid reader, and hiking enthusiast. Born and raised in Utah, she loves exploring the mountains, especially if she can bring her dog with her. She has a Bachelor's degree in English from Brigham Young University and a Master's of Business Administration from Utah Valley University. She loves writing sweet contemporary romance with a dash of humor and is the author of the Lost Roommates Series. You can learn more about Hillary and her books at authorhillaryslaughter.com.

www.ingramcontent.com/pod-product-compliance
Lightning Source LLC
Chambersburg PA
CBHW061949170626
46813CB00006B/2587